William Logan

The Early Heroes of the Temperance Reformation

William Logan

The Early Heroes of the Temperance Reformation

ISBN/EAN: 9783337189174

Printed in Europe, USA, Canada, Australia, Japan

Cover: Foto ©Andreas Hilbeck / pixelio.de

More available books at **www.hansebooks.com**

THE
EARLY HEROES

OF THE

TEMPERANCE REFORMATION.

BY

WILLIAM LOGAN,

EDITOR OF

"*The Moral Statistics of Glasgow,*" "*Words of Comfort,*" *etc.*

GLASGOW:
SCOTTISH TEMPERANCE LEAGUE.
LONDON: HOULSTON & SONS; AND W. TWEEDIE.
1873.

To

JOHN M'GAVIN,

GLASGOW,

ONE OF THE MOST EARNEST, INTELLIGENT, AND PRACTICAL

OF SCOTTISH TEMPERANCE REFORMERS,

This Volume is Inscribed,

WITH FEELINGS OF FRIENDSHIP AND ESTEEM,

BY

W. L.

PREFATORY NOTICE.

THE accompanying Notes and Recollections, concerning some of those with whom I have been privileged to associate in efforts for the advancement of Temperance, are the result of a sincere regard for those whose Lives and Labours I have imperfectly attempted to describe, and are offered to the public as a humble contribution to the early history of the Temperance Reformation.

It was no part of my design to compile a Dictionary of Temperance Biography, although there are not a few honoured names, both amongst the living and the dead, which are well worthy of recognition and remembrance; but I entertain the hope that the facts which are here recorded respecting some of the devoted men who bore the heat and burden of the day, may not only prove useful to the future historian of the temperance movement, but may also lead to increased efforts for the advancement of the cause on the part of those who are now engaged in promoting it.

The preparation of these Sketches, which has in all respects been a labour of love, has deepened my affection and respect for the earnest and disinterested men to whom we are indebted for one of the most important developments of benevolent effort that characterise the age in which we live. It has also strengthened my long-cherished conviction that the Temperance Reformation is the work of God, and that therefore it must prove ultimately successful. May the time soon come when Christian men and women everywhere, and the advocates of social as well as national reform generally, will see it to be their duty to do all they can to advance it !

W. L.

18 ABBOTSFORD PLACE,
GLASGOW, *October*, 1873.

CONTENTS.

——o——

CHAPTER I.

AMERICA.

PAGE

Origin of the American Temperance Society,   -   -   14

Dr. Lyman Beecher,   -   -   -   -   -   -   18

Beecher's "Six Sermons on Intemperance,"   -   -   18

CHAPTER II.

SCOTLAND.

John Dunlop,   -   -   -   -   -   -   25

Mr. Dunlop Visits Glasgow,   -   -   -   -   27

His First Temperance Lecture, -   -   -   -   31

Mr. Dunlop and the Divinity Students—Letter from

    Rev. James Towers, Birkenhead,   -   -   -   33

The Press on Mr. Dunlop's First Lecture,   -   -   37

CHAPTER III.

FORMATION OF FIRST TEMPERANCE SOCIETY IN SCOTLAND.

Societies at Maryhill and Greenock,   -   -   -   39

Mr. Dunlop Lectures in Edinburgh,   -   -   -   39

Visits Rochdale,   -   -   -   -   -   -   42

British Medical Declaration,   -   -   -   -   43

The Temperance Movement and Prayer, -   -   44

Mr. Dunlop Removes to London—his Labours there,   46

Mr. Dunlop's Writings,   -   -   -   -   -   47

Mr. Dunlop on Legislation,   -   -   -   -   48

His Last Illness and Death,   -   -   -   -   52

CHAPTER IV.

IRELAND.

Early History of the Temperance Movement—Letter

    from Mr. David Fortune,   -   -   -   -   53

CHAPTER V.

WILLIAM COLLINS.

Rev. Dr. Buchanan on Mr. Collins's Character, -   •   59
Dr. Chalmers and Temperance,   •   •   •   60
Signatures in First Temperance Roll-Book, Glasgow,   61
First Annual Meeting in Glasgow,   •   •   •   62
Mr. Collins Addresses Meetings in Glasgow and Edin-
    burgh,   •   •   •   •   •   •   63
First Temperance Tea Party, Glasgow,   •   •   64
Mr. James Corbett, Old Windsor,   •   •   •   65
Fac-simile of Admission Ticket,   •   •   •   67
Second Temperance Tea Party, in Baronial Hall,   •   67

CHAPTER VI.

WILLIAM COLLINS IN ENGLAND.

First Temperance Society in England,   •   • •-   69
Dr. Beaumont's First Temperance Lecture at Bradford,   69
Mr. Collins Addresses First Temperance Public Meet-
    ings in Liverpool and Manchester,   •   •   •   70
Mr. Archibald Prentice and the Press,   •   •   •   71
Mr. Collins Visits London,   •   •   •   •   •   72
First Public Meeting there,   •   •   •   •   •   72
Mr. Collins Lectures in Hamilton—Amusing Incident,   74
Mr. Collins before the Committee of the House of
    Commons on Drunkenness,   •   •   •   •   75
William Collins and other Temperance Worthies,   •   77
Letter from Mr. Robert Rae, London,   •   •   •   78
Death of Mr. Collins—Letter from Rev. Dr. Guthrie,
    Edinburgh,   •   •   •   •   •   •   •   79

CHAPTER VII.

ORIGIN OF TEETOTALISM.

Society at Skibbereen, Ireland,   •   •   •   •   81
Society at Dunfermline,   •   •   •   •   •   •   81
Society at Paisley,   •   •   •   •   •   •   •   82
Society at Glasgow—Mr. James Macnair,   •   •   82
Society at Greenlaw, Berwickshire—Letter from Rev.
    John Parker,   •   •   •   •   •   •   •   83

CHAPTER VIII.

TEETOTALISM IN PRESTON.

Joseph Livesey, - - - - - - - 87
Preston Teetotal Pledge, - - - - - - 89
The Preston Heroes Visit Towns in Lancashire, - 90
Mr. James Teare, - - - - - - - 90
Origin of the word "Teetotal," - - - 91
Dickie Turner at World's Temperance Convention, - 93
Mr. Livesey's Malt Lecture, - - - - - 93
His First Visit to London, - - - - - 94
His Second Visit to London, - - - - - 96
Mr. Livesey as a Temperance Worker, - - - 97
Mr. Livesey on the Platform, - - - - - 99
Mr. Livesey on Moral Suasion, - - - - - 102

CHAPTER IX.

ROBERT GRAY MASON.

Early Life of Robert Gray Mason, - - - - 103
Mr. Mason meets with the Rev. Richard Tabraham, - 105
Letter from Mr. Tabraham, - - - - - 107
Mr. Mason joins the Temperance Cause—Labours in
    Ireland, - - - - - - - 109

CHAPTER X.

MR. MASON VISITS SCOTLAND.

His First Temperance Meeting at Saltcoats, - - 111
Mr. Mason and the Saltcoats Publicans, - - - 111
Complimentary Address to Mr. Mason, - - - 113
Mr. Mason becomes a Total Abstainer, - - - 115
John Macintosh, the Teetotal Mail Guard, - - 115
Mr. Mason visits Hamilton, - - - - - 117
Mr. Mason in Edinburgh, - - - - - - 118
Encouraging Testimony to Mr. Mason's Labours by
    the Edinburgh Total Abstinence Society, - - 118
Mr. Mason in the North, - - - - - - 121
Wick Town Council present Mr. Mason with the
    Freedom of the Burgh, - - - - - 121
Farewell Soiree in Aberdeen, - - - - - 123
Mr. Mason as a Preacher, - - - - - - 126

CHAPTER XI.

MR. MASON IN ENGLAND.

The Press on Mr. Mason's Temperance Efforts, - - 128
His Labours Amongst the Young, - - - - 130
His Last "Yearly Epistle" addressed to the Editor
    of the *British Workman*, - - - - 131
Mr. Mason's Writings, - - - - - - 134

CHAPTER XII.

EDWARD MORRIS.

His Boyhood and Early Life, - - - - - 136
Removes to Scotland, - - - - - - 138
Mr. Morris as a Temperance Reformer, - - - 139
Mr. Morris on the Platform, - - - - - 142
His "Life of Henry Bell," - - - - - 144
His Open-air Sunday Services on Glasgow Green, - 145
His Closing Hours and End, - - - - - 147
Inscription on the Monument at his Grave, - - 148

CHAPTER XIII.

ROBERT KETTLE.

His Early Life, - - - - - - - 149
Removes to Glasgow, - - - - - - 152
Mr. Kettle and Dr. Chalmers, - - - - 152
Mr. Kettle and the Temperance Movement, - - 154
Adopts the Total Abstinence Pledge, - - - 157

CHAPTER XIV.

MR. KETTLE'S LITERARY LABOURS.

Edits *The Scottish Temperance Journal*, - - 159
Extract from his First Article—"Muzzled Dogs," - 159
Rev. Wm. Reid on Mr. Kettle's Capacity for Literary
    Work, - - - - - - - 161
Origin of the Scottish Temperance League, - - 162
Mr. Kettle as President of the Scottish Temperance
    League, - - - - - - - 163
Extract from his Last Article, - - - - 163

Mr. Kettle as one of the Adjudicators of the Prize
Essays on the Sabbath, - - - - - 165
His Last Days, - - - - - - - 166
The Editor of *The Scottish Guardian* on Mr. Kettle, - 167
Mr. Kettle's Funeral, - - - - - 168
Estimate of his Character, - - - - - 169

CHAPTER XV.

WILLIAM MARTIN AND FATHER MATHEW OF CORK.

Interview with William Martin, - - - - 173
Temperance Tea-party on St. Patrick's Eve, - - 175
Father Mathew sends for William Martin, and
adopts Total Abstinence Pledge, - - - 176
Father Mathew Visits Glasgow, - - - - 178
Banquet in the City Hall—Mr. Kettle presents an
Address to Father Mathew, - - - - 178
Father Mathew's Reply, - - - - - - 181
He Administers the Pledge in the Cattle Market, - 183
Results of Father Mathew's visit to Glasgow, - - 184
Interviews with Father Mathew in Cork, - - 185
Letter from the Right Hon. W. E. Gladstone, M.P.,
to Mr. Maguire, M.P., Biographer of Father
Mathew, - - - - - - - 186

CHAPTER XVI.

JOHN LAING OF KIRKCONNEL.

His Ancestors, - - - - - - - 188
John Inglis Reasons with Laing on Total Abstinence, 189
John Laing as a Temperance Worker, - - - 191
Letters respecting John Laing, - - - - - 192
First Interview with John Laing, - - - - 194
His Interest in the Young, - - - - - 195
His Last Illness and Funeral, - - - - - 197
A Touching Scene, - - - - - - 197

CHAPTER XVII.

MALCOLM MACFARLANE, GLASGOW.

His Early Efforts as a Sabbath School Teacher, &c., - 199
Refutes Feargus O'Connor in the City Hall, - - 200
Preaches to the Working Classes, - - - - 200

Competitor for the Prize Essays on the Sabbath, - 201
Advocates the Temperance Cause, - - - - 202
His Funeral, - - - - - - - - 204

CHAPTER XVIII.

JAMES MITCHELL, GLASGOW.

Adopts the Abstinence Pledge, - - - - 206
Letter from Mr. Dunlop, - - - - - 207
Estimate of Mr. Mitchell, - - - - 208
His Interest in various Temperance Associations, - 211
His Views on Legislation, - - - - - 212
Memorial over his Grave, - - - - - 215

CHAPTER XIX.

JAMES STIRLING.

The Turning-point in Stirling's Life, - - - 216
Joins the Total Abstinence Society, - - - - 217
Stirling's first Temperance Lecture in Glasgow, - 218
Mrs. James Stirling, - - - - - - 221
John Dunlop on James Stirling, - - - - 221
Rev. Dr. Wallace's "Gloaming of Life," - - - 222
Letter to Dr. Wallace on Stirling's Closing Hours, - 224
Stirling's Funeral, - - - - - - - 227
Rev. Wm. Reid Preaches Stirling's Funeral Sermon, 228
Stirling's Love of Nature—a Sabbath Evening at
 Dunoon, - - - - - - - - 228
Monument at his Grave, - - - - - 231

CHAPTER XX.

ROBERT SMITH.

Mr. Smith as a Citizen and Magistrate, - - - 232
As a Temperance Reformer and League President, - 236
Mr. Smith and his Family Circle, - - - - 240
Mr. Smith's Illness—Expression of Sympathy, - 243
Mr. Smith's last Appearance at the League Anniversary, 244
His Funeral, - - - - - - - - 248

EARLY HEROES

OF THE

TEMPERANCE REFORMATION.

CHAPTER I.

AMERICA.

T is a somewhat singular fact that every great
enterprise which has for its object the present and future welfare of those whom the
sacred writer designated "the common people," has
always been, in the outset, unpopular. This was
the case with the Sunday-school movement, with
home and foreign missions, with the efforts of
Howard, and others, to improve our prisons and their
inmates, with the anti-slavery movement, with the
ragged-school movement, with the agitation for cheap-
ening the people's food, and with the more recent
movement to reclaim fallen women. In all these
great movements the pioneers were in a minority. " I
do not hold," says George Gilfillan, the distinguished
writer, and author of *The Bards of the Bible*, "with
a certain wise sage, that minorities are always in the
right, but I believe they are more frequently in the

right than majorities.   Minorities had done the real work of the world, and they were doing that real work up to this hour.   Milton, when he retired into his cloudy tabernacle of darkness, was still, like Moses, in the midst of the darkness of Sinai.   John Hunter, the celebrated anatomist, announced a lecture on anatomy in London, and although he probably knew more about that science than any man in the city, yet when the hour of lecture arrived, he found nobody waiting to hear him.   That was being in a minority with a vengeance!   Yes, there was *one* person present—the door-keeper; and the Doctor addressing him, said, "John, take down that skeleton, and place it beside you on that seat, that I may commence my lecture with 'Gentlemen!'"

The temperance movement, we shall find, shared for a time a similar fate.   In glancing over the "Permanent Temperance Documents of the American Temperance Society," I find that in June, 1811, the General Association of Massachusetts appointed the Rev. Dr. Samuel Worcester, and others, to co-operate with committees of the General Assembly of the Presbyterian Church, and the General Association of Connecticut, for the purpose of "devising measures which may have influence in preventing some of the numerous and threatening mischiefs that are experienced throughout our country from the excessive and intemperate use of spirituous liquors."   This committee met at different times for consultation, and determined to make an effort for the formation of a State Society for the Suppression of Intemperance. A sub-committee, consisting of Dr. Worcester, Dr. Torrey, and Mr. Wadsworth, was appointed to prepare a constitution. This constitution was presented to the whole committee, and approved, and subsequently transmitted by them to a more general meeting, held in Boston on the 4th of February, 1813, now sixty years ago. On the following day a meeting was held at the State House, when the constitution was adopted, and a society formed, called *"The Massachusetts Society for the Suppression of Intemperance"*—the object, as stated in the second article, being "to discountenance and suppress the too frequent use of ardent spirits, and its kindred vices, profaneness and gaming, and to encourage and promote temperance and general morality."

In the same month, February, 1813, the Rev. Heman Humphrey, of Fairfield, Connecticut, commenced a series of six papers, in the *Panapolist* and *Missionary Magazine*, published in Boston, on "The Causes, Progress, Effects, and Remedy of Intemperance in the United States." Towards the close of these early papers, which many of us should like to peruse, Mr. Humphrey makes the following sensible observations, still much needed amongst ourselves at the present day:—"If farmers and mechanics would agree not to drink spirits themselves, and not to provide them for their workmen—if, instead of furnishing liquor, they would give additional compensation to labourers, a very large advance would be made towards banishing the fiery products of the distilleries from the field and the workshop. And this would be no inconsiderable part of that general reformation which is so loudly called for with regard to the use of ardent spirits."

It thus appears that the friends of moral reform in America, as early as 1811 and 1813, had made attempts, by means of united effort, occasional lectures, articles in public journals, and personal abstinence, to suppress the then fearful sin of drunkenness. During the next ten or twelve years little progress seems to have been made. The few in different parts of the country who were really in earnest, felt it to be very discouraging and up-hill work. Towards the close of 1825, "it was perfectly evident," writes one friend, " that unless a new movement could be started on a new plan, and one which should be commensurate in place and time with the evil—one which should strike at the root and exterminate it—drunkenness could never be done away with." A meeting of a few individuals was accordingly called to consider the following question:—"What shall be done to banish intemperance from the United States ?" After prayer and conference on the subject, the result was a determination to attempt the formation of an " American Temperance Society whose grand principle should be abstinence from strong drink ; and its object, by light and love, to change the habits of the nation with regard to the use of intoxicating liquors." The following are three of the six cogent reasons given for the adoption of the foregoing resolution:—" 1. To remove the evil, we must remove the cause; and to remove the cause, efforts must be commensurate with the evil, and be continued till it is eradicated. 2. We never know what we can do by wise, united, and persevering efforts in a good cause, till we try. 3. If we do not try to remove the evils of intemperance, we cannot free ourselves from the guilt of its effects."

Another meeting was held in Boston, composed of various religious denominations, on the 10th of January, 1826, and was opened with prayer by the Rev. Timothy Merritt, of the Methodist Episcopal Church. At the close, a committee was appointed to prepare a constitution, and the meeting adjourned till February 13, 1826. At the adjourned meeting a constitution was presented and approved, and a large and highly influential committee, lay and clerical, was appointed. The Hon. Heman Lincoln, of the Baptist Church, submitted the following resolution, which was unanimously adopted:— " That the gentlemen composing this meeting pledge themselves to the American Society for the Promotion of Temperance, and that they will use all their exertions in carrying into effect the benevolent plans of the Society." The executive committee consisted of the Rev. Dr. Leonard Woods, Rev. Justin Edwards, Hon. George Odiorne, John Tappan, and S. V. S. Wilder.

LYMAN BEECHER, D.D.

It was in 1826 that Dr. Lyman Beecher's well-known "Six Sermons on Intemperance" were delivered at Lichfield, and shortly after, I believe, in Boston. In August, 1846, it was my privilege to meet with Dr. Beecher in London, at the World's Temperance Convention. On that occasion there was a noble gathering of temperance worthies from many parts of the world in the metropolis; but, to me, the chief attraction was old Beecher, whom I had long esteemed as the father of Temperance Reform in America; and having seen and heard the venerable sage, and grasped his hand, I felt that the long journey had not been in vain. Dr. Beecher's appearance and manner were remarkably impressive. He had a sharp, intelligent, penetrating, benevolent eye; and he had not uttered more than a few sentences when one felt that he was listening to a man who was thoroughly in earnest. "I pant not," said Beecher, forty-seven years ago, at the close of his *Six Sermons*, "for fame or posthumous immortality, but my heart's desire and prayer to God for my countrymen is, that they may be saved from intemperance, and that our beloved nation may continue free, and become great and good!"

I gladly avail myself of the following unpublished remarks from the pen of a distinguished living writer:—"Dr. Beecher's 'Six Sermons on Intemperance' was, we believe, the first book of his that gained him a name in Great Britain. We remember reading them when a boy, and being greatly struck with their exceeding energy of style, boldness of imagery, pungency of illustration, and earnestness of tone. Intemperance—at that time, far more than now, the Great Moral Mischief of America—exerted almost a fascinating and fearful influence on Dr. Beecher's imagination. It seemed to him a black shadow breathed up from the pit, and darkening earth below, and beclouding heaven above. It rested like a nightmare upon the breast of his country. It sacrificed manly enterprise, it crushed manly energy, it withered manly health, it deadened religious enterprise, it formed a cloud between the Mercy-seat above and the Church of Christ below. It seemed the sum of all the evils of humanity, the master-stroke of demoniac skill and infernal ingenuity, the one great obstacle which prevented the earth from attaining the climax of all happiness, and Christianity the culmination of its triumph. All this, and more than this, Dr. Beecher enunciated with a vast force of conviction, *empressement* of feeling, and power of language. One passage especially we remember well, in which he described the earth as a vast whispering gallery, repeating the woes and horrors of intemperance, as peculiarly powerful and striking to young imaginations. Even those who may not agree with Dr. Beecher on every point cannot fail, we think, to do justice to the courage which led him, forty-seven years ago, to utter his mind so freely on the subject; to the magnanimity of soul which disdained reproach and despised contempt; to the honesty which marked all his statements, and the enthusiasm which inspirited all his language, and will not be slow to classify him with such benefactors of his race as Howard and Clarkson, Garrison and Livingstone—men whose greatness lay in their grappling almost single-handed with gigantic evils, or in seeking—with little support but that of God Himself—after godlike objects in which, even if they fail, their failure is more valuable, suggestive, and hopeful than any amount of secular success."

These sermons of Beecher, which were eminently practical in their cast, and yet at the same time glowed with eloquence, palpitated with earnest feeling, and glittered with poetical imagery, I have again perused, and regard as admirably suited to the present generation, and especially to young men and women, as they were to the people to whom they were delivered nigh half a century ago. I cannot close this chapter better than by giving from them the following brief extracts:—

"Oh! were the sky over our heads one great whispering gallery, bringing down about us all the lamentation and woe which intemperance creates, and the firm earth one sonorous medium of sound, bringing up around us from beneath the wailings of the damned, whom the commerce in strong drink had sent thither, these tremendous realities, assailing our sense, would invigorate our conscience, and give decision to our purpose of reformation. But these evils are as real as if the stone did cry out of the wall, and the beam answered it; as real as if day and night wailings were heard in every part of the dwelling, and blood and skeletons were seen upon every wall; as real as if the ghostly forms of departed victims flitted about the ship as she passed over the billows, and showed themselves nightly about stores and distilleries, and with unearthly voices screamed in our ears their loud lament. They are as real as if the sky over our heads collected and brought down about us all the notes of sorrow in the land, and the firm earth should open a passage for the wailings of despair to come up from beneath." . . .

"The science of self-government is the science of perfect government, which we have yet to learn and teach, or this nation and the world must be governed by force. But we have all the means, and none of the impediments, which hinder the experiment amid the dynasties and feudal despotisms of Europe. And what has been done, justifies the expectation that all which yet remains to be done will be accomplished. The abolition of the slave trade, an event now almost accomplished, was once regarded as a chimera of bene-volent dreaming. But the band of Christian heroes, who consecrated their lives to the work, may some of them survive to behold it achieved. This greatest of evils upon earth, this stigma of human nature, wide-spread, deep-rooted, and intrenched by interest and state policy, is passing away before the unbending requisitions of an enlightened public opinion.   •

"No great melioration of the human condition was ever achieved without the concurrent effort of numbers; and no extended well-directed application of moral influence was ever made in vain.   Let the temperate part of the nation awake, and reform, and concentrate their influence in a course of systematic action, and success is not merely probable, but absolutely certain. And cannot this be accomplished?   Cannot the public attention be aroused, and set in array against the traffic in strong drinks, and against their use?   With just as much certainty can the public sentiment be formed and put in motion, as the waves can be moved by the breath of heaven, or the massy rock balanced on the precipice can be pushed from its centre of motion; and when the public sentiment once begins to move, its march will be as resistless as the same rock thundering down the precipice.   Let no man, then, look upon our condition as hopeless, or feel, or think, or say that nothing can be done.   The language of Heaven to our happy nation is, 'Be it unto thee even as thou wilt;' and there is no despondency more fatal, or more wicked, than that which refuses to hope, and to act, from the apprehension that nothing can be done."   .   .   .   .

"Could I call around me in one vast assembly the temperate young men of our land, I would say—Hopes of the nation, blessed be ye of the Lord now in the dew of your youth. But look well to your footsteps, for vipers and scorpions and adders surround your way; look at the generation who have just preceded you, the morning of their life was cloudless, and it dawned as brightly as your own; but behold them bitten, swollen, and enfeebled, inflamed, debauched, idle, poor, irreligious, and vicious, with halting step dragging onward to meet an early grave. Their bright prospects are clouded, and their sun is set, never to rise. No house of their own receives them, while from poorer to poorer tenements they descend, and to harder and harder fare, as improvidence dries up their resources. And now, who are those that wait on their footsteps with muffled faces and sable garments? That is a father, and that is a mother, whose grey hairs are coming with sorrow to the grave; that is a sister weeping over evils which she cannot arrest; and there is the broken-hearted wife, and there are the children, hapless innocents, for whom their father has provided the inheritance only of dishonour, and nakedness, and woe.

"And is this, beloved young men, the history of your course? In this scene of desolation, do you behold the image of your future selves? Is this the poverty and disease which as an armed man shall take hold on you? And are your fathers, and mothers, and sisters, and wives, and children, to succeed to those who now move on in this mournful procession, weeping as they go? Yes, bright as your morning now opens, and high as your hopes beat, this is your noon and your night, unless you shun those habits of intemperance which have thus early made theirs a day of clouds and of thick darkness. If you frequent places of evening resort for social drinking, if you set out with drinking daily a little, temperately, prudently, it is yourselves whom as in a glass you behold."

CHAPTER II.

SCOTLAND.

ASSOCIATION for the purpose of promoting temperance, as we have seen, was first conceived and put into execution in the United States of America, where the inhabitants have been long advanced in the knowledge that "union is power," and in the practical skill necessary for applying coalition to a variety of purposes, both national and philanthropical. It is not, however, my object, at present, to trace the progress of temperance combination in that enterprising country. In Britain many of us have hailed with delight such early moral heroes of the cause from America as Lyman Beecher, Edward C. Delevan, Wm. Lloyd Garrison, Albert Barnes, John Marsh, E. N. Kirk, Henry C. Wright, William Patton, S. H. Cox, and more recently, Henry Ward Beecher, Theodore L. Cuyler, John B. Gough, Neal Dow, and Frederick Douglass, with not a few others, whose names are cherished as household words.

JOHN DUNLOP.

From forty to fifty years ago, few names were better known in benevolent circles in Glasgow and the West of Scotland than that of John Dunlop, brother of Mr. Dunlop, the late respected M.P. for Greenock. The temperance cause soon became very popular in America; the good news reached the United Kingdom, and attracted, amongst others, the attention of John Dunlop, a distinguished Christian patriot and philanthropist. He was born at Greenock, on the 2nd of August, 1789.

Prior to 1828, Mr. Dunlop had been extensively engaged in the West of Scotland in operations connected with the religious education of the young, and the scientific instruction of artizans, besides assisting in Bible, missionary, savings bank, and other societies of a benevolent nature. He, moreover, possessed enlarged opportunities of knowing the condition of the working classes, from having acted as an elder of the Church of Scotland and a Justice of the Peace. In following out these pursuits, he became deeply impressed with the notion that the great barrier to the progress of them all lay in national intemperance. In endeavouring to establish mechanics' libraries, he found that multitudes of young men could not afford periodical subscriptions, because they had to pay so many expensive "drink-footings;" and a still larger number were more concerned in making arrangements for coming drink usages and "sprees," than desirous of profiting by reading. Drunken parents were found remiss in keeping their children at Sunday-schools. The chief desecration of the Sabbath seemed to arise from general drunkenness, subsequent to the Saturday "pay night." The drunkard had no funds for the savings bank, and instead of sending his children to school sent them to the factory.

In the spring of 1828 Mr. Dunlop made a short tour in France, and interested himself in investigating the religious and moral condition of that kingdom, and in instituting comparisons between it and Scotland. He went to the Continent at that time under a firm conviction that his native country exceeded all others, not only in religious feeling and attainment, but in external morality. Yet after a candid investigation, so far as he was able to make it, of the moral state of the French, he was, with extreme reluctance, brought to the conclusion that he had formed a wrong estimate of the comparative merits of France and Scotland as regarded morality.

MR. DUNLOP VISITS GLASGOW.

In June, 1828, Mr. Dunlop visited Glasgow, and at a meeting of the Continental Society reported on the moral state of France, and urged the necessity of steps being taken in Great Britain as to the suppression of national intemperance. At this stage, Mr. Dunlop naturally, but erroneously, supposing that every benevolent and religious person would immediately become interested in the cause, occasionally suspended his operations, and waited from time to time till those gentlemen on whom he had in different places enforced the subject should propose to make some movement, especially his friends among the ministers of the gospel, whose especial duty this seems to be.   The principal points he had to prove were, First—The actual state of the country as regards intemperance ; the augmented consumpt of intoxicating liquors; the serious evils that in consequence pervaded the whole country, and more particularly the fearfully increased inebriation of *women and children.* Second—The American operations, the method of pledging and association, and the successful results. Third—That similar measures in this country would be attended with like prosperous results.   For after much labour and pains in demonstrating the two former propositions, the greatest scepticism prevailed as to the latter; and the difference as to the respective modes of life of the British and Americans was reiterated and urged continually in bar of any proposal to attempt temperance institutions in this country.

Mr. Dunlop, towards the end of 1828, paid a second visit to Glasgow, met by appointment several gentlemen, and spent the most of a day in conference on the subject. This meeting took place at Southcroft, Rutherglen, the residence of Mr. Basil Roberton, a pious, benevolent young gentleman of great promise, from whom Mr. Dunlop expected much assistance, but who was soon after called from this to the better land.

In August, 1829, he again visited Glasgow, and spent nearly two days in calling personally on a number

of the clergymen and laymen most likely to take an interest in a united effort to suppress the ravages of strong drink. The subject was favourably entertained by some, but the majority treated it as fanciful and visionary. On the afternoon of the second day, about twenty influential gentlemen met Mr. Dunlop at the Religious Institution Rooms, and received from him a statement as to the extent of intemperance in the country, with statistical details to support it; an account of the American Temperance Societies, and a proposal for a system of similar associations and pledge to be gone into in Scotland, comprehending the rejection of all wine as well as spirits, and an abrogation of the connection between courtesy and business and intoxicating liquor, since denominated "the anti-drinking usage department." Considerable interest was excited, and the discussion lasted about two hours. The only clergyman present had, before leaving his study, very wisely, as he thought, penned a resolution, and put it into his pocket, and it is evident that although an angel had come from heaven to address the meeting he could not have altered what was written. This solitary clergyman listened to what Mr. Dunlop had to say, and at the close of the address he rose, assumed a singularly solemn appearance, took the piece of paper from his vest pocket, and began to read nearly as follows :—
"That this meeting tenders its best thanks to Mr. Dunlop for his address with reference to the sin of drunkenness, but it is the opinion of the meeting that

no Temperance Association will ever work in Scotland!"
To the honour of Glasgow the resolution met with no
seconder. It was, however, rather a damper to Mr.
Dunlop, who thought to himself, " Well, if that is not
an extinguisher, it is something like it."

After a considerable pause, during which great
solemnity pervaded the meeting, Mr. William Collins,
the Glasgow publisher, prompted unquestionably by
the Great Mover of all, rose, and with considerable
emotion stated that the painful subject of intemperance
had occupied his mind for several years; that he had
had his attention strongly drawn to it in the district
he had charge of as an elder of the Church of Scotland,
and coadjutor with Dr. Chalmers, while he was a
minister in Glasgow; that the hopeless consideration
of the mournful case had not unfrequently kept him
from sleep during the night; that *now* he saw for the
first time, like a ray of light, that which by the Divine
blessing might lead to better things; and that he for
one should do every thing in his power to prevent the
reverend gentleman's resolution from taking effect.

These well-timed remarks of Mr. Collins produced
a deep impression. Other gentlemen followed, who
spoke strongly in favour of something being done, and
through this energetic interposition the meeting was
not allowed to disperse until Mr. Dunlop was requested,
on the motion of Mr. Collins, to continue his investi-
gations, and report to an adjourned meeting, to be
held a few weeks afterwards, in Glasgow.

MR. DUNLOP'S FIRST TEMPERANCE LECTURE.

John Dunlop having prepared his first lecture, on "The Extent and Remedy of National Intemperance," visited Glasgow for the fourth time in September, 1829, and found many individuals ready with flimsy objections, but very few willing to co-operate with him. It is somewhat startling, but nevertheless true, that no church or chapel in Glasgow would be granted to Mr. Dunlop for the delivery of his first temperance lecture! At length the amiable and accomplished Professor Dick, D.D., of the Secession, now the United Presbyterian Church, gave the use of his Divinity-hall, merely on the score of old acquaintanceship.

On a Saturday evening, Mr. Dunlop and a friend were busy writing notes to about forty ministers, requesting each of them to announce the lecture for the following Monday evening. A city porter was sent for to deliver the cards, but on presenting himself it was observed that the fellow was *drunk*. An intoxicated messenger to carry temperance notices! The thing was out of the question, and he was at once dismissed. Another porter was soon engaged,—"a clean, sleek, Methodist-looking person" (quoting Mr. Dunlop's own words); "his hair combed straight down his forehead, as sober as a judge, with a bright brass plate on his coat. As we had not quite finished writing, he happened to hear part of our conversation, and with

C

some interest modestly asked if we were taking measures about the introduction of temperance societies? If so, it would be one of the greatest blessings to the individuals who followed his occupation. A brother in America had written to him on the subject. This note was on the right chord. The voice of encouragement was new. In the midst of appalling and nearly universal opposition, this little adventure was a great comfort to us; and the worthy porter was so delighted with our business, that it was with difficulty we could persuade him to accept of one-half the usual fare."

With the exception of Dr. Wardlaw, and a few others, the majority of the clergy did not read the intimation, thinking the matter utterly vain and foolish. One divine had afterwards the candour to acknowledge to Mr. Dunlop, that when reading the announcement in one of the then most fashionable city churches, he had fixed his eyes doggedly on the paper, looking neither to the right nor left, lest he might be drawn to laugh outright, in case any of the audience should show symptoms of risibility! Thank God, that hardly such a minister would be found in any religious denomination at the present day! In proof of this, the noble utterances at many of the great May anniversaries in Exeter Hall need only be referred to; and none more appropriate than that of an esteemed President of the Wesleyan Conference, himself an abstainer, when he alluded in dignified yet reproving terms to ministers who fancied they could not preach two sermons on a Sunday without resorting to stimulants.

On the Monday evening Mr. Dunlop proceeded with "fear and trembling" to the lecture-room, and the first sight that met him at the door was half a dozen divinity students jocularly engaged in discussing the topic of discourse. The place was filled, and the lecturer's terse, thrilling statements rivetted the attention of all present. It was announced at the close that Mr. Dunlop would be in waiting at the Religious Institution Rooms, from ten to four o'clock on the following day, to answer questions and afford information. A few gentlemen from Glasgow, Paisley, &c., attended—among others, Patrick Letham, "the Gaius of Glasgow." A kind message was also received from the divinity students referred to, giving in their adherence, and offering to become members whenever a Temperance Society was formed.

MR. DUNLOP AND THE DIVINITY STUDENTS.

I have been favoured with the following interesting letter, dated May 28, 1873, from the Rev. James Towers, United Presbyterian Church, Birkenhead, one of the few survivors of those who had the privilege of listening to Mr. Dunlop's first lecture on the subject of temperance:—

My Dear Sir,—I have a pretty vivid recollection of the meeting which Mr. John Dunlop addressed in

Dr. Dick's Hall, in 1829. How the meeting was
announced I cannot remember, but somehow I was
anxious to hear the subject discussed, and went. The
room was respectably filled by a somewhat select
audience, and amongst others the Rev. Dr. Beattie was
there. Of my fellow-students I cannot recall one who
accompanied me, but I learned at the Synod this year
that the Rev. Dr. MacGill, our Foreign Secretary,
was present. Mr. Dunlop's facts and proposals seemed
to take all of us by surprise. We had all seen drunkenness, but, as he told us, we had laughed at it, instead
of laying it to heart. We knew that it wrought ruin
to multitudes, both in our churches and outside, but
we had not reflected that the usages of society, in connection at once with things secular and things sacred,
were insidiously producing the appetite, and begetting
the habits which entailed that ruin. Therefore, whisky
being *the* drink of the Scotch, he urged abstinence from
strong drink. From what I heard on retiring, and
from the fact of Dr. Beattie and others joining the
Society soon after, I am warranted in saying that many
left that meeting thoroughly persuaded that action
must be taken against this national vice, and admit-
ting that the pledge plan was excellent, if only it were
practicable. For myself, I determined to try abstinence, and became an *un*pledged abstainer, continuing
thus for about three months amid sneers and ridicule.
I was then invited, along with Mr. Middlemas, a
highly-respectable teacher in Glasgow, to dine with a

gentleman in the suburbs.   After dinner a tumbler was planted before each gentleman, that he might make toddy for himself and a lady.   I begged to be excused.   "What!" said the gentleman, "have you joined the Temperance Society?"   "No," I replied, "but I am an abstainer."   "Nonsense!" said the gentleman, "you cannot refuse to make toddy for a young lady."   When I tell you, my dear Sir, that I was then young—that I never had been in this house before—that in abstaining I was acting in opposition to the polite usages of society, and that an agreeable young lady was thrown into the balance in favour of the toddy, you will not greatly marvel that I made it, and shared it with my lady friend.   But there and then I resolved that, since by joining a society I might not only do good to others, but shield myself from the appearance of rudeness at a dinner table, I should be able to say, "I am a pledged abstainer."   Mr. Dunlop's lecture, therefore, led to my abstinence, and has had an influence on my practical every-day life from the hour I heard it to this day, although I never had the pleasure, so far as I remember, of meeting him in private.   We greatly err if we suppose that our lives affect only those who declare it in word or letter.

I need not tell you how, after a few years, it was discovered that abstinence from merely spirituous liquors was utterly inefficient to cure us of intemperance; nor how many even of our ministers, when total abstinence was adopted, went back and walked no more with us.   From the time I heard Mr. Dunlop, and especially when I listened to the comments made by the poorer classes on the professed self-denial of abandoning whisky while indulging wine-bibbing, the entire renunciation of all drinks which intoxicate as beverages seemed to be imperative.   And now when, after an agitation of forty years, the revenue reports disclose the tale of an additional five millions expended on drink—when drink starves children and murders wives, hinders education, opposes our Bible women and home missionaries' work—when drink is sent to our mission stations and makes poor heathens tenfold more the children of the devil than before—when it intrudes into pews and pulpits, and the preacher and the people fall before it, I ask all Christian men is not abstinence demanded?   If some brethren tell me it is not possible in their case, let me suggest that perhaps for Christ's sake and humanity's it might be.   Even an invalid has no excuse for *social* drinking.   I desire to judge no man—to his own master he standeth or falleth.   But since drinking usages are so fatal a stumbling-block, we may judge with Paul, that no man put such stumbling-block and occasion to fall in his brother's way.—I am, my dear Sir, yours very sincerely,

JAMES TOWERS.

A writer in one of the Glasgow newspapers refers in the following friendly terms to this first lecture of Mr. Dunlop—

"This introduces us to a topic to which we gladly advert, on account of its own individual importance —a topic to which allusion was made in one of your late numbers, in reference to the lecture of John Dunlop, Esquire. This respectable gentleman has the merit of bringing before us a subject of vast magnitude and importance, and we cannot help declaring the very great satisfaction we felt, in common with many others, in his excellent lecture on temperance. So many striking facts were detailed; in so affecting a manner did he describe the present crisis, in relation to the crime of intoxication; so rationally and temperately did he exhibit his plans, and he displayed, withal, so much dignified humanity, with so much modesty and Christian feeling, that few, we believe, left the meeting without an attachment to the speaker and a lively interest in the subject of the discussion."

The view which Mr. Dunlop took of the proper method of starting temperance associations in Scotland was, that it should be first considered and agreed upon by a number of influential individuals throughout the country; that, as a trial, a society should be established in Glasgow, to become the centre of operations for the West of Scotland, and that other large cities should follow in succession. Notwithstanding all his importunity, however, he found that the friends in Glasgow would not go forward, nor enter into such serious arrangements as temperance pledge and association implied, till they had a proof of the capability of the principle being worked on a smaller scale, and the real worth of the system demonstrated by positive existing examples.   Accordingly he was forced to retire upon his native town of Greenock, consisting then of about 30,000 inhabitants, to make the experiment there, for the grand objection among real friends now shaped itself into a doubt whether the same institution which had succeeded in America would be found suitable also for British society.

CHAPTER III.

FORMATION OF THE FIRST TEMPERANCE SOCIETY IN SCOTLAND.

T appears that the first Temperance Society in Scotland was established at Maryhill, near Glasgow, on the 1st of October, 1829, by Miss Graham and Miss Allan—two benevolent ladies who were ready to aid Mr. Dunlop in his efforts to elevate the inhabitants of Maryhill, where his family had long been "Superiors of the Manor." On the 5th of the same month Mr. Dunlop was instrumental in starting a Temperance Society in Greenock. He was convinced, from the outset of his benevolent mission, of the importance of the principle of abstinence from *all* intoxicating drinks, but finding many objections to united temperance action in any form, and knowing, moreover, that ale and porter were at that period but little used in Scotland, among the working classes especially, he did not insist on their being introduced into the Scottish pledge of 1829. For the accuracy of this I can vouch, as I oftener than once conversed with him pointedly on the subject.

In an important letter to a friend, forty-five years ago, Mr. Dunlop observes—"On the 5th of

October, 1829, after previous arrangements and prayer, I opened the temperance engagement book at Greenock (the pledge excluding all wines, as well as spirits). The society at Maryhill had been formed by two female friends some days before; and the two societies beginning immediately to flourish and do extraordinary good, proved the means, under Providence, of showing to the gentlemen now interested, in Glasgow and elsewhere, that there was a possibility of the plan succeeding if persevered in.

"About the middle of October, 1829, having received an invitation from Henry Wight, advocate [a zealous friend of Teetotalism, and latterly a preacher of the Gospel], and Alexander Cruickshanks [an influential member of the Society of Friends], for themselves, and on behalf of other gentlemen in Edinburgh, I went thither, residing with Mr. Wight. I held various conferences in different parts of the city, and, in a day or two, a select meeting of influential gentlemen, ministers, lawyers, and others, assembled at Mr. Wight's house. They seemed all deeply impressed with the subject of the general intemperance of the people, but could not make up their minds as to any sacrifice on their own part. The idea of giving up wine seemed quite inadmissible, and, on the whole, they appeared desirous of holding off till they saw how the system should work in the West of Scotland. Messrs. Wight, Cruickshanks, and some others, however, stood staunch. In the meantime the subject blazed abroad and became the sport of every table. All my own personal friends either stood aloof or condemned the business in unqualified terms. A person of the same condition and influence, of the same name, took pains to let it be known that it was not *he* that had astonished the public with this inconceivable folly! . . . The lecture was delivered next day. Some thought one thing of it, and some another : that wine must be excluded from any pledge, as well as whisky ; or that it was right, but would not work. All the friends, however, felt that something must be done. I was to breakfast on the morning after the lecture with Mr. Cruickshanks, who lived two miles distant. I was now quite in an unhinged state ; my nervous complaints, from over-anxiety, having supervened with greater influence. In proceeding along the streets in Edinburgh, the sight of a drunken man set me to bitter weeping. I was reluctant to be seen wailing in the open thoroughfare, and by strong exertion restrained the channels of grief while any people were passing ; but when I saw a hundred yards or two clear, I suffered the floodgates of the fountains to open up, and might have been one of the party who went up Mount Olivet with the King of Israel, having the head covered and the feet bare, recorded in 2 Samuel xv. 30."

The subject of temperance confederacy now fairly took wing; it was noticed by the press, and became the topic at all tables, and also in workshops, not only in Glasgow, but throughout the country. It was contemned and reviled in all the methods which ignorance, ill-nature, conviction, and startled conscience could supply; and though consigned to utter scorn by all parties, and its death-warrant signed a thousand times, still the people spake, debated, and commented upon it, and seemed fascinated to the hated topic as if by a kind of spell.

MR. DUNLOP VISITS ROCHDALE.

John Dunlop visited Rochdale in 1847, for the purpose of directing public attention to two of his favourite and very important branches of the temperance enterprise,—the "compulsory drinking usages," especially amongst working men, and the getting up of the Temperance Medical Certificate. On this occasion a meeting was held in the Public Hall, when the chair was occupied by Mr. Oliver Ormerod. Mr. Jacob Bright, now M.P. for Manchester, Mr. Dunlop, and others took part in the proceedings. The chairman had been identified with the movement from its commencement, and had the honour of accompanying Mr. (now the Right Honourable) John Bright, M.P., to a village in the neighbourhood of Rochdale, where the distinguished statesman first spoke in public on the temperance question, and where he was not so highly favoured with that fluency of speech which he now so richly possesses. Mr. Ormerod had also associated with Edgar of Belfast, Livesey of Preston, Henry Anderton, a well-known temperance poet, and other early heroes of the cause. He had heard that valiant temperance advocate, Cruikshank, the Dundee carter, in York, in 1831, and afterwards arranged for him to come and assist in forming the Rochdale Society.

The following is a copy of the medical certificate, to which Mr. Dunlop, with the assistance of fellow-labourers, obtained the signatures of about 2,000 physicians and surgeons, including the first medical authorities throughout England, Ireland, and Scotland :—

"We, the undersigned, are of opinion,

"1. That a very large portion of human misery, including poverty, disease, and crime, is induced by the use of alcoholic or fermented liquors as beverages.

"2. That the most perfect health is compatible with total abstinence from all such intoxicating beverages, whether in the form of ardent spirits, or as wine, beer, ale, porter, cider, etc.

"3. That persons accustomed to such drinks may, with perfect safety, discontinue them entirely, either at once or gradually after a short time.

"4. That total and universal abstinence from alcoholic liquors and intoxicating beverages of all sorts, would greatly contribute to the health, the prosperity, the morality, and the happiness of the human race."

In the course of a long and interesting interview which I had with Mr. Dunlop at Rochdale, the veteran moral reformer referred to a number of the formidable and almost insurmountable difficulties with which he had, single-handed, to grapple in the earlier stages of the movement. On that occasion I have a distinct recollection of his starting to his feet, raising his right arm, and exclaiming, with intense earnestness and deep emotion, "No person can have an adequate idea of the difficulties I had to encounter in the outset of this temperance movement. I felt at times as if I would have to abandon it in despair; everything seemed against me."

Fifteen years ago Mr. Dunlop presented me with a favourite copy of that interesting little volume, "The Gloaming of Life," a memoir of James Stirling, from the pen of the Rev. Dr. Alexander Wallace, Glasgow, at page 79 of which occurs the following striking paragraph—

"If ever," says Stirling's wife, addressing her husband, "a poor woman on earth got her prayers answered, I have got mine. When you used to be drinking, I used to be praying that God would stir up some good men to unite together, and try to put the evil down. Many are now engaged in the work; and, thank God, you amongst the rest. May He grant you a speedy victory."

Mr. Dunlop having underlined this passage with his own pen, had written on the margin of the volume the following suggestive, impressive, and, to the sincere follower of Christ, cheering words— "Few things have ever struck me so forcibly as the prayer here mentioned. At the outset of the Temperance Reformation, we were so opposed by rich and poor, religious and irreligious, spoken against, preached against, that we knew not where to turn. Some of our converts were dismissed from workshops—all conspired against and persecuted by the drink laws. We often thought of abandoning; but a strange, unaccountable, inward persuasion kept us to our task. We seemed not to be capable of giving up! Perhaps the source of our resolute advance lay in the prayers of this woman and such like. I was astonished when I first read this passage; it accounted for an apparently mysterious circumstance."

Mr. Dunlop had a deep and an abiding sense of the indebtedness of the temperance cause for its success to prayer, and the necessity of continuing to make it the subject of fervent supplication to God. When he had failed at an early stage of the temperance reformation in an attempt to form stated prayer-meetings for its advancement, he prevailed upon a number of private Christian friends throughout Scotland to make it the subject of secret petition at "the throne of grace" every evening at ten o'clock. This practice continued with some for a considerable time, and might still be profitably attended to by the friends of the cause, not only in the United Kingdom, but throughout the world. On this and kindred great questions pertaining to the present and eternal welfare of the human family, Christ still says to his followers, "Hitherto have ye asked nothing in my name: ask, and ye shall receive, that your joy may be full."

MR. DUNLOP REMOVES TO LONDON.

Mr. Dunlop having been led by Providence, as we have seen, to interest himself in the subject of British intemperance, and submit a plan of associated effort for its suppression, set the machine in motion, and devoted his whole time and labour and his moderate fortune, without reserve, to this admittedly momentous object.

In 1838 he changed his residence to London, in order that he might occupy a more central position for assistance and guidance in temperance operations. He continued absorbed in this work for thirty years, but in 1859 he was brought to a pause by increasing years and infirmities, and laid aside from further active service.

In August, 1862, in company with my friend Robert Rae, London, to whom the cause has long been greatly indebted, I visited Mr. Dunlop at his residence, Priory Road, London. We found the good man feeble in health, but as deeply and enthusiastically interested in the sacred cause of temperance as ever. He felt anxious to hear of the meetings of the Temperance Congress, which were then being held at Exeter Hall. On parting, he expressed his unwavering faith in the steady progress, and ultimate and complete triumph, of the temperance reformation. Standing in the doorway, and holding his two friends, one in each hand, the venerable Christian said, whilst his lips quivered with emotion, "Convey my warmest wishes to all my old friends and fellow-workers. Let us labour on, have faith in God, and pray earnestly for his blessing, and our children shall see the blessed results, if we do not.—Farewell."

Mr. Dunlop presided for many years over the principal total abstinence society or Union in London, and occupied the chair at other meetings throughout the city, but in no respect did he confine his labours to the metropolis. He went about in every direction, exercising a friendly influence over the societies in England and Scotland, and making for years regular journeys for that purpose to most of the large and middle-sized towns, as well as to many villages, in the kingdom, in all of which he was welcomed with great cordiality, and listened to with interest and attention. His correspondence was necessarily voluminous and extensive; most of the day and, on occasions of emergency, part of the night were thus occupied for lengthened periods of time.

Mr. Dunlop's writings on subjects connected with temperance were copious and continuous. He was a frequent contributor to newspapers and periodicals. The following are some of his separate works:—*National Temperance*, published 1829; *French and Scotch Morality Compared*, 1829; *Brandied Wine System of Great Britain*, 1832; *Essay on the Compulsory Drinking Usages of Great Britain*, 1850, 7th Edition; *Temperance Emigrants* (a Tale); *Semi-Antinomianism of British Churches*, 1846. He also wrote on National Education, Educational Parliamentary Suffrage, Sanitary Reform, the Philosophy of Human Association, and other topics. In 1863 he wrote a valuable and interesting paper, entitled, "The Moral History of Greenock," which was amongst the last from his useful pen.

MR. DUNLOP ON LEGISLATION.

Before closing this chapter, I shall quote a letter which I received from Mr. Dunlop in April, 1862, and in which he gave expression to the opinions he then held on the question of legislation. He said—

Dear Sir,—You ask my opinion of the present state of our temperance movement, which seems to consist of—

1. Associated exertion, in the way of moral suasion and abstinence, commenced in 1829, and advanced up to teetotalism in 1832; and

2. Associated appeal to the Legislature for prohibitory enactments, commenced in 1853—members, in the last, not being necessarily abstainers.

From the beginning of the movement, in 1829, I

have always had the hope of these two objects being conjoined. Because, although moral suasion may reach and influence the intelligent, the prudent, and the benevolent, yet in every community (that ever I met with) there exists always a great mass of *inertia*, stupidity, and brutish appetite, which will yield to nothing short of legal force. It becomes, therefore, necessarily part and parcel of temperance work, to prepare the minds of legislators and constituencies for direct enactment, and the minds of the public to submit to salutary restriction.

At a certain stage of this preparation, the point will be arrived at when enactment may, with safety and effect, be introduced. Near the middle of last century our Parliament made certain demonstrations of a prohibitory character; but the public not having been prepared by temperance organization and indoctrination, made such an outcry as to force Parliament to retrace its steps and rescind its statutes.

A Maine-law in all its wholesome rigour, laid on Great Britain at this moment (if it were possible such an enactment should pass the Houses), would have to be repealed in a few months; and Parliament must judge of the state of the public mind in this matter before even granting a permissive law.

The question, therefore, with such as me, is not so much whether a permissive Maine-law would be useful, as, how are we to prepare Government to enact it, and the country to submit to it?

There may be a danger in going to Parliament too soon, in which case the effort would be abortive—a mischance, always, if possible, to be avoided. At the same time it may be said, on the other side, we must commence proceedings towards prohibition at some period, and why not now, as there have been nearly thirty years of preparation by moral suasion?

He who demands a Maine-law, demands what would virtually force the commonalty to give up drinking intoxicating liquor altogether. But members of the "Alliance," who are not total abstainers, are not consistent here. And it may be asked whether, when any day of real contest comes, can these be relied on. Gentlemen, moreover, forget that, while they do not encourage abstinence by their example, they merely make it more difficult for the peasantry to enter upon the necessary course of denial. They thus try to raise up prohibition with the one hand, while by their example they keep up the old bulwarks of strong drink with the other.

If these views be correct, exertion towards abstinence, by moral suasion, is the generating power that is to produce, and also to maintain, prohibitory enactments; and to let the old teetotal societies go down now, would just deprive our present Maine-law attempt of all its peculiar and real nourishment.

On the other hand, there is something attractive to a band of earnest-minded men, to have an object for them to attain, of a fixed, tangible, and hopeful character, to be won by bold exertion, and where success would prove an extensive and glorious triumph. And I presume that the Maine-law agitation has introduced a great amount of energy and talent throughout the kingdom into measures favourable to general temperance.

In prosecuting the main point, how shall the nation be prepared for prohibitory enactments? I still persist in conceiving that the committees throughout the empire have, all of them, as yet greatly failed in never providing a regular systematic machinery for suppressing the fines, footings and other artificial and compulsory drink usuages. The senators of the land know nothing on this part of the subject at all; and ministers, magistrates, and other influential men rest equally ignorant. From my latest inquiries, I judge that three-fourths of these fatal drink laws are still in destructive operation.

I have a similar complaint to make in regard to the medical department. Not two dozen of our senators are conversant about the physiology of the case. How can these be expected to grant a Maine-law, when an enormous majority of them drink their little dose of poison daily as a necessary of life.

Since I met you at Rochdale, some years ago, little has been done by the committees in this department. A few individual medical authors have nobly assisted; but all procuring of useful medical certificates, in local districts, or indoctrinating the commonalty in the true laws of health and fullest physical enjoyment, has been long since suspended.

If those who demand an immediate Maine-law were to receive a check in approaching Parliament, it might perhaps lead them to investigate the roots of the matter, and to adopt more fundamental operations than mere petitioning an unprepared Legislature, and a species of surface agitation,—efforts which might easily be joined in by crowds of persons who would give no essential assistance by their own self-sacrifice to that state of national adaptation which is clearly a prerequisite for any effective prohibitory law.—Dear Sir, yours truly,   JOHN DUNLOP.

During Mr. Dunlop's somewhat lingering illness, his son sent a note to Mr. Robert Rae, from which I quote the following closing words—"My father is now quite unable to see his friends, even should they do him the favour to call, but he begged of me to tell you this,— 'To ask an interest in your prayers.' " On the morning of Saturday, the 12th December, 1868, this Christian patriot and philanthropist, having entered on his eightieth year, " after he had served his own generation by the will of God, fell on sleep." There have been few more active, disinterested, unwearied, and successful workers in public affairs in Great Britain, or in Europe, than John Dunlop. His name will be long an honoured and fondly-cherished household word, not only in Scotland, but far beyond it.

CHAPTER IV.

IRELAND.

IN 1829 the American plan of temperance association was introduced, as we have seen, into Scotland by Mr. John Dunlop, and in the same year into Ireland by Professor Edgar, D.D., of the Royal College, Belfast, and the Rev. G. W. Carr, who seemed to have acted in entire ignorance of each other's movements.

My friend, Mr. David Fortune, Secretary to the Irish Temperance League, Belfast, has sent me the following communication, dated Belfast, June 2, 1873, relative to the origin of temperance agitation in Ireland:—

The facts regarding the early history of the temperance movement in Ireland are briefly as follow:—In July, 1829,* a public meeting was held in Belfast to devise ways and means for preventing the profanation of the Sabbath; and, in order to this, for preventing on that day the sale and use of ardent liquors. Some present advocated an

---

* Although from this it would appear that the Temperance agitation in Ireland began in 1829, still it is on record, as will be seen in a subsequent chapter, that an Abstinence Society was formed at Skibbereen as early as 1817.

agitation to secure a Public-House Sunday-Closing Act (such as Scotland has for the last twenty years been blessed with), while others were more reliant on moral effort.   Amongst the latter was Professor Edgar.   He was appointed to prepare an address to the public on the subject.   While engaged at this he was visited by an old friend, the Rev. Joseph Penney, an Irish Presbyterian, who had emigrated to America, and had returned at this time with glowing accounts of the organization and success of the Temperance Reformation in the United States, and full of zeal for the establishment of temperance societies in his native country.   Professor Edgar was deeply impressed with his reports and arguments, and entered promptly and heartily into the cause.   He inaugurated his splendid temperance career by opening his parlour window, and pouring out, into the court before his house, the remaining part of a gallon of old malt whisky, purchased some time before for family consumption.   A few days after this decisive act, he prepared the appeal to the public (the first appeal on the temperance question to the Christians of Europe), and requested its insertion in two local papers, the *Guardian* and *News Letter*.   The editor of the former flatly refused to insert it, assigning as his reason that he considered the writer demented!   It was, however, accepted by the proprietor of the *News Letter* (a shrewd Scotchman), and inserted in that journal of date 14th August, 1829.   It is impossible to describe the excitement which the letter produced, not only in Belfast but throughout the kingdom, as a number of newspapers copied it from the *News Letter.* This was followed by another letter, even more decided in its tone, which appeared in the *News Letter* of the 4th and 11th September. An important fact is noted in the postscript to this letter. Dr. Edgar remarks— "I have most satisfactory evidence already that the appeal to the public on the subject of temperance has not been made in vain. Accounts from different parts of the country assure me 'that the cause has only to be presented, and it meets the approbation of the benevolent and the wise.' A most interesting communication has been sent to me by Rev. George Whitmore Carr, of New Ross, giving an account of the formation of a Temperance Society in that town last week, under the most auspicious circumstances." A letter of Mr. Carr, dated 4th December, 1829, says—"On the *20th of August* last, the New Ross Temperance Society was established at a full meeting, held in the Quakers or Friends' Meeting House."

On the 24th of September, 1829, I find that a select meeting was held in the Belfast Religious Tract Depository, at which the Ulster Temperance Society was formed. Professor Edgar, Rev. Mr. (now Dr.) Morgan, Rev. Thomas Hincks (curate of Belfast), Rev. M. Tobias, of the Wesleyan Church, Belfast, and Rev. Thomas (now Professor) Houston, of the Reformed Presbyterian Church, Knockbracken, were the first to subscribe to the pledge of the new society, and all rendered important service to the cause. Drs. Morgan and Houston are still recognised as amongst the most influential temperance divines in Ulster. In October, 1829, Professor Edgar delivered his first temperance sermon, in the Methodist Chapel, Donegall Square, Belfast. The second of the series was preached by the Rev. Dr. Morgan.

Before the end of the year Professor Edgar was able to report that the cause was extending rapidly in Ireland, and that from different parts of Scotland and England he had very cheering intelligence. Twenty-five societies, containing 800 members, had been established in Ireland in four months, and early in 1833 upwards of 150 societies were instituted in the province of Ulster alone, containing 15,000 members.

I presume you have the details of the Herculean labours of the father of Irish Temperance Societies, already embodied in your sketch—details of his energetic prosecution of the great cause by writing, preaching, speech-making, and organizing societies in Ireland and elsewhere—during twelve of the most active years of his life. It has been well remarked that "Wesley himself, in his best days, scarcely laboured more vigorously than did Dr. Edgar during this part of his temperance career." And although he did not appreciate the *total* abstinence movement so freely and fully as could have been desired, yet this brave apostle of temperance served his generation with marked faithfulness, and has left behind him an honoured name—not because he was a highly-gifted orator, or a profound theologian, or a scholar of unrivalled excellence—but because he diligently improved the opportunities of usefulness presented to him, and was instant in season and out of season in doing good—because he laboured fearlessly and perseveringly for the overthrow of intemperance and the regeneration of his drink cursed country.

The career of this good and truly great man closed in the home of a loving friend, Mr. Hugh Moore, Rathgar, on the forenoon of Sabbath, 26th of August, 1866. Not only in the Church—whose Professorial Chair he had for nearly forty years adorned, and whose schemes he had promoted with unequalled success—but in almost every field of philanthropy and Christian enterprise, his noble and influential presence was deeply missed. His funeral, which took place on the 29th of August, was attended by a vast concourse of people, including professors, ministers, magistrates, bankers, merchants, and other prominent citizens of the commercial metropolis of Ireland. Rich and poor alike mourned his loss, as that of a personal friend, and one of the greatest benefactors of his country. At its first meeting after, the General Assembly of the Irish Presbyterian Church passed a special minute, expressing its profound sorrow at the death of its gifted professor, and its tender sympathy with his bereaved widow and family.

Dr. Edgar was buried in the Malone Cemetery, about three miles from Belfast, and a monument of chaste design marks the spot where the remains of this eminent Christian philanthropist now rest in peace. It bears the following simple inscription :—

JOHN EDGAR, D.D.
DIED AUGUST 26, 1866.   AGED 68 YEARS.
FOUNDER OF THE TEMPERANCE REFORMATION.
" The memory of the just is blessed."

Since Mr. Fortune's letter was in type, death has removed the Rev. Dr. Morgan, Belfast, who, from the day in which, with Edgar and Hincks, the old temperance society platform was erected, until the close of his ministry, ever remained steadfast and consistent in his advocacy of the temperance cause. At a meeting of the Directors of the Irish Temperance League, held in Belfast on the 9th of August, 1873—Dr. Murtry presiding—the following resolution was adopted :—

"That this Committee desire to record their deep sense of the loss sustained by the Temperance movement and the Irish Temperance League by the death of the Rev. James Morgan, D.D. Almost from its institution he proved himself a staunch and most devoted friend and supporter of the League, and was long recognised as one of its most influential vice-presidents. He took a warm interest in all its movements, and from year to year enriched the pages of the *Journal* with valuable contributions in advocacy of the principles of total abstinence and prohibition, and in hearty appreciation of the progress of the cause with which, from its earliest history, he had been so honourably identified. His distinguished piety, his eminent services to the Church, his unwearied interest in various schemes of practical benevolence and philanthropy, and his ardent attachment to the temperance movement, endeared him to all who had the privilege of knowing him; and this committee feel that they have to mourn not only a friend and supporter, but a truly great and good man. They desire further to record their profound sympathy with his sorrowing wife and family in their great bereavement."

CHAPTER V.

WILLIAM COLLINS.

WILLIAM COLLINS, the well-known Glasgow bookseller and publisher, was born at Eastwood, on the 12th of October, 1789, and died on the 2nd of January, 1853. The Rev. Dr. Robert Buchanan, of the Free College Church, Glasgow, in an appropriate discourse preached on the occasion of the death of Mr. Collins, entitled " The memory of the just is blessed," thus writes—"That intense desire to do good to others, which was the prominent characteristic of his after life, began very soon to show itself. Having obtained a situation in a large factory at Pollokshaws (near Glasgow), in which many young persons were employed, and where education, both secular and religious, had been much neglected, he addressed himself immediately to the task of their intellectual and spiritual improvement. By week-day, evening, and Sabbath schools, conducted chiefly by himself, a reformation was ere long produced, so great and so manifest that workers from that establishment were held to possess a recommendation in the very fact of their belonging to it. When about 24 years of age he came to Glasgow, and within little more than twelve months thereafter was ordained an elder in the Tron Church.

From the day when Dr. Chalmers succeeded Dr. Macgill in the Tron Church, in 1815, Mr. Collins was ever foremost in carrying out the plans of that greatest reformer and evangelist of modern times. It was Mr. Collins who opened the first Sabbath school conducted on that local system which Dr. Chalmers originated, and which has since spread over the whole city. When Dr. Chalmers removed, in 1819, to St. John's parish, he was followed into that new field of labour by his faithful elder."

And here, in passing, I may refer to the illustrious Chalmers and the temperance movement. Shortly before the Doctor's lamented death, in 1847, the Rev. William Reid, Edinburgh—an old, zealous, and useful friend of the cause—had several interviews with him on the subject of temperance. Mr. Reid refers as follows to one of these visits, in the *Scottish Temperance Review* for July, 1847—"'So much am I impressed,' said Chalmers, 'with the importance of what you say, that I think I shall make my next quarterly address to the West Port folks on the temperance question;' and then," says Mr. Reid, "with one of those peculiar flourishes of the left hand which all who have heard Dr. Chalmers must remember, he exclaimed, with an energy that would have electrified an audience of ten thousand people, 'The Temperance cause I regard with the most benignant complacency; and those who stand up in their pulpits and denounce it I regard as a set of *theological greybeards!'"*—a large jar still too often used in Scotland for holding intoxicating liquors.

The name of William Collins is the first on the long and honoured list of male members, numbering 4,568 in the original roll-book, which I have examined, of the "Glasgow and West of Scotland Temperance Society," dated 1829. In close proximity to the name of Collins stands that of another genuine, unassuming friend, to whom the cause has been much indebted, "George Gallie, 48 Glassford Street," now of the well-known bookshop in Buchanan Street. The latter part of the same roll-book is occupied with the names of the female members of the society, numbering 2,918. The first two names in this list are those of Miss Graham and Miss Allan, the benevolent ladies who co-operated with Mr. Dunlop in commencing the first Temperance Society in Scotland, at Maryhill, near Glasgow, on the 1st of October, 1829. The first page of the same book contains the names of Mrs. William Collins, Mrs. William Wardlaw, Mrs. Patrick Letham, with those of other Christian female worthies, whose good deeds amongst the poor are still gratefully remembered in Glasgow. It is pleasant thus to note the early interest that women took in this great and blessed temperance movement. Since then the cause has been greatly indebted to them, and they in return, in various ways, owe not a little to it. Their quiet, unostentatious, and very valuable services were never more needed than at the present day. May the Lord enable them faithfully to follow in the footsteps of those who "stood by the cross of Jesus," and who came "early, when it was yet dark, unto the sepulchre!"

FIRST ANNUAL MEETING.

The first annual meeting of the "Glasgow and West of Scotland Temperance Society" was held on Monday, the 20th of December, 1830, in the late Rev. Dr. William Anderson's Church, John Street, at one p.m., and continued, by adjournment, at seven in the evening; the committee having previously held a meeting in the morning for prayer, to implore the Divine blessing on the day's proceedings. The meetings were enthusiastic and deeply interesting. The chair was occupied by William Collins, one of the vice-presidents, and the following took part in the proceedings:—Rev. Dr. Hamilton, Strathblane (father of the late Rev. Dr. James Hamilton, London); Rev. Dr. Baird, Paisley; Rev. Dr. Burns, Kilsyth (father of the late Dr. Islay Burns, Free Church College, Glasgow); Rev. Dr. William Anderson, Messrs. Robert Kettle, Patrick Letham, Treasurers; William Wardlaw, Charles Ritchie, M.D., John Kerr, Secretaries, Glasgow, &c.; all of whom, with one or two exceptions, have been called from earth to heaven.

"On the 12th of November, 1829," says the Report, "after repeated discussions, a constitution was drawn up at Glasgow, and signed by one of the secretaries and nine individuals; and thus the basis was laid of the Glasgow and West of Scotland Temperance Society. One of the earliest measures pursued by the committee after their appointment was to diffuse as widely as possible, by means of the press, information respecting the principles and objects of temperance societies. And here they consider themselves called upon to express, in the strongest manner, the obligations under which they lie to Mr. Collins for his unwearied and disinterested exertions in distributing the publications issued by the Society; and for having allowed them for so long a period, without any remuneration whatever, the use of his premises as a depository, and the assistance of his own invaluable personal services. They consider that the cause of Temperance in Scotland owes much of its present prosperity to the entire devotedness of heart with which he has sought its advancement, and to the numberless channels which he has opened up in all parts of the country for the circulation of the Society's publications." The total number of temperance tracts and larger publications issued in Scotland during 1830 was considerably more than half a million.

Mr. Collins was the mainspring of the old temperance agitation in Scotland. He took a prominent part at the first public meeting of the society, held in the Trades' Hall, Glasgow. His stirring speech was published, and upwards of 15,000 of it put into circulation. As a fair sample of the best kind of argument

E

that the Glasgow publicans could then furnish—and they have made no perceptible progress throughout Great Britain and Ireland since—they sent a couple of drunken men, who attempted in vain to upset the proceedings. Mr. Collins was also one of the chief speakers at the first meeting of the Edinburgh Association for the Suppression of Intemperance, and during 1830 more than 30,000 copies of his Edinburgh address were printed and circulated. This meeting was productive of much good in Edinburgh, and for the purpose of sustaining and extending the interest excited, the committee sent an order to Glasgow for 80,000 temperance publications. About this time a short series of popular Sunday evening discourses was delivered, under the auspices of the Glasgow Temperance Society, in St. George's Church—now so ably occupied by the Rev. John Barclay—by clergymen of various religious denominations. From some unforeseen circumstance one of the preachers did not make his appearance, when Mr. Collins, at the urgent request of the committee, occupied St. George's pulpit, and delivered an able discourse, which was listened to by a very large audience.

FIRST TEMPERANCE TEA PARTY.

In 1830, about thirty temperance friends held their first "social meeting," as it was called, or tea-party, which was presided over by William Burgess, a member of the Rev. Dr. Mitchell's congregation, and one of the oldest Sabbath-school teachers in Glasgow. This memorable tea-meeting was held in the commodious school-room under the then Wesleyan Methodist Chapel, in Bridge Street, the site now occupied as the booking office of the Glasgow and South-Western Railway.

As considerable interest clusters around this soiree, from its having been the first, it is believed, of all public tea meetings, a glance at its history may not prove uninstructive. It originated at one of the meetings of "The Tradeston Temperance Society," when a question arose as to the most innocent and refreshing beverage to be used by those who had pledged themselves to abstain from ardent spirits. A young man, with his eyes sparkling with hilarity and glee, proposed that the committee have a tea meeting; but this novel proposition was received with a loud burst of laughter. The president, though somewhat taken by surprise, said that he liked the idea, but saw no reason why such a social meeting should be confined to the committee—why it should not be extended to the whole society. This was approved of, and accordingly the meeting was held, and, though much fear was entertained as to success, it nevertheless passed off very favourably. "Thus," says one who was present, and to whom I shall immediately refer, "on a cold and stormy evening in the month of December, in the year of our Lord one thousand eight hundred and twenty-nine, a new idea was born—a seed was sown, weak and unpromising at first, but there was vitality in that seed to produce a plant; the plant grew and flourished, and brought forth fruit, yielding seed after its kind. And from that single idea what a vast amount of pure and innocent enjoyment has resulted to all classes of the community, more especially to those who earn their daily bread by the labour of their hands, as well as to their wives and families!"

In reference to this same tea meeting, the following is a letter, which lies before me, received by Mr. Robert Rae, Secretary to the National Temperance League, from Mr. James Corbett, a venerable temperance reformer, who died in the summer of 1868 :—

"OLD WINDSOR, 30th March, 1863.

"DEAR SIR,—I beg to enclose herewith, for your acceptance, one of the original tickets of the *first* public tea meeting, which was held in the school-room of the Methodist Chapel, Bridge Street, Glasgow. The tickets were executed by a young man whose name, I think, was Henry Airlie. He was a calico printer, and being a member of committee, he very generously volunteered to cut a block with his own hands, and thus save the expense of printing—a matter of no small importance, as many of us were ridiculed and laughed at by our friends at the folly of getting up a '*tea fuddle*.'

"I was employed for the prime of my life as a Civil Officer of Her Majesty's War Department, and during the time I was stationed in Canada (about the time of the Rebellion) I delivered a number of lectures at London, Canada West—then a village chiefly occupied by two regiments of infantry and a battery of royal artillery. One of the lectures I delivered to a large audience was on temperance; and at its close one of its principal innkeepers stood up and offered five dollars towards the printing. A thousand copies were sold; but I have not one left."

The ticket to which Mr. Corbett refers, and of which the following is a fac-simile, was carried about with him like a charm for more than thirty years—

In consequence of the success which attended the first tea party, the friends were encouraged, early in 1830, to hold a second social meeting, in the Baronial Hall, Laurieston, Glasgow, which was attended by about 200 persons. Mr. Collins, who occupied the chair, and the Rev. Dr. William Anderson, of Glasgow (who was detained from the first tea meeting by public engagements), were the only speakers. The Dr. had to deliver three speeches in course of the evening. Mr. Macmillan, "the temperance poet," as he was called, gave a humorous recitation of one of his own poems. There was also music at intervals. The meeting was highly successful. One of the Glasgow papers gave a favourable report, and called the "social meeting" a "*soiree.*" During the next few weeks about a hundred *soirees* were held in different parts of Scotland, and excited great interest. The *soiree* spread like wildfire, and speedily became an "institution,"—people wondering how they could spend an evening so happily without intoxicating liquors.

The first public breakfast party, under the auspices of the Glasgow Temperance Society, was held in the Assembly Rooms, now the Glasgow Athenæum, and addresses were delivered by Professor Edgar, D.D., of Belfast; Mr. William Collins, and others. The company, which was an influential one, numbered 200.

CHAPTER VI.

WILLIAM COLLINS IN ENGLAND.

T the formation of the first Temperance Society in England, which took place at Bradford, Yorkshire, on Monday, the 14th of June, 1830, Mr. Collins delivered a powerful speech. Henry Forbes, of the well-known firm of Milligan, Forbes, and Co., had joined the Temperance Society when on a business visit to Glasgow—"Henry Forbes, Bradford," being the fourteenth name in the original Glasgow roll-book—and on his return home was instrumental in starting the Bradford Society. The chair at this first temperance gathering in England was occupied by John Rand, J.P., an influential and highly esteemed member of the Church of England. The Rev. Dr. Edgar, of the Royal College, Belfast; the late revered and accomplished Dr. Benjamin Godwin, of the Baptist College, near Bradford (who often spoke to me in pleasant terms of the address then delivered by Mr. Collins); the Rev. W. Morgan, M.A., Incumbent of Christ Church, Bradford; and Dr. Thomas Beaumont, took part in the proceedings. William Wilson, who spent hundreds of pounds sterling in circulating religious and temperance tracts, David Harris Smith, and other members of the Society of Friends, were also present.

On the evening of Tuesday, the 7th of December, 1830, Dr. Beaumont delivered a lecture in the Corn

Exchange, Bradford, on "The Nature, Uses, and Effects of Ardent Spirits," which was published, and rendered at that time important service throughout the kingdom to the temperance reformation. The temperance cause in England, and especially in Yorkshire, had been much indebted, for thirty years, to the venerated Wm. Morgan, and the intelligent and generous-hearted Thomas Beaumont, both of whom, I doubt not, are now in heaven.

Mr. Collins was one of the principal speakers at the first public meeting of the Liverpool and Manchester Temperance Societies, and his speech was published, and obtained a circulation of 13,000. The Commercial Travellers' Temperance Society was established about the same time in Manchester, and was productive of good results. In October, 1830, a large and influential gathering was held in the Friends' Meeting-House, Manchester, a report of which appeared in the *Manchester Times*. The chair was occupied by Samuel Fletcher, one of Manchester's benevolent Christian "merchant princes," who, after a few remarks, introduced Mr. Collins. His address was an eloquent and argumentative one, and occupied about two hours in the delivery. In the course of it he called upon Christians of all denominations to aid in the great work of opening up a way to the regeneration of the human race, and to set an example *themselves*, as it could not, in the nature of things, be expected that preaching only against the vice of drunkenness would have any permanent effect. He appealed especially to Christian ministers, as they valued the eternal salvation of the souls committed to their care, to think seriously on the subject. He contended that there was no drawing a line of distinction between moderate and excessive drinking; the moderate drinker having, in many cases, from placing too much reliance on his principles, become a notorious drunkard.

Mr Henry Forbes, Bradford, was next called upon. In a perspicuous manner, and with great effect, he dwelt upon the baneful drinking customs amongst commercial travellers, especially at the dinner table, and urged the formation of a Commercial Temperance Society, as not only a means of relieving themselves from tyrannical practices, but as an indispensable security to their employers.

In consequence of the non-arrival of Dr. Edgar, from an irregularity in the Dublin steamer, Mr. Collins was again called upon, and spoke for upwards of an hour. At the close of the meeting a cordial vote of thanks was proposed to the speakers, by the Rev. Dr. M'All, then one of the most powerful and popular preachers in England. At the termination of the proceedings a number of gentlemen enrolled themselves as members of the society, amongst whom were several of "the fourth estate" from the *Manchester Times*, the *Chronicle*, and *Courier* offices. The *Manchester Times* was conducted for many years by Archibald Prentice, who, during the closing years of his ever active and useful life, was one of the most grateful and sincere friends of the abstinence cause, and did not a little, by means of his pen, for its advancement. Mr. Prentice was present, shortly before his death, at one of the Sunday evening services, in the City Hall, Glasgow. The preacher was the Rev. William Reid of Edinburgh, and the hall was densely crowded. The old director of the Anti-corn-law League had witnessed many a great meeting, but none more so, for moral power, than that in the City Hall. When the vast assembly arose to sing Jehovah's praise, accompanied by the organ, the veteran reformer was deeply moved, covered his face, and said, in a whisper, "Thank God for such a magnificent temperance gathering—worthy alike of Glasgow and the eloquent preacher !"

MR. COLLINS VISITS LONDON.

Mr. Collins visited London, and was instrumental, after great exertion and discouragement, in establishing the original "Metropolitan Temperance Association," afterwards called "The British and Foreign Temperance Society." The first public meeting was held in Exeter Hall, on Wednesday, the 29th of June, 1831. Sir John Webb, Director-General of the Army Medical Department, occupied the chair ; and after he had spoken, the meeting was addressed by the Bishop of Chester, the Solicitor-General for Ireland, Rev. Dr. John Pye Smith, Professor Edgar, D.D., Belfast ;

Dr. Hewitt, from America; Rev. Dr. Bennett, London; Rev. George Clayton, London; Rev. G. W. Carr, New Ross; Mr. William Allen, Dublin, and Mr. Collins. The few words uttered on that occasion by Mr. Collins are too valuable to be lost sight of:—He stood, he said, on that platform with deep emotion, to witness the first public meeting of the Temperance Society in this metropolis, because he claimed to himself the high honour of being the founder of that institution. He came to London, and, after trying for several weeks, he could not get a single person to join him. He left London, and, when he was fifty miles off, God put it into his heart to turn back, and make another attempt. But his second attempt was not more successful than the first, and he again left London. He went to Bristol, and succeeded in forming a Temperance Society there. This success induced him to return again to London, and make a third attempt, in which he rejoiced to say that, under the blessing of Divine Providence, he was successful. He concluded by remarking that no one who had witnessed the operations of Temperance Societies could resist the conviction that they were extensively beneficial to the best interests of mankind. At an adjourned meeting of the London Society, Mr. Collins delivered a logical, telling address on "The Claims of Temperance to Scriptural Authority," which was afterwards published and extensively circulated.

" Mr. Collins," says the late Edward Morris, in his " History of Teetotalism," " was the life and soul of the temperance movement in Glasgow. He was of that moral temperament, that whatever he took in hand must be done with energy. These are the men that God raises up in all ages and in all lands to improve society. It ·was from hearing, for the first time, a very excellent lecture on Temperance from the late Mr. Collins, in December, 1830, that I was convinced of the full importance of temperance associations, and when the good man, now in heaven, had done speaking, I put down my name on the members' roll."

It was my privilege to hear, in 1830, in my native town of Hamilton, one of the many lucid, instructive, thrilling temperance addresses delivered by Mr. Collins. On that occasion I was not a little surprised and puzzled on observing the church officer walk into the place of meeting with a fine white pillow under his arm. In the lecturer's zeal to direct public attention to the fearful ravages of strong drink he was then addressing meetings, in different parts of the country, almost every night, and had somewhat inflamed his hand; hence a considerate friend had suggested the use of the pillow. Mr. Collins placed it on the desk before him, in order to protect his hand, which, in the great earnestness and enthusiasm of his advocacy, he brought so frequently, and with such force, upon the desk that but for the pillow between him and the hard board it would probably have been lacerated. Very soon the feathers in the pillow were driven to each end, whereupon he took it up in both hands, shook the feathers hastily together, and proceeded with his address. This he did several times, until ultimately, as if impatient of such repeated adjustment of the pillow, he doubled it up, and, keeping hold of it by the two ends with one hand, knocked away with the other; and before he had reached the last half of the lecture he became so animated that the pillow was abandoned altogether. It was apparent to all that the good man's own soul was on fire, and he set and kept others on fire too. He was intensely earnest—he believed what he said—and hence he prevailed upon vast numbers to follow his praiseworthy example. May his mantle fall on every temperance reformer of the present day, and especially upon the rising generation !

Mr. Collins was one of the most important witnesses examined by the Committee of the House of Commons on "drunkenness," in June, 1834, of which the late lamented James Silk Buckingham, M.P., was chairman. The valuable evidence given by Mr. Collins before that Select Committee occupies upwards of 28 octavo pages. In reply to the last question put by the Committee—"Have you any suggestion that you wish to make in conclusion?"—Mr. Collins answered in the following terms :—"The only statement I have to make is to implore the Legislature to suppress entirely the distillation and sale of ardent spirits, as being the source of almost all the crime, and misery, and wretchedness which exist; and as, in short, the mightiest evil which at present afflicts and destroys the people. Let them effectually chain up this destroying angel which is passing over the land, withering and laying waste all that is fair and good among the people; let them fearlessly and conscientiously do their duty to God and to their country; and the Legislature which will effect this will achieve a mightier good for their country than all the statesmen and all the legislators who have presided over the councils of our nation have been able to effect for this country for these hundred years."

The editor of the *Temperance Society Record*, in reviewing one of Mr. Collins's pamphlets in May, 1833, says:—"The author is a gentleman who has both spent and been spent for the benefit of his fellow-men, and to whom the Church of Christ are under deep obligations for his unremitting zeal in the cause of morality and religion, while promoting the interests of temperance societies."

In addition to the time and labour which Mr. Collins devoted to the cause of temperance, it appears from the list of annual subscribers to the Glasgow and West of Scotland Temperance Society, that he was one of its most liberal supporters. Although the receipts for 1830 amounted only to £447, of which the small sum of £148 was obtained from subscriptions and donations, Mr. Collins subscribed £25, and in the following year he gave £50.

On the 1st of June, 1830, the first number of a monthly periodical was published by Mr. Collins, entitled *The Temperance Society Record*, which was conducted with great spirit and considerable ability, and contained a vast amount of important information. The pages of this early *Record* ever and anon testify to the disinterested efforts of William Collins, John Dunlop, Robert Kettle, Wm. Smeal, James Playfair, William B. Hodge, Wm. P. Paton, Rev. William Anderson, Loanhead; Dr. Richmond, Paisley; William Wardlaw, Rev. Dr. Hamilton, Strathblane; Rev. Dr. Symington, Glasgow; Rev. Dr. John Ritchie, Edinburgh; Professor Edgar, Belfast; Rev. Dr. Baird, Paisley; Rev. Andrew Scott, Cambusnethan; Rev. Dr. John Bruce, Newmilns; Rev. Peter M'Dowall, M.A., Alloa; Rev. James M'Gill, Hightae; Rev. Dr. William Smart, Paisley; Simon Kemp, Edinburgh; John Bowes, Dundee; Rev. Thomas Struthers, Hamilton; Rev. Dr. William Anderson, Rev. Dr. John Robson, Glasgow, and other kindred spirits. The last number of the *Record* appeared on the 1st of December, 1835. The editor thus concludes his valedictory address:—"It is the indifference of Christians to these noble institutions which has hindered their progress and delayed their triumphs. On them lies the awful responsibility of the intemperance of our country, that gigantic evil which is laying waste all that is fair and good among our people. And never till, in the true spirit of that self-denial which the gospel enjoins, they deny themselves the use of ardent spirits, which does themselves no good, but is productive of immeasurable evil to others, will they succeed in delivering our country from this sore and desolating evil—an evil, the extent and malignity of which, none but the Infinite mind can possibly comprehend."

Several years ago my old friend, Robert Rae, London, favoured me with a note respecting Mr. Collins, from which I quote the following:—"I had several interviews with the late William Collins, during a six weeks' residence at Rothesay for the benefit of my health, in the spring of 1852; only a few months, if I remember correctly, before Mr. Collins's death. During these interviews Mr. Collins manifested the greatest possible interest in the temperance movement, both in its earlier and later stages, and nothing seemed to give him greater pleasure than to hear of its progress. He mentioned to me one day that he had just sent off his subscription (of £100, I think) to the Rev. Dr. Buchanan, for the Glasgow Evangelization scheme at that time promoted by the Free Church, and he said he had with great earnestness and at considerable length expressed his opinion, that the proposed efforts in behalf of the sunken masses would prove almost entirely useless, unless a Temperance Society were planted alongside of every Territorial Church. On this point he seemed to entertain a very strong conviction. On another occasion the conversation happened to turn upon the question of legislative action for the suppression of intemperance, and he remarked that his opinion on that subject had undergone a great change since the time he had been examined before the Parliamentary Committee in 1834, when he expressed an opinion in favour of such action."

From failing health this "man of God" could not devote that time to the temperance question which he had formerly bestowed on it. His pamphlet on "The Harmony between the Gospel and Temperance Societies," published by the Scottish Temperance League, is one of the most explicit and convincing little treatises on the religious aspect of the question that could be met with, and is as much needed at the present time as when it was first published. This eminently useful servant of God now "rests from his labours, and his works do follow him."

In a letter which I received from the late Dr. Guthrie, Edinburgh, in April, 1862, respecting my notes on the Temperance Pioneers, Mr. Collins is thus referred to:—"I was especially glad to see my old and noble friend, Collins, holding such a conspicuous place in your story. The part he played, in being the first to throw himself into the breach, was quite like the man. The pity is that the Church has so few like him; but let us be thankful, the tide is wearing in. It is strange how far the seed in that respect, like the thistle-down, may travel."

F

CHAPTER VII.

ORIGIN OF TEETOTALISM.

IN preceding chapters we have seen that when the temperance agitation commenced, the pledge adopted prohibited ardent spirits, but allowed the "moderate" use of ale, porter, and wine. This movement soon became very popular in Scotland, England, and Ireland, and a number of influential clergymen of all denominations, as well as laymen, threw themselves heartily into it. But whilst the old temperance principle was good, it was soon found that it did not go far enough. Those who entered on the path of reformation by joining the Temperance Society, discovered that it was just as bad, in some cases worse, to get drunk on beer or porter, as upon rum, gin, brandy, or whisky. Besides, there was something absurd and ridiculous in the sight of members of a "Temperance Society" sitting at one end of a table in a public-house drinking ale and porter —of which I happened to be an eye-witness some forty years ago—and a number of old half-tipsy topers at the other end indulging in whisky! The old temperance principle was, doubtless, a most important step in the right direction, still it was far from embodying all that was necessary; and subsequent experience has amply proved that the only effectual cure for a man or woman addicted to intoxicating drink, and the only safe course for a moderate drinker, is to abstain altogether.

In a paper prepared for the "Temperance Congress of 1862," Mr. Robert Rae, Secretary to the National Temperance League, gave an account of some documents in his possession, which went to shew that an Abstinence Society had been formed as early as the year 1817 at Skibbereen, County Cork, which continued in active operation until it was absorbed by the more comprehensive movement of Father Mathew in 1838. The founder of the society, Mr. Jeffery Sedwards, a nailer in that town, died in 1861, at the advanced age of 85. The society's meeting-house, with its books and records, were destroyed by fire in 1854; but several of the first members, who were still alive in 1862, maintained that total abstinence was their bond of union from the beginning, and that the first rule of the society was expressed in the following words:—"No person can take malt or spirituous liquors, or distilled waters, or anything inebriating, except prescribed by a priest or doctor."

So far as my information goes, the next "total abstinence," "teetotal," or "nephalist" pledge, is to be traced to Dunfermline, in Fife. When visiting Dunfermline in 1847, Mr. John Davie, merchant, informed me that on the 21st of September, 1830, he and a few friends signed a declaration, as members of the "Dunfermline Association for the promotion of Temperance by the relinquishing of all Intoxicating Liquors." Mr. Davie—an earnest, liberal, warm-hearted teetotaler—has the sheet with the original signatures in his possession. The second total abstinence pledge, then, can be fairly traced to the ancient city of Dunfermline, but the friends there made no special effort to make it public.

On the 14th of January, 1832, Dr. Richmond, Mr. William Melvin, Mr. David Melvin—all of whom survive, and remain faithful friends of the cause—together with five others, established a society in Paisley, on the total abstinence principle, and the following are the first two regulations :—"1. That this Society shall be denominated the Paisley Youths' Society for promoting Temperance and the principle of Abstinence from all Intoxicating Liquors. 2. That this Society shall consist of such persons as shall voluntarily agree to abstain from the use of all Liquors containing any quantity of Alcohol, except when such are absolutely necessary."

On the 15th of January, 1832, Mr. James Macnair, with a few others, established, in a school-room in Oxford Street, Glasgow, the "Tradeston Total Abstinence Society." Mr. Macnair had, from a very early period, been deeply impressed with the ravages of intemperance, and, when resident in Greenock, pled, I understand, in favour of abstinence from all intoxicating liquors. He also specially interested himself in the wine question, and brought it before the Church Court with which he was then connected. A few years ago he was admitted as an occasional communicant to the Rev. Dr. Alexander Wallace's Church, Glasgow, and greatly rejoiced at having this opportunity of sitting down at the Lord's Table where unfermented wine alone is used, seeing that he had, from conscientious conviction, been deprived for many years of observing this ordinance in other churches. Although well advanced in years, he still continues to take a warm interest in all that pertains to the overthrow of the drinking system and the advancement of the temperance reformation.

FORMATION OF A TOTAL ABSTINENCE SOCIETY AT GREENLAW.

In a letter of June 11th, 1862, to Mr. Robert Rae, London, the Rev. John Parker, United Presbyterian minister, Sunderland, writes :—

"In reply to your kind letter I send you the accompanying extracts from the minute book of the Greenlaw (Berwickshire) Temperance Society, instituted on the 19th January, 1832. While attending the Divinity Hall, in Glasgow, in 1831, I was opposed to temperance societies, not from any liking to intoxicating drinks, but because I thought such institutions unscriptural and absurd. One evening I went accidentally to hear Cruikshank, I think they called him, the Dundee carter. To his simple, earnest, and telling advocacy of the cause I owe the liberty which I have enjoyed ever since, and the part which I have acted in connection with our noble cause. I cried to myself, as he went on, 'I have found it, I have found it,' and from that moment I have waged war against all intoxicating drinks as poisons, and have carried my principles so far (and for which I have been much censured) that, with the exception of two or three times, when it would have been reckoned cruelty to keep them from brethren who never abused themselves, they have never entered my door; and then a small quantity was given as any other medicine, and as if it were a crime I was committing. To this I confess during a term of twenty seven years, though my house all that time has been a home to hundreds of brethren, and other relations and friends. And only once or twice have I tasted brandy as a medicine, when pre-scribed under an attack of British cholera. On the evening of the 19th January, 1832, the inhabitants of Greenlaw were convened in the old Court-room to form a Temperance Society. Then and there I insisted upon a second horn to the altar, which was only allowed out of deference to a well-meaning but weak brother, and generally laughed at. My own name stood at it alone for some weeks, and then my sisters adhibited theirs. The Temperance Society occasioned for a time great excitement. I laboured hard as its secretary, but in all my addresses came out with the long pledge. After receiving licence at Coldstream in 1834, and ordination here in 1835, the Society fell off, and subsequently (I do not know the date) the present Greenlaw Abstinence Society, to which you refer, was formed on my own principle, and by the very parties who had tried to laugh it down. On one of my visits I had the old minute book presented to me by my successor in office, a book which I now regard with affection and gratitude."

The following is the minute referred to:—

"Greenlaw, 19th January, 1832.

"A meeting of the friends of Temperance Societies was held in the Court-house, at half-past six in the evening. Mr. George Clazy, of Eccles, opened it with prayer, and then, in a speech of considerable length, showed the great and increasing evils of intemperance, and argued that temperance societies were a wise, reasonable, and Scriptural means of eradicating it, particularly by keeping men temperate, and also in many instances of reclaiming the drunkard. Mr. John Parker, in his address, attempted to remove objections frequently urged against temperance societies, and concluded with some remarks introductory to the principle stated in the eighth regulation.

"JOHN PARKER, Sec."

We quote the rule referred to:—

"VIII. Finally, that as some wish the 'other liquors,' the moderate use of which is allowed in the second article, placed upon the same footing with ardent spirits, as best suiting their peculiar views and circumstances, the society do not think this prejudicial to the cause. And looking upon the temperance and total abstinence principle as parts of one great whole, provision is here made for acting upon the latter. All, therefore, who do so shall be considered members of this society; and those wishing to avail themselves of this article shall be required to sign the following declaration:—

"'We do resolve that so long as we are members of this association we shall abstain from the use of distilled spirits, wines, and all other intoxicating liquors, except for medicinal and sacramental purposes. Adherence to this principle will be notified by prefixing a * to the name.'

"P.S.—Gratefully do I, at the distance of upwards of thirty years, look at that star which I prefixed to my name, now brighter than ever, and which, I have no doubt, will shine brighter and brighter, till my country be freed from the curse of intemperance.—J. P."

CHAPTER VIII.

TEETOTALISM IN PRESTON.

JOSEPH Livesey, of Preston, appears to be the natural connecting link between the old temperance agitation for abstinence from ardent spirits and the simpler and safer principle of total abstinence from all intoxicating beverages. This modest, indefatigable, disinterested, and singularly useful temperance reformer, was born at Walton-le-Dale, near Preston, on the 5th March, 1794, so that he has now (1873) completed his 79th year. He was left an orphan at the tender age of seven years. In 1828 Mr. Livesey was one of the founders of the Preston Mechanics' Institution, and acted for many years as its treasurer. It is a somewhat remarkable coincidence that Mr. Dunlop and Mr. Livesey should have been directing their attention to kindred objects in 1828, and that the drinking system should have presented itself to both as the great barrier to their philanthropic efforts for the elevation of the working classes.

In giving a bird's-eye view of Mr. Livesey's connection with the temperance movement, I may notice the incident, as related by himself, which first led him to become an abstainer. It was in the year 1830, a year or two before the subject, in its earliest

phase, was introduced into Preston.   Having business
to transact with a tradesman, they called at the house
of a Scotch friend, who, according to custom, brought
the whisky bottle on the table, and invited Mr.
Livesey to take a glass, which he did, filled up with water.
He took only a single glass, yet he felt much the
worse for it, and in the evening was very unwell.   As
the father of a family, and as one connected with
several useful movements, and having a strong feeling
on the then prevailing intemperance amongst all
classes, he considered that he should be doing best to
abstain all together, and next morning he made a vow
to that effect, which he has solemnly and religiously
kept to the present day.   When the subject of temperance societies was introduced into Preston about
the close of 1831, Mr. Livesey, along with the late
Mr. James Teare, and others, gave every assistance to
those who came to lecture and circulate tracts on the
subject.

In 1832, Mr. Livesey commenced the printing
business.   The first work of any note which issued
from his press was a monthly periodical, entitled *The
Moral Reformer*, which contains several excellent
papers from his own pen on the temperance question.
In a suggestive and characteristic preface to the first
volume of *The Moral Reformer*, in December, 1832, the
editor thus writes :—" I am often asked how I find
time for all my work, and my answer is, the time which
others spend in the 'pot-house,' or in visiting and

attending parties, I spend in active pursuits; and, never taking any liquor at home or elsewhere, my head is seldom out of order. I lose no time in the evenings to extinguish my reason, or in the mornings to try to regain it; and, thanks to a kind Providence, my health was never better for many years than it is at this day."

It is stated in Mr. Joseph Dearden's interesting *Brief History of Teetotalism*, that "on the 1st of January, 1832, a few young men in connection with Mr. Livesey's Sunday-school, in Preston, formed themselves into a Temperance Society." Many young men, who were afterwards successful in life, attribute their first step in mounting the ladder to the education they received at Mr. Livesey's Sunday-school. He selected some of the more promising of the scholars to form a class for the study of English and grammar, and taught them at his private residence on the week-day evenings.

On the 22nd of March, 1832, an adult Temperance Society was established in Preston. Mr. Dearden states, in his *Brief History*, that "on Thursday, Aug. 23, 1832, Messrs. John King and Joseph Livesey signed a total abstinence pledge in Mr. Livesey's shop, Church Street. On Saturday, 1st September, 1832, some of the leaders of the society called a meeting to be held at the Temperance Hall, and at this meeting John King, Joseph Livesey, John Gratrix, Edward Dickinson, John Broadbelt, John Smith, and David

Anderton, signed the following pledge, viz.:—'We agree to abstain from all liquors of an intoxicating quality, whether ale, porter, wine, or ardent spirits, except as medicine.'" To the propagation of this newly-adopted principle, Mr. Livesey, with a small but noble-hearted band of fellow-labourers, devoted much time and effort.

No sooner had the seven teetotal Preston worthies adopted the more thoroughgoing abstinence pledge than they felt wishful that others should participate in its blessings. "Anxious," says Mr. Dearden, in his *Brief History of Teetotalism*, "to spread the principles of abstinence which had been of so great benefit to the town of Preston and neighbourhood, and to stimulate others to increased exertions, Thomas Swindlehurst, Joseph Livesey, James Teare, Henry Anderton (the temperance poet), and others, belonging to the Preston Society, undertook a missionary tour. They started from Preston on Monday, July 8, 1833, and visited Blackburn, Haslingden, Bury, Heywood, Rochdale, Oldham, Ashton, Stockport, Manchester, and Bolton, and held meetings every day during the week. They took with them 9,500 tracts, about 6,000 of which were distributed gratuitously."

Mr. James Teare, in his *History of Total Abstinence*, refers, in glowing terms, to this early Lancashire teetotal crusade. "In all places," says this departed, and early, indefatigable, and useful advocate of the cause, "we had large and crowded meetings, indoors and in the open air, and advocated thorough-going teetotalism, and did all in our power to show the people the inefficiency of the moderation system. During the week we divided ourselves into two parties. On Tuesday evening, Messrs. Teare, Anderton, and Swindlehurst went on to Rochdale, but the people there would not give any countenance at that time to the total abstinence principle. We could not get a school or chapel in which to hold a meeting. The day after, however, we all met together at Rochdale, drove the car round the town, got the bell, and gave notice to the inhabitants that a temperance meeting would be held at the ' Butts,' in the open air, at noon, where we had a large concourse of people."

During my residence for some years as a missionary for Messrs. John Bright and Brothers, in Rochdale, where the good resulting from the disinterested efforts of those enthusiastic temperance pioneers is still to be met with, I not unfrequently heard this noble tee-total gathering referred to in pleasant terms.

ORIGIN OF THE WORD "TEETOTAL."

Mr. Livesey referred in one of his speeches at the anniversary of the Scottish Temperance League, held at Glasgow, in May, 1862, to "Dickie Turner," and the origin of the now far-famed term Teetotal. "I have been asked several times," said Mr. Livesey, "if I could give any explanation of the origin of the word

Teetotal. Now I can assure you, if any authority be required as to the origin of that word, none higher can be given than myself, for I was present when the word originated. It was first pronounced by a man named Dickie Turner. At that time (1832) there were temperance societies based upon the principle of abstinence from all spirits and great moderation in all fermented liquors. Dickie attempted at a meeting to show the difference, deprecated the practice of drinking fermented liquors in moderation, and enjoined that of abstinence, when he came out with the expression that gave rise to that notable term, *Teetotal*, which, since then, has gone throughout the world. He said that we should be 'te-te-tee-total.' We all took up the word at that moment, and were glad of it, for the designation 'abstinence from all intoxicating drinks' was cumbersome. We said that was the thing; and from that moment till now, the word *Tee-total* denotes abstinence from all kinds of intoxicating drinks in opposition to moderation in all fermented liquors."*

* Mr. Joseph Dearden, Preston, in his pamphlet, published June, 1873, entitled "The Dawn and Spread of Teetotalism," thus refers to Dickie Turner signing the pledge—"It was in that month [October, 1832] that Dickie Turner first signed any pledge. On the second Thursday in October, he strolled into the meeting at St. Peter's Schoolroom, where he signed the moderation pledge. I was present and urgently pressed him to sign the pledge of total abstinence, which he then did, and kept it consistently till the day of his death. At this meeting Mr. Thomas Swindlehurst occupied the chair."

This famous Dickie Turner I once, and only once, had the pleasure of meeting, at the World's Temperance Convention, held in the Literary Institution, Aldersgate Street, London, in August, 1846. On that occasion I occupied a seat in the gallery, and before long, I observed a short, dark-complexioned man enter and seat himself by my side. Taking advantage of a pause in the proceedings, we entered into conversation, and I soon found, to my surprise, that underneath a somewhat childlike and simple exterior, beat a heart as warmly as heart could beat in attachment to the teetotal cause. This was none other than Dickie Turner, who, in proof of his gratitude for what the pledge had done for him, had walked all the way from Preston to be present at that gathering. He died 27th October, 1846, aged 56. His funeral was a public one, and was attended by upwards of 400 persons, from various parts of the country.

As the favourite drink of the working classes in England was malt liquor, Mr. Livesey hit upon an admirable method of convincing them that their high opinion of this beverage for giving strength and sustaining labour was a great delusion. In his valuable lecture on "The Properties of Malt Liquor," which has gone through many editions, amounting to more than 100,000 copies, he showed by ocular demonstration that there was more real nourishment to the body in a pennyworth of bread than there was in a gallon of ale. In 1834 this popular lecture was delivered in

many towns in Lancashire and Yorkshire, in the
county of Durham, in Birmingham and London, and
produced great numbers of converts to the abstinence
cause.

MR. LIVESEY'S FIRST VISIT TO LONDON.

Mr. Livesey was the first to introduce the total
abstinence movement into London, in June, 1834.   I
was present at the annual meeting of the National
Temperance Society, held in Exeter Hall, in May,
1845, and have still a vivid impression of the graphic
description Mr. Livesey then gave of his first visit to
London, but prefer quoting his own account of it, as
related at the anniversary of the National Temperance
League, in Exeter Hall, in May, 1862—Edward Baines,
M.P., in the chair. "I came to London," said Mr.
Livesey, "single-handed, and at my own expense,
when I could not very well afford it, and spent nearly
a fortnight before I succeeded in getting a place to
meet in.   I then got some large and small placards
printed. I remember taking the small bills and some
wafers, and going round the Bank of England and
various other places, and sticking them up, thinking
that somebody would see them.   The fact is, I was so full
of it, that I thought I was going to produce a revolu-
tion in this great metropolis, and to exercise a power
even beyond that of the *Times* itself, so vain was I
and so ignorant of this great city, and of the feelings of

the people on the subject.   I also engaged two men to parade, with announcements, in front of the place during the day before the meeting was held.   The place was a sort of cellar-chapel, about three steps underground, in Providence Row, Finsbury Square, capable of holding from three to four hundred people, and I expected that it would be full to overflowing. The evening came, the hour arrived, and to my astonishment I was honoured by the attendance of about five-and-twenty people!   It was the Malt Lecture I delivered, which many of you, I daresay, have read.   So much, my friends, for the origin of Teetotalism in this great city.   If there is a man under this roof who has reason to be glad, and I might say proud, of the success of Teetotalism in London, and in other parts, from the influences emanating from this great metropolis, I am that man."   Mr. Livesey's reception at this noble Exeter Hall assembly was of the most encouraging and enthusiastic description, and furnished evidence the most satisfactory, that the veteran's self-denying and persevering labours were highly appreciated by a metropolitan audience.

Much good resulted from . the delivery of Mr. Livesey's Malt Lecture to that comparatively small company in Finsbury Square.   One brewer resolved to give up the use and sale of ale from what he had heard and seen that evening.   Another intelligent person said that if Mr. Livesey would re-deliver the lecture, and make it as plain to Londoners in general, he

G

would cheerfully give £1000. A London chemist, however, on that occasion, not possessed of a very sensitive conscience, actually charged Mr. Livesey half a sovereign for distilling a small quantity of ale that he required to illustrate his malt lecture. From this humble and obscure meeting emanated the first Teetotal Society in the metropolis.

On the first of September, 1835, Mr. Livesey, accompanied by his earnest and devoted fellow-labourers, Swindlehurst and Howarth (the latter better known as "Slender Billy"), paid a second visit to London. They held their meeting in a not very popular hall in Theobald's Road, off Holborn. At the hour when the meeting should have commenced the number of persons present was small. To assist in gathering an audience, Messrs. Livesey and Howarth left the hall, got hold of a hand-bell, and began announcing the lecture in the neighbouring streets, Mr. Howarth ringing the bell and Mr. Livesey inviting the people to the meeting. They had not, however, gone far with this novelty to London people before a police officer tapped one of them on the shoulder (Howarth, I believe), and stated that if they did not stop he would be obliged to take them into custody. The result was that the meeting was an excellent one; not a few were made teetotallers, amongst whom was William Inwards, brother of Jabez Inwards, who, to the present day, has rendered, as is well known, signal service to the cause as a lecturer. From that day till the present the teetotal cause has been steadily progressing, not only in London but throughout the country, till it can now, thank God, count its members by tens and hundreds of thousands.

MR. LIVESEY AS A TEMPERANCE WORKER.

Joseph Livesey has continued, with slight intermissions, his gratuitous and self-denying temperance labours till the present day. From the commencement of the movement his press was employed in printing tracts, and for some time during the early days of teetotalism all parts of the country were supplied with the Preston tracts. The *Preston Temperance Advocate* issued from the same press: it continued under Mr. Livesey's management from 1834 till 1837 inclusive, and greatly assisted the temperance reformation. I have gone over every page of that *Advocate*, and have no hesitation in stating that it contains the fullest and most important particulars of the early progress of teetotalism of any work extant, and does great credit alike to the heart and head of its unassuming editor.

So recently as November, 1869, Mr. Livesey published an earnest letter on "Visiting and Tract Distribution," in which he observes, "The fact is, that religious people depend too much on the pulpit, and teetotallers on the platform. Unless there is a greater mixing of the classes—the rich and the poor, the wise and the ignorant, the good and the bad, and the abstainers with the drinkers—we may go on as we have been doing, lamenting the awful amount of crime and drunkenness, but making very little real progress. We should never forget that passage—'He *went about* doing good;' that going about on the temperance mission in a promiscuous way, both on Sunday and at other times, is an important part of our work." This is wise counsel, and ought not only to be pondered over but energetically acted upon. From the commencement of Mr. Livesey's benevolent career he has given special attention to the visitation of the poor in their own dwellings, where his friendly advice has been productive of great good.

It has not unfrequently been alleged that temperance reformers are men of one idea. This charge cannot be brought against Joseph Livesey. He has always been ready to lend a helping hand to every movement which has for its object the elevation of the people.

Skibbereen, Dunfermline, Paisley, and Greenlaw, as we have seen, had the honour of originating the first societies on the out-and-out principle of total abstinence, but Preston has the indisputable title of commencing the movement on a truly aggressive and national scale; and Joseph Livesey wears the proud distinction of being its father and founder, and one of its most devoted and energetic promoters.

Not uncommonly is it urged that the teetotal movement is the effervescence of mere juvenile fanaticism, furnishing a fitting arena on which "a pack of lads," for the most part, who must needs throw their corks somewhere, may deliver themselves of their pent-up noise and froth. The "atrocious crime of being young" once did of necessity attach to our movement, for we know of no way of becoming old except by first being young. But that charge can no longer be preferred with any show of truth. Here is a man who was young when it was young, who has grown with its growth, and on whose head there have now gathered the snowy honours of nearly fourscore years.

As a man Mr. Livesey is eminently lovable and interesting. You discern in him at once the simple-minded, transparent, truthful Englishman, in whom there is no "blarney," and in whom there is "no guile." His most prominent feature is honest geniality and benevolence. As a speaker, Mr. Livesey is easy and artless, often elegant without designing it, and always attractive and effective. One can readily discern in the veteran the fire, and fervour, and unquenchable zeal of the temperance reformer in his earlier prime. He has the gift of language naturally in a superior degree; and he has that best secret of successful speaking—earnestness of purpose. There is a silvery melody in his tones which makes his speaking very enjoyable, and which insures his being heard in the largest halls. Mr. Livesey is entitled to all the honours that the temperance public can show him, for his has been a pre-eminently practical career. He is no mere Corinthian pillar to bring round to the front on special occasions, but a true and indefatigable worker, who spared no pains at a time when pains were thankless, and who underwent no small share of sharp persecution. Very interesting and suggestive on this head are some of the facts related in his " Reminiscences of Early Teetotalism," in the *Staunch Teetotaller*, the first number of which appeared in January, 1867.

It gives me pleasure to quote the following inspiring words in the " Prefatory Remarks " to Mr. Livesey's *Staunch Teetotaller*:—"Committed as I have been to the temperance cause for five-and-thirty years, and feeling, as I do now, that I cannot reasonably calculate upon a long series of action in the future, I am anxious, if possible, again to speak to the country, and to my brother teetotallers on this important subject, through the medium of another periodical. If my health sustains me to complete a twelvemonth's volume I shall be content; if longer, still more grateful. I now feel it a task to leave home to lecture, but can pleasantly fill up part of my time in writing for the press. . . . In this undertaking I expect no gain, but rather a loss, but still, I hope, a gain of something better than money—a gain to the cause of sobriety and human enjoyment. I shall print at least 10,000 copies monthly, and if they are not sold they shall be distributed gratuitously. My success depends entirely upon my health ; if that breaks down it may stop the work ; but if I remain as well as I am at present I hope I may be able to make some impression upon the public, and to stimulate to greater activity the efforts of my friends, thus humbly assisting to hasten the triumph of that blessed cause which is dear to the heart of every honest teetotaller."

For about two years Mr. Livesey was able to edit the *Teetotaller*, and his own contributions were characterised with all the fire, energy, and enthusiasm of former years. When addressing a temperance meeting in Preston, towards the end of October, 1869, he adverted to the services of his medical attendant, and observed that his faith in the principles of entire abstinence from alcoholic liquors, either as food or medicine, had been fairly tested. When at the worst, and deemed by his medical attendant to be in a dangerous state, the doctor said he could not be responsible for the consequences unless he (Mr. L.) would consent to take brandy or some other alcoholic stimulant. This he refused to do; and, solemnly addressing the audience, said :—"I was prepared to die, if need be, but I was *not* prepared to dishonour the glorious cause to which I am attached, and for which I have laboured so long."

On the 19th of May, 1869, Mr. Livesey was called to part with his beloved wife—one who was in the broadest and best sense of the term a worthy "helpmeet" to him, not only on the temperance question, but on every other which had for its object the present and future welfare of the human family.

Whilst I write, (June, 1873,) Mr. Livesey is as energetically employed, chiefly with his pen, in furthering the temperance cause as when he started in 1832. In proof of this I find, in a letter addressed by Mr. Livesey to the editors of *The Leeds Mercury*, May 27, 1873, on the subject of the Permissive Bill, the following paragraph:—Now that Government tell us they have gone as far as they can at present in legal restriction, that section of temperance reformers who have *not* placed their hopes upon Parliament have this consolation, that we have a power which neither Government nor politicians can impair or interfere with, and that is the power of diffusing true temperance principles among the people, enlightening their minds, appealing to their convictions, and captivating their affections by a good example and by the ties of brotherly social interest. Public-houses, no doubt, stand, and always have stood, in our path; but while we cannot violently and compulsorily close them, we must work in the only proper way to lessen their evil influence. True abstinence will not only become at once a blessing to thousands, but, if ever legislation is to advance, it will qualify them to help its progress. This is our work, and if we had continued in this during the last twenty years as we did at the beginning, our cause, I am confident, would have been in a far more flourishing condition than we find it at present.

CHAPTER IX.

ROBERT GRAY MASON.

I HAVE no hesitation in placing Robert Gray Mason amongst the early moral heroes of the Temperance Reformation. He was born in the town of March, in the Isle of Ely, and county of Cambridge, on the 18th of November, 1797; departed this life on the 31st of August, 1867, in the seventieth year of his age; and was buried in the beautiful cemetery at Bolton, Lancashire, where an impressive and appropriate service was conducted by the Rev. William Roaf, of Wigan. In the town of March he received an English education, at the expense of his mother's father, John Gray; but he learned nothing of Latin or Greek, and for the accuracy which he afterwards acquired as an English speaker he was chiefly indebted to the circumstance of having mingled a good deal in respectable society, where the language was correctly spoken.

Young Mason's maternal grandfather chose his calling, and at the age of fourteen he was bound apprentice to the trade of a carpenter and builder, and served his time at the village of Nordolph, in the county of Norfolk, where, to quote his own words, he "learned to fell timber, erect houses, build bridges, and do everything that could be done with wood and stone."

To the mortification of Mason's grandfather, it turned out that Robert had been apprenticed to a rigid Wesleyan Methodist, who monthly entertained the travelling preachers, and weekly the local preachers. He was also the principal man of the society, a class-leader, and built for them a commodious chapel. Mason relates that up till eighteen years of age he was trained for a pugilist, and "to this day," he says, "many of those who reside in the place of my birth are well aware of what I was fifty years ago. And such was then the darkness of my mind and the depravity of my heart, that I would have thought it an honour to have died fighting. This was, however, the crowning criminality of my conduct, and the crisis of my foolish ambition. When all with me—in a spiritual sense—was as dark as midnight, the Sun of Righteousness began to approach the horizon, and not long afterwards became visible to mortal eyes. A great ball was to take place at an hotel a short distance from the dwelling in which I was born, and during the dance a dreadful quarrel took place. As I was there, they engaged me to keep the door, knowing that none would then attempt to enter without my permission. I had ere this, however, heard the sound of the Gospel trumpet, and had, I trust, experienced a portion of the Spirit's enlightening influence. And the more I gazed on that frightful picture before me at that ball, I felt it to be a sort of hell upon earth! So deep was the lesson on my mind, and the impression on my heart, that I was afraid that God, in His righteous vengeance, would swallow up the wicked multitude with an earthquake. Under this alarming conviction I rushed from the inn, without the utterance of a single word to any one, and at an hour or two past midnight ran off as fast as if the devil was intent to stop me. Indeed, I made a physical effort, for hearing a tempting uproar behind me, as if to allure me back, I gave a kick at the enemy of souls, after the manner that one horse would kick at another, and away I ran till I became breathless, and the bond was, I trust, broken for ever. To God alone be all the praise for what I felt and did at that decisive hour; for from that moment I never any more mingled with one of my companions in sin. No, the snare was broken, and I had 'escaped as a bird out of the snare of the fowler.' I had twelve miles to walk to the place of my apprenticeship, in the darkness of the night, over a solitary road, where all was silent as the grave, but I took courage and pressed onward till I reached home. Nearly fifty years have run their course since that memorable midnight, and what scenes have I witnessed since, which I could not forget if I would !"

MR. MASON MEETS WITH THE REV.
RICHARD TABRAHAM.

It was at this remarkable crisis in Mason's history that he providentially met with the Rev. Richard

Tabraham, a highly-esteemed and useful Wesleyan minister—one whose honoured name has long been familiar to Temperance Reformers as a devoted friend and an able advocate of the cause. This zealous servant of Christ was then minister of Wisbeach Circuit, to which the village of Nordolph (where Mason resided) belonged, and having been brought into contact with Mason at his master's residence, he unfolded to his benighted mind the good tidings of the Gospel. "He was the first Christian man," says Mason, "who spoke to me words 'that accompany salvation,' and I shall ever remember with gratitude the happy and holy hours I spent with him on the banks of the river which flows from Nordolph to Wisbeach. Oft have I accompanied him half-way over the road, after hearing him preach, that I might open my whole heart to him as a penitent seeking the Saviour, and be directed to go to Him simply as a sinner. He was affectionate and kind to me, and his loving-kindness won my heart and made me long for his company and conversation; for I derived both instruction and consolation from the good man. I think I still hear him, in sweet, soothing strains, saying, '*Robert, don't forget that you are a sinner.*' He seemed anxious, above all things, to impress that important sentiment on my soul, and thus prevent me from building on a sandy foundation."

Three years ago I received the following letter,

dated London, January 26, 1870, from the now venerable Richard Tabraham :—

DEAR MR. L——, Fifty-two years since, in my
third year in the Wesleyan ministry, I found our
mutually loved and honoured friend, Robert Gray
Mason, apprenticed to a worthy Wesleyan carpenter
at Nordolph, on the Wisbeach Circuit, at whose
house I visited when I preached there.   One morning
I stepped into the workshop, and had a pleasant conversation with him and his fellow-apprentice.   God
was pleased to bless the word to their spiritual good.
Some years after he met me in London, and told me
that God had made me the means of his salvation.
This issued in a mutual attachment, till he passed to
that heaven where I hope to meet him ere long.

I have been an avowed enemy to drink, tobacco,
snuff, and fashion, more than seventy years; have
borne some losses, crosses, and scorn for teetotalism,
nearly forty years, and now I see it crowned with
laurels, its professors honoured, its universal spread
in the distance, and am sometimes able to lecture
for it five times in the week, in my seventy-eighth
year, and hope to die and be buried an out-and-out
teetotaller.   Go on prosperously.—Yours in Jesus,

RICHARD TABRAHAM.

After completing his seven years' apprenticeship,
Mason went to Cambridge, where he joined the fellow-
ship of the Wesleyan Church, and after being there
for two or three years, was urged to become a local

preacher, and acted as such for six or seven years, one of which was spent at Burslem, in Staffordshire. While at Burslem, he was sent to Macclesfield, in the same county, to preach anniversary sermons in the Wesleyan Chapel, in which he discoursed alternately with "Billy" Dawson, for many years one of the most popular and useful lay preachers amongst the Wesleyans. In Mr. Mason's audience at Macclesfield was the town-clerk, John Clulow, who was so much pleased with him as urgently to request that he should labour as a missionary in three of the alleged spiritually darkest English counties, those selected being Stafford-shire, Cheshire, and Shropshire. In this capacity he was employed for about two years, visiting and preaching, when at the expiry of that period, his kind patron, the town-clerk, died. At this time there appeared in the *British Seaman's Magazine*, an advertisement for an assistant minister and travelling secretary to the British Seaman's Society. Mr. Hall, Frodsham, Che-shire, having seen this advertisement, and considering it "just the place for friend Mason," without consult-ing him, wrote to the committee in London, stating that there was a person whom he knew, that he believed to be the very kind of man required, and succeeded in procuring him the situation. Having received a letter from Mr. Hall, Robert Gray Mason proceeded to London, and there, as he expressed it, "felt himself perfectly at home." This was in 1829. For twelve months he continued to labour chiefly among sailors, holding meetings, distributing tracts, and doing all in his power to elevate this important and still too much neglected class of our fellow-countrymen.

Whilst Mr. Mason was engaged as a missionary amongst the sailors in London, intelligence of the Temperance Reformation reached this country from America, and the question was at once taken up by philanthropic men in Bradford, Manchester, Bristol, and London, one of the first meetings in the metropolis being presided over by James Silk Buckingham, M.P. Mr. Mason warmly espoused the cause, and afterwards, in visits to the seaports of England, and subsequently the seaports and barracks of Ireland, strongly advocated its claims. The clergy of Ireland had taken a lively interest in the movement, and finding that the racy, impressive anecdotes which he related of the losses that had taken place at sea through drink told well upon the audiences, his services were permanently secured. He preached to the coast-guards and their families, and embraced every favourable opportunity of giving an address on the evils of drunkenness, and advocating the principles of temperance. During Mr. Mason's residence for three years in Ireland he advocated the claims of temperance in nearly every county of "beloved Hibernia." At that time it was total abstinence from spirits only, but as the labouring classes there drank no fermented liquors, "Temperance in Ireland," says Mr. Mason, "was Teetotalism in England."

At this period cholera was raging in Dublin, and our friend Mason stepped boldly forward and acted the part of a true hero. In a communication to a correspondent he observes—"I remained in Dublin as long as the pestilence prevailed, and an awful visitation it was! I am inhaling an infected atmosphere, beholding death on every side, and standing in jeopardy every hour; yet I am not alarmed. I have visited the streets where the disease is most prevalent. I have stood by one writhing in agony on a bed of straw; accompanied another to the crowded hospital, where there are nearly 600 patients; and followed a third to the open grave; and through divine mercy I am yet alive. It is a remarkable fact that, so far as I can ascertain, not one member of the Temperance Society (out of some thousands) has yet become its victim."

That good man, Father Mathew, at the close of a letter to Mr. Mason, from Cork, in December, 1844, thus writes—"Your great and successful labours are well known throughout all our societies, and your honoured name is a familiar household word amongst us. Ever cherishing the recollection of your solicitude and efficacious patronage, I am, with high respect, dear friend, yours affectionately, THEOBALD MATHEW."

CHAPTER X.

MR. MASON VISITS SCOTLAND.

IN September, 1836, Mr. Mason paid his first visit to Scotland, where he set to work in real earnest as a preacher of the Gospel and a lecturer on Temperance. When he reached Glasgow, "the prevalence," said he, "of intemperance struck me with horror. The very atmosphere seemed to be polluted with the odours of alcohol, and every ship which sailed appeared to me a sort of whisky shop."

The first temperance meeting was held at Saltcoats, in Ayrshire. It was a "fair" or market day, when there was a large number of people assembled. Strong opposition was experienced, the opponents of temperance being determined to put down the friends of that cause, and from the difficulty of obtaining a place of meeting it was found necessary to erect a tent. The erection of the tent raised the ire of the Saltcoats publicans, and one of their leaders, a rhymster, got out a placard, which opened with the following doggrel lines, which may be taken at the present day as a fair sample of the mental calibre of those engaged in the traffic—

"On the day of our Fair, on the green there will preach
A Mason on Temperance, our heathen to teach;
But I fear by the heat of the day they'll turn dry,
And his nonsense at night set them all on the fly."

Whilst the temperance friends were engaged in erecting the tent, Mason was busy preparing a reply in rhyme to the publican's burlesque effusion. The piece, extending to neary 300 lines, was delivered at the *soiree*, and took the good people of Saltcoats and the neighbourhood by surprise. Hear a few lines of it, entitled " A Publican's Prayer":—

"O bless me in body and mind and estate,
    And aid me, that I may more drunkards create,
    More families beggar, more blasphemy cause,
    More hatred occasion to heavenly laws,
    More hospitals fill, and more prisons erect,
    More pot-houses crowd, and more churches neglect!
    O may I still scatter, as long as I've breath,
    Disease and disorder, destruction and death ;
    Give tears to the wretched, and chains to the slave,
    And guests to the madhouse, and food to the grave !"

Towards the end of the piece occur the following patriotic lines—

"Our work is a warfare—our weapon is truth;
    Our warriors wait, in the pride of their youth,
    To receive from their captain the word of command,
    At which they'll come forth—an invincible band.
    To arms, then, ye heroes!—for freedom ye fight!
    The foe's in the field, and the battle's to-night;
    No longer submit to a spirit that reigns,
    Holding all that is dear in the direst of chains.
    Did Wallace and Bruce ever yield to the foe?
    Your rocks, glens, and mountains re-echo—No, no !
    And firm as the base of your mountains and rocks,
    'Gainst the proudest usurper stood Melville and Knox.
    Then let us still labour our land to restore,
    And fight till we conquer, like victors of yore."

On the day following the *soiree*, the committee of the Saltcoats Temperance Society presented Mr. Mason with an address, accompanied with a fine copy of Bagster's Polyglot Bible.

As a sample of a large number of complimentary addresses presented to Mr. Mason by the friends of temperance throughout Great Britain, I cannot do better than quote from one of them the following extract, which does credit to the pioneers of the cause in Saltcoats, from whom it was received :—

"HONOURED SIR,—We have great pleasure in embracing this opportunity of expressing our high estimation of your character and talents, and our sincere admiration of your laborious and disinterested exertions in the diffusion of Gospel truth, and the establishment of temperance societies. You have recently witnessed one of the happy fruits of your generous efforts in our soul-cheering soiree, where everything bright and beautiful was harmoniously blended with the powers of oratory, the charms of poetry, and the melody of song; and where two hundred and fifty persons, of various sentiments, enjoyed the 'feast of reason and the flow of soul,' without the slightest aid of the intoxicating cup. We trust that the meeting of last night will be long remembered with unmingled pleasure, and that its influence upon the community in general, and our society in particular, will be of great and permanent advantage. You will be delighted to hear that, after defraying all expenses in erecting the pavilion and supplying the guests, we have the surplus of a few pounds for the distressed families of our unemployed operatives; and as we are convinced that poverty, as well as crime, will vanish from our beloved country, in proportion as intemperance is diminished, we cannot but rejoice in the prospects of our noble institution. As members, therefore, of the Saltcoats Temperance Society, we desire to present you with this address, expressive of our warmest gratitude for the services you have rendered us. With pleasurable emotions we inform you that our excellent society has received an accession of nearly three hundred members since you came among us; all of whom have in this holiday season nobly resisted the sneers of interested opponents, as well as the wiles of seducing associates. Our sole object in addressing you, is to strengthen your hands in one of the most laudable undertakings in which a Christian philanthropist can be engaged; and we humbly trust, that all your future exertions will be crowned with success, similar to what has attended your efforts in this place.—ROBERT WALLACE, President."

After leaving Saltcoats Mr. Mason continued his labours for some time in Ayrshire, unconnected as an agent with any association, preaching twice, but generally three times, each Sabbath, in the pulpits of the different churches and chapels, and lecturing during the week. From Ayrshire he went to Iona, and spent a week on that famed island. The clergyman was most obliging, and the inhabitants felt interested in listening for the first time to the advocacy of temperance principles.

MR. MASON BECOMES A TOTAL ABSTAINER.

Like a number of the early friends of the cause, Mr. Mason acted for several years on the old temperance principle before adopting the more thoroughgoing pledge of abstinence from all intoxicating liquors. The teetotal pledge was adopted by him on the 25th of Dec., 1836. "On that day," as I have heard him state, "I drank my last drop of beer." His adoption of the pledge was brought about in the following somewhat singular manner :—Mason had been driven to Dumfries by a drunken coachman—in those days a circumstance of too frequent occurrence. On reaching the end of the journey, addressing the driver, he said, "Sir, you have placed my life in jeopardy, and perilled the lives of all the passengers. You are unfit to have the charge of horses, much less of men. Take my advice and give up your drinking." "Coachey" was very civil, expressed thanks for the advice, and departed. Shortly after this interview the coachman met John Macintosh, then the well-known and respected guard of the Edinburgh and Dumfries mail, and thus accosted him, "I think that I have met one of your sort to-day, John." This zealous, weather-beaten teetotaller, resolved to lose no time in calling on

Mason at his lodgings, which he did on the day following, being Christmas. Mr. Mason had just finished dinner, and had been using beer. When Macintosh's eye caught the glass he was taken somewhat aback; but as they were alone, he, in the most respectful manner, said, "You are an intelligent man, Mr. Mason, a public character, have access to pulpits and platforms, and must know that the drinking customs of this country are polluting society to a dreadful extent, and the difference between your giving your countenance to these customs and fighting against them, when weighed in the balance of eternity, an angel cannot guess!" These pointed words deeply impressed Mason; and when he thought on what that man had to meet with on the road from the public and from tippling associates on account of his teetotalism, and when he reflected on how for more than three years the total abstainers had looked at that man and at himself, he dashed the goblet from him and never again touched a drop of any kind of intoxicating drink.

Mr. Mason was struck with the general appearance of John Macintosh. He was, he said, the finest stalwart Scotsman he had ever seen. His open, modest countenance was covered with smiles. Mason always spoke of Macintosh in the most grateful terms as his "teetotal father." I had only once the pleasure of meeting with this retiring yet true hero in Glasgow. His intelligent, benevolent eye beamed brightly, as he raised his right arm, and recounted a few of his early struggles in advancing the temperance movement. In 1860 he met with a melancholy and fatal accident in the discharge of his duty as one of her Majesty's mail guards, on the Edinburgh and Glasgow Railway. When in the act of exchanging a mail-bag at one of the stations he was instantly launched into eternity! His name is still lovingly remembered by the older teetotallers in Edinburgh, Glasgow, Dumfries, and other parts of Scotland. For thirty-six years he held the responsible situation of mail guard, and her Majesty's Ministers granted, what is seldom done, an annuity of £25 to his widow.

It was my privilege to listen to Mr. Mason for the first time in the Rev. John Inglis' church, Hamilton, on Monday, the 27th of October, 1837. On that occasion he gave a clever, fascinating, instructive, and, at times, eloquent lecture on the then not very popular doctrine of total abstinence from all intoxicating liquors. Towards the close he made an earnest and telling appeal on behalf of teetotalism. Thirty-five of the members of the old Temperance Society rallied round the good man, and formed, at his suggestion, the first Hamilton Total Abstinence Society. The pious John Naismith, James Hamilton, Francis Wilson, and others who joined that evening have been called to heaven, and some still remain faithful friends of the cause.

Mr. Mason was the principal speaker at the first

annual *soiree* of the Glasgow Total Abstinence Society, which was held in the Lyceum Rooms, Nelson Street, on the 2nd January, 1837. The meeting was a very interesting and successful one. The chair was occupied by the venerable John Dunlop, of Greenock.

MR. MASON IN EDINBURGH.

After visiting and forming total abstinence societies in various parts of the West of Scotland, where he accomplished much good, Mr. Mason, in the summer of 1837, proceeded to Edinburgh, and there fixed his head-quarters. The Edinburgh Total Abstinence Society was instituted on the 27th of September, 1836. The second annual meeting was held in the Freemasons' Hall, on the 26th of December, 1838. At page 14 of the report submitted by the Secretary, Mr. George Agnew, I find the following cheering reference to Mr. Mason, which will, I doubt not, be perused with interest and profit alike by friends on both sides of the Tweed, and far beyond—

"The Committee have the happiness of adding, that our encouraging success has by no means been confined to the Scottish metropolis; but that, through the indefatigable and disinterested exertions of the Society's excellent travelling agent, wonders have been achieved in almost every part of our beloved country. They cannot, therefore, send this report into the world without offering a due tribute of praise to the Rev. Robert Gray Mason, to whose generous and valuable

services they are so much indebted. Seeing the
wickedness and wretchedness produced in every
direction by the desolating ravages of intemperance,
he came nobly forward, in the true spirit of a Christian
philanthropist, in order to diminish, if possible, the
havoc of the Destroyer. Uncheered by the least
prospect of worldly emolument, he sacrificed the offer
of other respectable and lucrative situations for the
purpose of devoting his energies to the removal of our
nation's reproach. He has now been engaged in the
warfare for nearly two years, and he has the consolation of knowing that, though great have been his toils
and trials, his triumphs have been still greater. In
the short space of twelve months Mr. Mason has held
meetings in 180 places, preached 150 sermons, delivered
300 lectures, formed 120 societies, and added 30,000
members to the total abstinence ranks. To accomplish
this he has travelled thousands of miles, sacrificed
many a comfort, and endured many a storm; and
when your Committee take into consideration the
tracts he has distributed, the letters he has written,
and the schools he has visited, in addition to getting
up meetings and forming associations, they are confident the Society will be able to appreciate the
importance of his work.

"Your Committee, however, regret to state that,
unremitting as Mr. Mason's labours have been, he
has not been able to procure more than the bare
expenses of his mission, and, in many cases, not

even these. He has, in fact, delivered lectures at more than sixty places in the course of the past year, at which he received nothing; and the whole of his receipts have not amounted to more than £70, while his expenses have been upwards of £80. The cause of his receiving little or nothing in many places which he has visited, has, your Committee believe, originated in an impression that he receives a salary from the Edinburgh Total Abstinence Society, under whose sanction he labours. This erroneous impression they are bound to correct, and to state honestly that, owing to the want of adequate funds, the Society is not able to support a salaried travelling agent. The Committee declare this truth to the honour of the Society's champion; for, had he not gone boldly forward, expecting no recompense from them, they have every reason to believe that, instead of boasting of three hundred total abstinence societies in Scotland, they should have had little more than one hundred. Under these circumstances, your Committee cannot but rejoice that Mr. Mason has been prevailed upon to continue his important services in connection with the Edinburgh Society; and he goes forth, at the commencement of another year, cheered on by the good wishes of all who are acquainted with the value of his work; and the earnest prayer of your Committee is, that many thousands of our degraded sons and daughters, who are at present unfortunately under the influence of that most delusive, degrading, and soul-destroying vice of intemperance, may be arrested in their fatal career, and restored to their proper senses, by the influence of his forcible appeals; and that the blessings of many who were ready to perish may prove the recompense of his reward."

This single extract, in my opinion, from whatever point it is looked at, speaks volumes in favour of our departed friend, and will itself stand as a memorial of his unwearied and self-denying labours for generations to come.

MR. MASON IN THE NORTH.

Robert Gray Mason was a special favourite throughout the North of Scotland, and by many friends even in England and Wales had long been familiarly known as "The Father Mathew of the North." In Inverness, Elgin, Aberdeen, Kirkwall, and many other parts of the country, I have often heard the name of Robert Gray Mason referred to in the most cordial terms by the friends of temperance. His disinterested labours were also favourably recognised outside the temperance ranks. In Wick, for example, the Magistrates and Town Council unanimously agreed to present him with the freedom of that ancient royal burgh. At a special meeting of the Town Council, in March, 1841, the following resolution was adopted :—

" Taking into consideration the great and incalculable benefits conferred on this community by the Rev. Robert Gray Mason, whose forcible, impressive, and convincing lectures, in favour of the noble principle of total abstinence from all intoxicating drinks, have had a powerful tendency in restoring domestic comfort to many families, and arresting the progress of vice and immorality—the Town Council resolve, as a mark of the sincere esteem in which they regard that gentleman's valuable services, to present him with a burgess ticket of this royal burgh."

The meeting at which the burgess ticket was presented was a numerous and highly respectable one. In reply Mr. Mason embraced the opportunity of delivering a faithful and impressive address, which was afterwards published in a neat pamphlet of forty-eight pages, entitled an *Epitome of Genuine Temperance Principles and Triumphs*. The Committee of the Wick Total Abstinence Society also presented Mr. Mason with an Address, on which occasion the Earl of Fife spoke as follows:—

"When I reflect on the evils that have been removed, and the benefits that have been conferred by the establishment of your excellent Association,—when I remember the obstacles you have had to surmount, and the enemies you have been called to encounter, in the prosecution of your laudable labours,—I feel the fullest assurance that history will record the noble deeds, and posterity revere the honoured name, of your energetic and philanthropic Mason."

I have perused with interest a tractate in which a graphic narrative is given of Mr. Mason's labours in

Thurso, Dornoch, Tain, Invergordon, Dingwall, Fort-
rose, Inverness, Aberdeen, &c.   In the granite city he
spent a month, and delivered many sermons and lectures
in the different churches.   The city was stirred, and
hundreds were added to the temperance ranks.   Large
and enthusiastic meetings were likewise held in Buchan
district, Inverury, Keith, Elgin, and other northern
towns.   As an illustration of the intelligent and
comprehensive view which Mr. Mason at that early
period took of the subject, I quote the following
outline of one of his lectures delivered to 700 people
in the Rev. Mr. Lind's church, Elgin—1st, Our
labour is one of disinterested patriotism and philanthropy.   2d, Our *sphere* is chiefly among the working
community and the rising generation.   3d, Our *object*
is to preserve the sober, and reclaim the drunken.
4th, Our *principle* is entire abstinence from every
pernicious and intoxicating article.   5th, Our *aim* is
GOD'S HIGHEST GLORY, AND OUR COUNTRY'S GREATEST
GOOD.

FAREWELL SOIREE IN ABERDEEN.

After Mr. Mason had spent seven years in advocating
the cause of Teetotalism throughout the length and
breadth of Scotland, he arranged to return to England.
Of a large number of valedictory *soirees* held in honour
of Mr. Mason in various parts of the country, I shall
only refer to one which took place in Aberdeen

on November 15, 1843. The chair was appropriately occupied by George Maitland, an old staunch friend of the cause, now gone to his happy rest and reward. The meeting was a numerous and influential one, and was addressed by the late Rev. R. Forbes, the Rev. John Kennedy, D.D. (now of Stepney, London), and others.

In course of the evening Mr. Mason delivered an earnest address, towards the close of which he gave utterance to the following cheering words :—

"I have had the honour, Mr. Chairman, of holding meetings in eighteen of your city churches, and the pleasure of seeing fifteen of your ministers enrolled in our ranks. . . . . In reference to my humble services in your cause, I thank God for enabling me to say to his glory, in this parting address, that I have been graciously enabled to finish the work I began, and have held no fewer than five thousand meetings in fifteen hundred places, scattered over all the three-and-thirty counties of beloved Caledonia, since I gave my name to the temperance pledge. To speak of the difficulties and dangers associated with a tour over all the Highlands and Hebrides of Scotland, and the exposure and expense connected with the delivery of seven hundred lectures in one hundred islands—in addition to my various labours in nearly every town and village in the Lowlands—would be superfluous. Every sensible person must be aware that such an undertaking could not be accomplished without much

pain and peril, toil and trial; but suffice it to say, it
has been achieved, and, as far as good has been
wrought in the work, to God alone be the praise."

Here I may introduce a note in which Mr. Mason
refers to his early friend, the Rev. Richard Tabraham,
and their manifold self-denying labours—

"Strange to say," observes Mason, "that good man,
Richard Tabraham, has been as far north as the stormy
Shetland Isles; and so have I, and over all of them,
which he has not. And I have likewise visited them
twice over, and gone to the most distant and dangerous. I have also occupied every one of their Established churches, and likewise the Free, United Presbyterian, Congregational, and Wesleyan. Then, again,
Mr. Tabraham has, for nearly thirty years, advocated
the cause of Temperance; so have I, and to an extent
far beyond that of any other person, and in hundreds
of churches in Scotland and chapels in England. And
it may be truly added that my meetings, whether
sermons on the Sabbath, or lectures through the week—
the one on Righteousness, the other on Temperance—
have been in every county, every city, and every chief
town in England, Scotland, and Wales, and nearly the
same in Ireland, together with the Channel Isles, the
Scilly Isles, the Orkney Isles, and the Isles of Man,
of Wight, and of Anglesea. Thus I exceeded my beloved friend Tabraham, but I am glad to find that he
far excels the great majority of his brethren as a
Temperance Reformer."

As the plan which Mr. Mason adopted in getting up meetings and arranging for Sunday services was somewhat original, it may briefly be referred to. He called upon the different clergymen of the places he visited on Saturday, and readily obtained the use of their churches for the Sabbath. Having succeeded in this, he announced from the respective pulpits that he would lecture during the week; if the people were interested by his preaching they came to hear his lecture, and the collections then obtained "carried him on his way." He depended chiefly for his success in obtaining places of worship on letters of introduction which he received from ministers of all denominations. His Sabbath audiences were generally large, and those in the evening often crowded. The interest excited by his preaching on Sunday opened up the way for the people listening to Temperance during the week. The subject of Total Abstinence, however, was not even introduced into his sermon, and he made it a point never to do so. "This is not the time or the place," I have not unfrequently heard him say in England and Scotland, "for me to advocate the temperance question, although I feel deeply interested in it, but I shall be glad to see you at such a meeting to-morrow evening, when you shall hear my views on the subject."

During the week Mr. Mason spoke almost every night. When he visited any town, the inhabitants generally heard for the first time the principles of teetotalism promulgated; and in most places at that time throughout Scotland he was instrumental in forming the first Total Abstinence Society. In many parts of Scotland the name of Robert Gray Mason is still, and will long remain, an honoured household word.

CHAPTER XI.

MR. MASON IN ENGLAND.

SUBSEQUENT to 1843 Mr. Mason returned to England, and from that period, with short intervals, laboured under the auspices of the British Association for the Promotion of Temperance, now known as the British Temperance League, the executive of which meet in Bolton, Lancashire. For a time after his return to England he followed the arrangements made for him by that Association; but for many years he preferred to work in his own way, arranging for and delivering his sermons on Sunday, and his temperance lectures during the week, as he had done in Scotland.

It would serve no useful purpose to follow our friend minutely in his varied fields of usefulness throughout England. This would be, to a great extent, simply a repetition of what has been said respecting his labours for about seven years in Scotland.

From a host of complimentary notices which I find in temperance journals and newspapers, I select the following lines from the *British Temperance Advocate* and the *Guernsey Comet:*—

"The Rev. R. G. Mason has for some time past traversed this extensive union—East Norfolk—

preaching from two to four sermons on the Sabbath, in most of the principal places of worship, to the delight and profit of the numerous congregations, and delivering five or six lectures on temperance weekly, generally to large audiences, in nearly all the principal towns and villages of Norfolk and a part of Suffolk. It is little to say that a man of his urbanity, intelligence, talent, piety, and zeal, has won golden opinions amongst those who have heard him, and left a highly favourable impression, both of himself and his cause, in all the places he has visited."

Having frequently heard Mr. Mason in England and Scotland, I can cordially endorse the following paragraph from the *Comet:*—

"Mr. Mason's style is very familiar and truly impressive. There are no satirical or ill-natured reflections thrown upon those who differ from him, and nothing calculated to exasperate or injure a single individual. On the other hand, there is everything to soften down and win over the most hardened inebriate and the most hostile opponent. He seems to possess an almost inexhaustible stock of *arguments* the most convincing and conclusive, *anecdotes* the most numerous and pathetic, *figures* the most appropriate and diversified, and *facts* the most numerous and instructive; so that it is scarcely possible that any one can sit under his lectures without being greatly edified and highly benefited. Still, we are of opinion that he shines more in the pulpit than on the platform, and seems more at home in proclaiming the glad tidings of salvation than in advocating the cause of temperance."

In another paper, a Norwich correspondent justly observes that Mr. Mason's numerous Sunday services *were all perfectly gratuitous, a fact which does him great honour.*

HIS LABOURS AMONGST THE YOUNG.

Mr. Mason took a special interest in the rising generation, and displayed not a little tact and skill in addressing them. He had long made it a part of his work to visit and address not only Sunday Schools, but Day, Ragged, and the National or Parish Schools. It had been represented to him that, as the National Schools in England were under Government pay and clerical control, he would not get access to them; but though attempts were made to discourage and even debar him, he tried the experiment, and the cheering result was that out of about 350 schools, in thirteen different English counties, only one refused to receive him.

Mr. Mason continued to pursue his disinterested labours till about the month of May, 1861, when he was seized with a slight stroke of paralysis, which put a check upon his exertions. The most eminent medical authorities in London were consulted, who strongly advised him to avoid late and long meetings, large audiences, and everything likely to cause excitement. This he felt for a time to be rather a hard task; but, to quote his own words, "Providence bent the back to the burden." From that time he chiefly resided in Bolton, where he was watched over with tender care by his attached friend, John Cunliffe (since then deceased), and where he spent part of his leisure time very profitably in domiciliary visitation throughout the villages and hamlets of that thickly-populated part of Lancashire. He also embraced every opportunity of delivering short addresses to the boys and girls in the respective schools, where he always met with a cordial reception.

For many years Mr. Mason was in the habit of issuing a yearly epistle, in which he gave an epitome of his labours. I have re-read four of them, the first three respectively addressed to his old friends, George Maitland, Aberdeen; George Gallie, Glasgow; and the Rev. Wm. Reid, Edinburgh. The fourth, and the last, I believe, he ever penned, dated December 5, 1863, was inscribed to T. B. Smithies, the genial editor of the *British Workman* and *Band of Hope Review*. The following is a copy of this, to me, very suggestive and interesting epistle, which is earnestly commended to the attention of the devoted friends of the young:—

"DEAR FRIEND,—By the blessing of the Most High, my health is considerably improved, and my strength abundantly renewed. With a few exceptions, I feel nearly as hearty and healthy as I did when in the meridian of manhood, while holding nine or ten meetings per week. Under God, I ascribe this welcome change to my three months' tour in beloved Scotland, where I breathed the purest air and enjoyed the rarest exercise. My lot for the last two years has been cast in the most populous county of Great Britain, and my general residence at Bolton-le-Moors. Finding the surrounding districts of this important town to abound in villages and hamlets of a tolerable size, and with schools and chapels very numerous and well attended, I made up my mind to visit them. Feeling a warm interest in the education of young people, I felt it my duty and delight to devote my energies to their welfare. Having of late—as you have probably heard —had a stroke of *paralysis*, and being urged by medical authority to avoid all long and loud speaking, especially in large and crowded assemblies, I have felt it my duty to take their advice. This, however, is to me a very severe trial, and one which I have brought upon myself by laborious exertions of an exciting nature. And this also has induced me to play a more prudent part, and I have therefore directed my attention to the rising generation. Remembering that these are to live and move when I am dead and gone, and to occupy the places which their teachers now occupy, I feel it a position of very great, and even infinite, value.

"Then, first of all, I tried the experiment of ob-taining access to the chief National schools of the southern counties of England, and the following are a few of the principal towns and cities :—Brighton

Hastings, Salisbury, Southampton, Reading, Yeovil, and Guildford; Exeter, Barnstaple, Ilfracombe, Dorchester, Winchester, Bath, and Bristol; and (previously) those of Portsmouth, Monmouth, Weymouth, Sidmouth, Exmouth, Dartmouth, and Plymouth; besides Falmouth, Yarmouth, and Teignmouth, Canterbury, Rochester, Wells, and Windsor; and I may add Dover, Ramsgate, Maidstone, Chichester, Chatham, Pembroke, and St. David's. And having succeeded in securing the chief schools and chapels of these towns and cities, I feel very thankful and content. To impart seasonable and salutary instruction to 43,000 scholars of 396 schools, in 168 towns of 15 counties, was no mean undertaking. And these I had in places 300 miles from Bolton, where I now reside; and since then I have been nearly 300 miles in the north, and addressed various schools beyond and at Edinburgh, Glasgow, Kirkcaldy, Gourock, Greenock, Leith, and Paisley. I am, however, once more in populous Lancashire and prosperous Bolton—a town with 33 places of worship, with both day and Sabbath-schools. These, with but one exception, I had the privilege of addressing: and at the last of them we had of scholars and teachers nearly 1600; and in all combined, 16,000.

"At many of the places I have visited there are four or five schools, and in several of the schools two or three departments, namely, boys, girls, and infants, and each of these I usually addressed; and I may likewise add that I was more than once at some of the same places. The whole multiplied by three would amount to 500 addresses, and all, save Wigan, were gratuitous.

R. G. M."

MR. MASON'S WRITINGS.

In a few closing sentences I shall refer to Mr. Mason's literary productions. His poetical address, "The Broadside," and an "Epitome of Genuine Temperance Principles," have already been referred to. He also published a number of tractates, bearing the titles of "The Temperance Cause in Ireland;" "An Urgent Appeal to Christian Ministers on the Disuse of Strong Drinks;" "Rational Defence of Temperance Principles;" "New Year's Address, or the Glorious Triumphs of Genuine Temperance," delivered in January, 1839, at the annual soiree of the Glasgow Total Abstinence Society; "A Friendly Farewell to the Aberdeen Temperance Association," &c. In poetical pieces, Mr. Mason published, amongst others, the following :—"The Publican," extending to 296 stanzas; "The Brewers of Burton," containing 97 stanzas; "The Old Domestic Oak," 97 stanzas ; "The Flight of Years, or Farewell to Fifty-two;" "The Cypress Wreath ;" and "The Scottish Sabbath, and other Poems," &c. Mr. Mason has also published a neat little volume of hymns, which is divided into three sections : first, "Hymns for Temperance Meetings," numbering 182; second, "Religious Hymns," and "Sacred Pieces," &c. Many of these pieces have long been in general use, and highly appreciated in not a few temperance meetings, especially in England and Wales, where the singing has always occupied its proper place at temperance gatherings.

In these chapters I have referred chiefly to the unwearied and disinterested services of Robert Gray Mason in Scotland, and more briefly to his "works of faith and labours of love" in England. He never recovered from the paralytic stroke of May, 1861, which ultimately told to some extent on his over-wrought and naturally busy brain. His call by the blessed Master whom he had so long and faithfully served was somewhat unexpected. On the 31st of August, 1867, in his 70th year, he entered on the "rest" which remaineth for the people of God. The funeral was a large and highly respectable one. There were friends present from various parts of Lancashire and Yorkshire, and one from Glasgow. The burial service was conducted at Bolton Cemetery, by the beloved William Roaf, for thirty years the devoted and useful minister of the Independent Chapel, Wigan, who, in March, 1870, was himself called to join the "ransomed of the Lord" in glory. The remains of Robert Gray Mason were carried to the grave by the loving hands of his self-denying fellow-labourers, the agents of the British Temperance League, and there interred in "sure and certain hope of the resurrection to eternal life."

CHAPTER XII.

EDWARD MORRIS.

EDWARD MORRIS—the brave, enthusiastic, laborious, and useful temperance reformer —was born at Shrewsbury, Shropshire, on the 20th of April, 1787, and died at Glasgow on the 1st of August, 1860, in his 74th year. Like a large number in England, he was greatly indebted to the praiseworthy efforts of the Sunday-school teacher. Miss Mary Hughes, an intelligent and benevolent lady, had commenced a school in connection with the parish church. "All who came to the school," says this lady, "were admitted without any other inquiry being made than the name and residence of the applicant. Many came from a distance of several miles, bringing their dinner with them; and, when the weather was fine, it was pleasant to view them in cheerful groups, sitting on the grave-stones, enjoying their frugal meal in a pretty country churchyard."

Shortly after this well-conducted school was opened, the zealous teacher called on the mother of young Morris, and urged her to send all her children to the school. Edward had reached his ninth year without having learned the alphabet, and felt ashamed to accompany his sisters to this Sunday-school. Ere long, however, he presented himself for admission, and soon became a special favourite. When he left the church, on the evening of the first Sunday, he had mastered the alphabet, and continued to make rapid progress. Edward was employed during the week at a woollen factory, and his hours were so long that he could not take advantage of a free class taught by Miss Hughes. When only about fourteen years of age, he was sent out as a commercial traveller, and his journeys kept him, at times, for two or three weeks from home. In this responsible situation he conducted himself to the entire satisfaction of his employer. Every spare hour was now assiduously devoted to self-improvement. At the Sunday-school he had been rewarded for his excellent behaviour with a Bible, which he always took with him as a travelling companion, and at that early age manfully endeavoured to follow its moral precepts.

In consequence of dull trade, young Morris had reluctantly to leave the parental roof and remove to the neighbourhood of Manchester, where he met with a good situation in a spinning mill. In the village where he resided it was almost impossible to obtain lodgings with a sober family. Even the mothers of helpless infants would leave their tender charge at night, and squander away the time in dissipation at the beershop. At such seasons Edward not unfrequently left his own bedroom to lift a helpless crying babe from an adjoining room, and, carrying it downstairs to the deserted kitchen fire, warmed and soothed the little one to sleep, and then, with a tenderness which would have done credit to the unnatural mother or sottish father, replaced the infant in its cradle. In a short time the book-keeper and Edward opened a Sunday-school for the instruction of the children employed at the factory, and soon had an attendance of sixty.

By and by young Morris removed from Lancashire to the works of the New Lanark Spinning Company, of which Robert Owen was then one of the active partners. Shortly after entering on his new situation at the mills, an incident occurred illustrative of the sterling honesty and determination which ever characterised him in after life. Edward had charge of the store, and had got a hint that a certain farmer, instead of supplying the company, according to agreement, with the best flour, was suspected of leaving an adulterated article. The farmer accordingly called, and was about to leave his flour as usual, when young Morris cast his coat, turned up his shirt sleeves, and plunging his hand into one of the sacks, found all right at the top, but a little further down discovered some of inferior quality. He then held up the bad flour in presence of the interested onlookers, and ordered the dishonest farmer to replace every bag upon his cart, and be off with them, adding—" We pay for the best flour here, and won't take that rubbish." This little circumstance not only delighted Mr. Owen, but justly gained for the " young Englishman " great favour with the large number of hands employed at the works. He remained in the service of this company for nine-teen years, four of which were spent at the works near Lanark, and the remainder as salesman at Glas-gow. Although Edward differed widely from Robert Owen on questions of vital importance, he always spoke of him as a most upright and kind master.

On the very first Sabbath after his arrival in Glasgow, we find him taking an active part in the Wesleyan Methodist Sunday-school, where his labours were highly appreciated. When visiting absent scholars at their homes, he met with many adults who were suffering severely from want of work and high-priced provisions. At the suggestion of Edward, six or seven young men formed a society for the relief of "Aged Men," each one subscribing a small sum quarterly, and visiting in turn such cases as their little fund enabled them to assist. This led, I believe, to the formation of the Old Man's Asylum, now one of the many useful city charities in Glasgow.

MR. MORRIS AS A TEMPERANCE REFORMER.

I shall now refer more particularly to Edward Morris as a temperance reformer. It appears that he joined the Old Temperance Society on the 5th of December, 1830, after having listened to a stirring lecture by Mr. William Collins, in Glasgow. He had no sooner adopted the principle than he threw himself heartily

into its advocacy.   Early in 1831 he commenced to
travel in Scotland and the north of England to solicit
orders for a fine work entitled, *Select Views of the
Lakes of Scotland*.   In the different places visited
he embraced every opportunity of advocating the
newly-adopted principle.   In Callander, Dumfries,
Annan (at which place he was warmly welcomed by
Mr. James Simpson, banker, still a staunch teetotaller),
and many other Scottish towns, his lectures excited
considerable interest, and were productive of much
good.   The journey was extended as far as Preston,
where he met with a cordial reception from Joseph
Livesey, Joseph Dearden, and others.

As a proof of the deep interest taken in this early
visit to Preston, I shall quote a few lines from a note
received from Mr. Dearden, still an earnest friend of
the cause:—"In Livesey's *Moral Reformer* for November, 1832, you will find an original poem by Edward
Morris, which to this day we sing at many of our
public temperance meetings.   It was composed when
he visited Preston, and is dated October 18, 1832.
In the December number of the same year appears an
address of his to the young men and women of Preston,
which contains good teetotal and religious advice.   Mr.
Morris spoke at several meetings in Preston, and was
at our meeting in St. Peter's schoolroom when 'Dickie
Turner' signed the pledge.   There are several still
living who remember with great pleasure his visit to
Preston."

The following are the first three verses and the last of the hymn referred to by Mr. Dearden, and addressed "To the Members of the Preston Temperance Society"—

"What evils, Intemp'rance, with thine can compare?
What wailing, and anguish, and wide-spread despair
Abound in thy dwelling! Thy region is death,
And poison comes forth from thy terrible breath.

"Ah, cruel deceiver! thou'st smitten our isle;
The red Rose of England refuses to smile,
And Scotia's proud Thistle bows low in the gale,
And Erin's loved Shamrock droops sad in the vale.

"But see! a new Banner is lifted on high,
Its beauty and glory are seen in the sky;
And Preston, this banner is precious to thee,
Thy sons and fair daughters around it I see.

   *   *   *   *   *

"That Being who sits on the throne of the sky,
And bends o'er all creatures a pitiful eye,
Beholds with approval. His blessings we own,
And He more abundant our labours will crown."

Like not a few of the early friends of the temperance movement, Mr. Morris very soon discovered that there was something awanting in the pledge, which required abstinence from ardent spirits only, and accordingly, before long he was found advocating total abstinence from all intoxicating liquors. In October, 1834, he delivered a lecture in the Seaman's Chapel, Brown Street, Glasgow—reported at the time in the papers—in which he "urged," says the *Temperance*

Journal, "the adoption of the new, or teetotal pledge, then in full and successful operation in Preston."

MR. MORRIS ON THE PLATFORM.

In October, 1836, an important discussion took place in the Lyceum Rooms, Glasgow, between Mr. Morris and Mr. Gray—Mr. M. defending teetotalism, and Mr. G. moderation. The discussion, which extended over three nights, excited much interest in the city, was favourably noticed by the Press, and the champion of teetotalism, by an overwhelming majority, came off victor. During the same month, at the request of Mr. John Dunlop, then resident in Greenock, Mr. Morris visited that town, and held a discussion with another advocate of the drinking system, and defeated him likewise. In those early and stormy stages of the temperance agitation in Glasgow and elsewhere, our hero occupied, in his own sphere, a prominent, honourable, and useful position.

The first time it was my privilege to hear Mr. Morris, he was addressing an attentive meeting on the temperance question, in 1842, in Cowcaddens, Glasgow. He was then employed as clerk at the Canal Office, Port Dundas, where he was well known and highly respected. I gladly avail myself here of a note received from the Rev. Peter Mearns, for a number of years employed as a zealous city missionary at Port-Dundas, now successor to the revered Dr. Adam Thomson, of Coldstream:—"I knew Mr. Morris very well, and respected him as an earnest and unflinching advocate of abstinence. He was very sharp and fearless in reproving sin. When he was clerk at the passengers' room, Port-Dundas, a man, who was much intoxicated, one day came forward with those who were applying for tickets, and after waiting a little fell down drunk. Mr. Morris went forward to him when all were served, and asked him what he wanted. He said, 'I want a ticket.' 'But you're drunk,—you can't go into the boat.' 'O, yes! I've only got a *refreshment*.' 'A refreshment! it's a *defreshment* to you, and I advise you to take no more.' And he gave him time to get sober. Our friend had a good deal of ready humour, which always served him when advocating temperance at a time when it was unpopular. One day he was giving good advice to people waiting in the passengers' room, when a gentleman stepped forward, and abruptly said, 'Mr. Morris, do you say there is any harm in my taking a glass of wine?' Mr. Morris promptly replied, 'I shall answer your question, sir, by asking you another, after the Scotch fashion,—Is there any harm in my letting it alone?' Not expecting this, the gentleman was nonplussed, and turned away amid the derisive laughter of the bystanders."

The following note from Mr. Robert Rae, London, of September 23, 1864, will be read with interest—

"I have pleasure in sending a note respecting our old friend, Mr. Morris. The first time I saw Mr.

Morris was in the winter of 1841-2, at a temperance meeting in Canon Street Chapel, Glasgow. At that meeting he was the principal speaker, and spoke, as he often did at that time, with extraordinary energy, eloquence, and power. I shall never forget the enthusiastic appreciation, indicative of the true poet, with which, when referring to the 'Marriage at Cana,' he quoted the beautiful line, 'The conscious water saw its God, and *blushed*.' I co-operated with Mr. Morris for several years in the Committee of the Cowcaddens Total Abstinence Society, and was often struck with the single-minded earnestness, combined with shrewdness, sagacity, and good temper, that he always brought to the transaction of the society's business. The temperance movement had taken a deep hold of his ardent, pure-minded, guileless, and generous nature, and he deemed no sacrifice too great to make for its advancement. Mr. Morris well deserves an honourable place in your gallery of temperance heroes."

In 1843, Mr. Morris published the *Life of Henry Bell, the Practical Introducer of the Steam Boat into Great Britain*. This little volume, of 180 pages, attracted considerable attention when it appeared, and in the list of subscribers I observed the Duke of Argyll, Sir James Campbell, and a number of influential gentlemen. The book does much credit alike to the heart and head of its author. If Edward Morris had done nothing more than produce that little volume, and bring to light the claims of that retiring but great public benefactor, Henry Bell, his memory ought to be long and gratefully remembered, not only by the citizens of Glasgow, but by the promoters of steam navigation generally.

In 1847, Mr. Morris published a poem of 400 pages, on which he bestowed much time and labour, entitled, *The Glorious Isle; or, a Glance at the Leading Features of British History.* In 1855, he brought out the *History of Temperance and Teetotal Societies in Glasgow.* He was one of the early friends of the United Kingdom Alliance, and remained till his death its enthusiastic supporter.

Whilst Mr. Morris felt specially interested in the temperance enterprise, he was ever ready to lend a helping hand in forwarding every question calculated to elevate the "toiling millions" of his fellow-creatures. So far back as March, 1834, we find him delivering a series of lectures on the necessity and advantages of Early Closing, which excited considerable attention. He frequently contributed terse and important letters to the newspapers on topics of public interest, and in his earlier days often assumed the *nom de plume* of "Brittanicus."

For a number of years Mr. Morris conducted an open-air service on Glasgow Green, east of Nelson's monument, commencing about five o'clock, with devotional exercises. There he stood, with open Bible in hand, pleading in fervid, and at times eloquent, impressive terms, in behalf of Christianity, temperance, and kindred subjects. His homely words of advice were listened to with respectful attention, and by many of the working classes, who seldom or never attended any place of worship. He continued to preside at these Sunday evening meetings long after his health had considerably failed; and when urged by friends to cease taking part in these gatherings, he would say in his own earnest way, "I *must* speak a word, however feeble, for religion *and* temperance, so long as the Lord gives me health and strength to do so." On such occasions he was generally assisted by friends, and I felt honoured in standing by his side and taking part in the proceedings.

I shall never forget the last time he visited his favourite spot on Glasgow Green. He was not able to say much. The service was somewhat shorter than usual. It was my privilege to walk home, arm-in-arm with him, on that beautiful autumnal Sabbath evening. He felt it necessary to halt every now and then to gain strength. His love of nature was intense. When he had reached the end of Oxford Street, on the south side of the Clyde, the eye of the "old man eloquent" kindled as he caught the setting sun, and fixing his gaze in the direction of the glowing west, he exclaimed, "What a glorious orb!" and, after a pause, added, "and how much more glorious must be the Sun of Righteousness! Yes, the Sun of Righteousness shall arise with healing in his wings!" The good man's public work was finished.

The few closing months of his eventful life were spent in peace and quietness under his own roof, with his beloved wife and daughter. His time was chiefly occupied in poring over a well-thumbed Bible, and a few of his old favourite authors, such as a translation of Homer, Milton, Cowper, and Shakspeare, with a few of the more modern poets. His heart always warmed when his old favourite topic of teetotalism was introduced, and he felt great delight in referring to the old friends with whom he had long associated in the temperance enterprise.

On the evening before he died, observing an old picture on the wall, he raised his right hand and said with emotion, "Ah! don't take down or remove my dear old mother!" a wish which was sacredly complied with. A beautifully touching and instructive lesson this, especially to the young, to honour and comfort their parents whilst they have them, and, when gone, to cherish their memory.

When asked shortly before his death, if his prospects were bright for eternity, he exclaimed, "Yes! thank God, I am going to glory;" and then raising his voice to an unusual pitch, said, "and O, I could like to drag *the whole human race along with me!*" laying emphasis on the words "the whole human race." In reply to the question, if he had anything to say to those near and dear to him? he commenced to quote a few lines of the hymn —

> "I leave the world without a tear,
> Save for the friends I held so dear."

His last words were these—"Love one another! love one another!" and the happy spirit was wafted by angels to the realms of the blest.

His funeral was attended by a numerous class of mourners from various parts of the city and elsewhere. The burial service was conducted by Rev. Dr. Alexander Macleod, of John Street United Presbyterian Church, of which Mr. Morris had for several years been a member.

As a proof of the estimation in which Mr. Morris was held by his fellow-labourers, a beautiful monument of Sicilian marble, in the form of an obelisk, was erected at his grave in the Glasgow Southern Necropolis. The following is a copy of the inscription, from the pen of the Rev. Dr. Alexander Wallace, Glasgow :—

"Sacred to the memory of EDWARD MORRIS.   Born on the 20th April, 1787; died on the 1st of August, 1860.

"Ardent and enthusiastic in his nature, and with the heart of a true patriot, he warmly identified himself with the temperance reformation at its commencement, and continued abundant in labours for the promotion of this and other kindred movements till the close of his long and useful life.

"With few educational advantages in his youth, he was a striking example of what diligence and a brave heart will accomplish in the work of self-education. He was a firm believer in the truths of the Gospel, and his motives for action in the cause of social progress were drawn from THE CROSS.   His hoary hairs were found in the paths of righteousness, and his latter end was peace.—Erected by a few friends."

CHAPTER XIII.

ROBERT KETTLE.

THE late Robert Kettle was a good but not a "goody" man. It is long since Coleridge distinguished between the two; and a well-known writer some time ago in an Edinburgh Magazine thus draws out and illustrates the distinction:—A good man, we take to be a man whose goodness is unpretentious—who wears it as a humble though comely garment, not as a flaunting scarlet robe; a goody man is proud of his small virtues and decorums, and seems to ask at every one he meets—"Don't you know me, Mr. So-and-so, the celebrated goody man." The good man has his faults and errors, and does not seek to disguise them, feeling that the acknowledgment of an error is the pledge of an effort to get rid of it—nay, is that very effort begun; the goody man has reached a sort of stinted perfection—the sun of his virtue is so small that its spots are hardly visible, and the faults he has he hides under loud sounding professions, and a great outcry against the same as they occur in the lives of others. A good man is largely charitable to others, while sternly condemnatory of himself; the goody man has little approbation or charity to spare except for himself, and others like him, or for those rich and great personages who, if not goody men, have a profound respect for those that are. A good man, in general, has nothing particular to distinguish him in his dress, manners, or mode of speech; a goody man, wishing to be traced and noticed in every step of his imaginary way to heaven, elongates his countenance, and solemnizes his style till it seems the echo of the grave.

Out of good men have come martyrs, poets of progress, modest philanthropists, statesmen, many hard working ministers, and others. Robert Kettle belongs to that class of good men justly described as modest philanthropists, and it is in this light that I mean principally to view him in the following pages.

In 1853, the Scottish Temperance League published a memoir of Mr. Kettle, by the Rev. William Reid, Edinburgh, and I shall avail myself of the privilege frankly granted by the author to quote occasionally from his interesting narrative, now out of print.

Robert Kettle was born on December 18, 1791, in the village of Kintillo, near the foot of the Ochils, Perthshire, a place described as one of great loveliness. His father was a small farmer, and his mother a woman of sense, good temper, beauty, and excellent character. Robert, like many boys who afterwards became distinguished men, was a solitary, self-involved youth, fond of musing and reading in lonely spots. Yet he was not at all unsocial or proud. In proof of this we are told that, there being in the school a half-witted lad, whom all the rest despised, Robert manfully came up to his side, assisted him in reading, and encouraged him by all the means in his power. The master praised him as his model scholar. From the parish school he passed to labour at the loom, while his leisure he employed in reading and reflection. But even previous to this we are told he had, when only twelve years, written a small volume on the subject of prayer. At fourteen he lost his mother, whom he tenderly loved and long deplored. He was very pious in his early as well as in his latter days—had a profound reverence for the Sabbath; and although, when ill with fever, and thought dying, he felt, in his true modesty, unprepared for death, and told his father so, I believe that few young men were in reality readier for that mysterious change.

He felt a strong desire to be a minister, but was prevented by the circumstances of his father, and compelled to betake himself to mercantile pursuits. Probably he became a far more useful man in his secular vocation than if he had, after severe struggles and pinching poverty, extending not to himself only, but to his relations, mounted a pulpit, sunk, perhaps, into a second-rate position, and gone to a *starving* instead of a "living," within the Church. He became a clerk to Mr. Kennedy, the manufacturer in Perth, where he continued for five years.

MR. KETTLE REMOVES TO GLASGOW.

In 1815, Mr. Kettle came to Glasgow, and soon obtained a situation under Messrs. W. Kelly & Co., an extensive firm in the cotton trade. Mr. Reid quotes some letters of Kettle, written at this time, describing his lodgings and landlord, and his first impressions of Glasgow preaching, which show a largeness and liberality of mind not common in that day, along with great acuteness of remark and a spice of quiet humour. He gives almost a ludicrous account of the manner in which the psalmody at family worship was performed in those days, when, instead of singing, there was a kind of monotonous humming, like the purring of a cat.

About this time Chalmers burst like a thunder-clap on Glasgow, and Mr. Kettle became one of his most devoted admirers, although it sounds strange to hear him saying that "the doctor was no orator," and that his preaching "is more calculated to lead the judgment than to touch the feelings." A good elocutionist Dr. Chalmers certainly never was, but neither, it is thought, was Paul; and if oratory means the power of deeply impressing the public mind, he has had few equals in any age. His admiration of this great man led, by and by, to personal intimacy. Chalmers discerned Robert Kettle's worth at a glance, and got him to accept the office of a deacon in his church. There he laboured with great assiduity, and often accompanied

Chalmers in his visitations from house to house—the Doctor once remarking to him as they hurried along, with only the possibility of a few serious words in each house from him—" Ye'll be saying this is laying the butter rather thinly on."

He was scarcely in Glasgow till he began, "with fear and trembling," to teach a Sabbath school, but soon he found it of vast weight in confirming his religious impressions, in keeping him from temptations, and in securing him valuable friendships. One of his intimates at this time was Edward Irving, who was then the "uncelebrated Irving," and, according to Carlyle, far more interesting than afterwards when he attained that meteoric and unhealthy reputation, which first raised and then ruined him in the Metropolis. Kettle admired this noble man to enthusiasm, and loved him as an elder brother. Altogether, the extracts given from Mr. Kettle's letters, written at this period of his life, give us the impression of a man of singular strength of judgment, clear in his vision, and vigorous in his language, although with some of the defects as well as merits of self-taught men.

In 1829, Mr. Kettle commenced business for himself as a cotton yarn merchant—a business in which he prospered. While never a slave to trade, he was proud of the honourable profession of a merchant—gloried in its shame, and pursued it as "ever in his Great Task-master's eye." No man more valued the leisure hours it allowed or improved them better, and he wrought the harder till four o'clock in the warehouse, that he might in the evenings, as he says himself, "cultivate those thoughts, feelings, and affections, which become our condition as social, rational, and accountable beings." While thus engaged in city business, and feeling its anxieties as well as its gratifications, its trials and its triumphs, his heart had never travelled from his native Ochils, and every year he was in the habit of visiting Kintillo, where his father was still living with a good female cousin, whom Mr. Kettle greatly esteemed, keeping his house, and when there he would sit in the "old arm chair"—look out at the beautiful and well-known scenery around; and at other times would hold prayer meetings and give affectionate advices in the parish school-room to the people of the village, who hailed the annual visit of their excellent friend and fellow-villager as a great event. He was also very kind to young men in Glasgow hailing from Kintillo, and while promoting their material did not forget their spiritual interests.

MR. KETTLE AND THE TEMPERANCE MOVEMENT.

When the temperance cause was introduced into Scotland in 1829, it was some little time before Mr. Kettle saw it to be his duty to join the movement. The Rev. William Reid, referring to a striking incident in Mr. Kettle's life, which appears to have happened about this time, states—" Being on board a steamboat along with some friends, according to a custom still lamentably common with steamboat travellers, Mr. Kettle joined with them in partaking of toddy. On afterwards passing along the deck he missed his footing, fell down the trap into the engine-room, and made a narrow escape of falling into the furnace. The only injury he sustained was a bruise on the knee. · The circumstance, however, impressed him deeply, and brought him instantly to decide in behalf of the temperance cause. Relating the accident one day to us, he observed—'Had I been killed, no one would have attributed it to the drink which I had taken, and yet I am firmly convinced it was the drink that did it. No one might have observed me walk-ing unsteadily, but yet my feet were not so capable of their duty as they ought to have been. My con-viction is that hundreds of accidents are the result of drinking alcohol, without alcohol ever getting the blame of it. I was just (said he with emphasis) in that slightly elevated state of mind in which many think and act in a manner they would be ashamed of in their perfectly sober moments.' "

In a letter to a friend, dated July 27, 1830, Mr. Kettle states—"I send you some temperance tracts, which you must read and ponder, previous to my seeing you, as I mean to make an attack on your appetite. I have not yet put down my name, but I mean to do so im-mediately. I have been a conscientious member all this year, and have had no cause to regret my abstinence. My conscience does not even allow me to give it, so you may expect cold cheer when you visit this quarter."

In proof of the fact that he soon identified himself with the cause, I find him at the first anniversary of the Glasgow and West of Scotland Temperance Society, held December 20, 1830, acting as one of its treasurers. Shortly after, he became one of the secretaries of the same institution, then designated the Scottish Temperance Society, an office which he filled till the society was dissolved in 1836. In glancing over the pages of *The Temperance Society Record*, which was started in June, 1830, and stopped in December, 1835, the honoured name of Robert Kettle frequently turns up, especially in connection with the practical working of the movement.

" In September of 1836 (says the Rev. Wm. Reid), Mr. John Finch, of Liverpool, a man of great energy of character, visited Glasgow. At the first meeting held thereafter, he delivered a most interesting and convincing lecture. Mr. Morris acted as chairman, and declared that it was now high time to re-construct the Temperance Society on the Preston plan, and moved accordingly. The proposal was most cordially responded to, and at the close of the meeting thirty-seven persons came forward and joined. Their names are before us, and from the trades to which they belonged, the localities in which they resided, it appears that God in this cause also has chosen 'the

weak things of the world to confound the mighty.'
The weaver from his shuttle, the smith from his anvil,
the shoemaker from his stool and awl, were amongst
the first in Scotland to declare war with 'everything
by which the devil makes drunkards everywhere.'"

Mr. James Mitchell, painter, King Street, Glasgow
(an ardent friend of the cause, who was one of the first
to agitate in favour of what is now known as the
Habitual Drunkards Bill, and who died 16th February, 1873, aged 70), showed me the card he received
when he joined, in October, 1836, the Glasgow Total
Abstinence Society.

Although Mr. Kettle did not for some time see his
way to adopt the more thoroughgoing principle of
abstinence from all intoxicating liquors, he continued a
zealous advocate of the Temperance Society. As soon,
however, as he had made up his mind on the subject,
he threw himself heartily into the cause. Accordingly,
when writing to a friend, on the 31st of March, 1838,
I find him saying, "I have been up and down the
country speaking on teetotalism, yet I can hardly say
I have had the cold all winter, and I used to have it
almost every second week. I was at Kilsyth two
nights ago, and although I spoke an hour and three
quarters in a crowded meeting, I feel none the worse
for it. You must all give up the use of *Satan's tea*,
and banish the foul fiend from the midst of you."

In September, 1838, forty-one delegates, represent-
ing thirty societies, met in Glasgow, and formed "The

Scottish Temperance Union," of which Mr. John Dunlop was appointed president, and Mr. Kettle chairman of the executive committee. Out of this Union sprang, in June 1839, "The Eastern and the Western Scottish Temperance Unions," the head-quarters of the former being in Edinburgh, and of the latter in Glasgow. Again, we find Mr. Kettle acting as chairman of the executive in the Western metro-polis. Not contented with the mere honours of an official, he became an unwearied advocate of the cause, lecturing long with great energy in various places, avoiding, too, all ribaldry and personalities, and using only the weapons of reason, persuasion, and argu-ment. A good joke is told about his reply to a gentleman, who quoted the words of Paul, " Use a little wine for thy stomach's sake." "Many people," retorted Mr. Kettle, "complain of their stomachs; but if the truth were known, their stomachs have more reason to complain of them." Even when Mr. Kettle did use hard words and was disposed to be severe to the brink of uncharitableness, and to approach what might have seemed offensive in other men, it was pardoned in him on account of his great sincerity and simplicity of character, and his well-known philan-thropic and Christian exertions in other fields. Dr. Chalmers, though he never went theoretically as far as his old friend Kettle, yet heard of his labours in this direction with great interest, and heartily wished him " God-speed."

CHAPTER XIV.

N January, 1839, *The Scottish Temperance Journal* was started. For a few months it was edited by the Rev. J. H. Roebuck, a very promising and zealous young Methodist minister in Glasgow, who was, however, soon called to his rest and reward in heaven. His funeral sermon was preached by the Rev. Dr. William Anderson, Glasgow. Amongst the first acts of the Executive of the Western Scottish Temperance Union was, it appears, the appointment of Mr. Kettle as editor of the *Scottish Temperance Journal*. The first article in the monthly issue of that periodical for September, 1839, was from the editor's own pen, entitled " Muzzled Dogs." I have re-perused that paper with much interest, and think the whole of it might be read with profit by all temperance reformers of the present day. I quote the closing paragraph, not to excite controversy, but to cause reflection :—

" We are not very partial to legislative measures in the matter of drinking, as a means of redeeming our country from the dominion of drunkenness. As an ulterior and secondary means they will doubtless be both necessary and highly proper ; but in the present state of matters we must endeavour to get all

the religious, and many of the more rational of our
people persuaded to muzzle themselves for the promotion of personal safety or the public good, as the
individual may incline.   As long as our false notions
of intoxicating liquor and domestic drinking habits
continue, sound and salutary legal restrictions upon
either cannot be expected; and, although they were
imposed, they would remain a dead letter in the
statute book.   Let public opinion become leavened
with our principles, and public spirit strengthened by
their practical operation, then legislation will lend its
willing and able assistance in purging out of our land
the deadly *virus* of dissipation, and in protecting our
people from all the licensed plunderers, and all the
legalised patrons of the immorality which at present
prey upon them.   All that we expect from 'the
powers that be,' in the meantime, is a review of principles, and an honest endeavour to exhibit consistency
in their attempt to remove the causes of disease and
crime from the community.   Should they give attention to our advice, we may live to see the day when a
muzzled dog and a muzzled dramseller will pass along
our streets, the living illustration of that wise legislation which applies the principle of prevention to
those evils that are either inveterate or incurable in
their nature, and whose instrumental cause is well
known and placed entirely under the control of man."

Mr. Kettle continued to occupy the post of Editor
of the *Scottish Temperance Journal* till shortly before

the close of its career in March, 1847. "Its pages," the Rev. William Reid truly remarks, "were frequently enriched with his own contributions, whose clear, vigorous, and racy style always attracted attention, and not unfrequently awakened delight with his inoffensive humour. Perhaps no unprofessional man has written so largely upon the principles of the temperance movement, certainly none have written more ably. How few ' trained,' as he himself said, ' amid the dry details of business,' could take so masterly a grasp of a controverted subject, and express their thoughts upon it with so much propriety and force? What was said of the author of *The Protestant*, might, with equal propriety, be said of him, that the same dip of the pen which settled a bargain finished a paragraph that was to shake the strongholds of iniquity; indeed, his published articles were generally written at his counting-room desk during the intervals allowed him in the transactions of business. Like Chalmers, who could snatch half an hour by a wayside inn and add a page to the sermon that was next Sunday to thrill the crowds in the Tron Church, he could pass from the subject of spindles and hanks to a teetotal improvement of the last striking incident he had read of in the papers. There he stood, with pen in hand, humming, as was his wont, a tune, and all the more briskly when the thoughts flowed freely, and ready to receive the next caller, and talk of yarns with as much freedom as if he had just been making out an invoice. ' It is that iron-headed man I mean,' said an Englishman, who had forgot his name, when talking to another of his labours in the Sabbath Essay Scheme. Nor was it unusual, such was the simplicity and kindliness of his character, to look across the desk to his youthful clerk, when he had finished an article, and asking, 'What do you think of this?' read it aloud." It may be interesting to some of our readers at a distance to know that "the youthful clerk" here referred to was our friend Mr. A. H. Maclean, now at the head of the old firm of Messrs. Robert Kettle & Co., of Glasgow, one of our prominent and staunch abstainers.

The *Temperance Journal*, under Mr. Kettle's judicious management, rendered important service to the cause. Not a few of his articles were reprinted as four-page tracts, and circulated in tens of thousands: such as "A Kind Word to Working Men," "The Broken Pledge," " I can Temper Mysel'," "Appeal to Christians," &c. His services, too, as editor, were cheerfully given without pecuniary fee or reward.

The Scottish Temperance League was formed, as is now well known, at a meeting held at Falkirk, on the 5th of November, 1844, by the following gentlemen— James Ballantyne, A. D. Campbell, James A. Johnston, George M'Whirter, William Menzies, M.D., from Edinburgh; Andrew H. Maclean, Robert Reid, William T. Templeton, and myself, from Glasgow. After the Edinburgh and Glasgow friends had said " good night " to each other at the railway station, I

remember Robert Reid remarking, as the train started
for Glasgow, and in a somewhat more impressive tone
than usual—" Well, I firmly believe that in the formation of the Temperance League a step has been
taken that will tell for good upon old Scotland, and
far beyond, not only in our own day but after we are
gone." I give, I believe, Mr. Reid's own words.
May they be signally realised!

In July, 1848, Mr. Kettle was appointed president
of the Scottish Temperance League, an honour to
which, as a temperance reformer, he was justly entitled. "In this position," observes the Rev. Mr. Reid,
"he lent the efficient aid of his name, talents, and
pecuniary means. He presided at the business meetings of the association, and by the suavity of his
manner, the prudence of his counsel, and the weight
of his experience, guided the deliberations of the
assembled members in the paths of practical wisdom.
So much, indeed, were the friends of the temperance
reformation pleased with the benevolent and enlightened presidency of Robert Kettle, that in the month
of July, 1850, they presented him with his portrait,
painted by Daniel Macnee, the eminent artist."

Mr. Kettle was an occasional contributor to the
Scottish Temperance Review. It was edited at first by
the Rev. William Reid, afterwards by Mr. A. H.
Maclean, who was succeeded by the Rev. Dr. James
Paterson. The first number appeared on October 1,
1845. The last article from Mr. Kettle's terse, useful,

and genial pen, appeared in that ably-conducted publication in March, 1852, very shortly before his death, and was entitled, "The State of Maine Anti-Liquor Law." The following are a few of its closing sentences, which show that he had no stereotyped opinion on the moral and legal aspects of the question—

"We have read this wise and well made law, and have listened to its practical details with unmingled pleasure. We are quite satisfied that it will do ten times more good than our Sanitary Improvement, Health of Towns, Poor Law Amendment Bills, and all such like will ever achieve. When our legislators gather more sense and courage, we trust that they will follow the example of Maine, and, like her, break the eggs of the cockatrice, in place of hatching them, and then hunting the venomous brood. In the meantime, let all teetotallers exert themselves for the spread of our principles, that our people may not only be prepared to acquiesce in such a law, but like 'the common people—*the voters*' of Maine, demand it, and then it cannot be withheld from them, in spite of all that interest, appetite, and corrupt custom may say to the contrary."

I have sometimes thought that the republication of some of the more striking articles of the *Review* would be a useful contribution to the Temperance Literature of the present time. The vigorous moral suasion advocacy of its writers would, in my opinion, be a healthful change from the now too absorbing pursuit of legislative action.

Mr. Kettle had much pleasure in acting as the principal adjudicator in the case of essays on "The temporal advantages of the Sabbath," for which prizes had been offered by the late John Henderson, of Park, a gentlemen of far-famed benevolence. These essays extended to 1043, every one of which he read once, and many of them twice and thrice over. The examination of these occupied him for fifteen months, and he was often engaged with them from an early hour in the morning till late at night. He was proud of the essays sent in, not merely from his deep interest in the subject, but from the evidence they furnished of the growing intelligence of that working class from which he had himself sprung, and which had always continued dear to his heart. This was the last great public work of his life. When conversing with the good man on this point, he frankly, yet in his own modest way, admitted to me, that he believed that it had injured his health, thereby shortening his days.

Long before this Mr. Kettle (in 1832) having been led by the Voluntary Controversy to re-consider the question of Establishments, had left the communion of the Church of Scotland, and become a dissenter. Two years afterwards, having adopted Baptist principles, he was admitted to the church assembling in Hope Street, under the pastorate of Dr. James Paterson, where he made himself very useful, and was greatly beloved.

MR. KETTLE'S LAST DAYS.

Mr. Kettle's last public appearance was at a meeting in the City Hall, Glasgow, for the purpose of bringing the subject of Savings Banks under the notice of his fellow-citizens. This was on the evening of the 10th February, 1852. He then addressed an audience of from 2000 to 3000, chiefly composed of the more intelligent portion of the working classes, with great effect; the speech unfortunately, however, has not been preserved.

But the time for the termination of his useful life had now arrived. On Sabbath the 7th of March he attended Church as usual. In the evening he complained of cold. On Monday he rallied and continued to attend to business till Wednesday, when he went home for the last time, and by Thursday fever had commenced. During his short illness his disease permitted him to say but little. "He bore all," says the Rev. Dr. Paterson, "with patience, firmness, resignation. He summed up his feelings in reference to what he was passing through, by saying on one occasion, '*I am sair forfaughen*'—tersely and idiomatically conveying, 'I am sorely fatigued in this conflict!' On the Sabbath before his death, when asked by a friend how he felt, he replied—'Perfectly happy; resting upon the Rock of Ages.' He inquired once what day it was, and on being told it was the Sabbath, he lifted up his eyes and clasped his hands in prayer. Hearing a little after the Sabbath bells, he inquired what sounds these were, and on being told, he again lifted up his hands in prayer. All he could do he said, in dying circumstances, was 'simply *confessing* and *adhering* to Christ.'" On the morning of the 23rd of March, his ransomed spirit winged its way to the Throne of the Eternal.

In reference to Mr. Kettle's death, the editor of *The Scottish Guardian*, in March, 1852, said —

"Those who knew him best and came most in contact with him as a merchant, speak with admiration of the inflexible rectitude of his transactions in business, and the incorruptible integrity of his character. Nothing could disturb the equanimity of his temper, or sour the genial kindliness of his heart. His liberal soul was constantly devising liberal things. 'Large was his bounty and his soul sincere.' In the death of Mr. Kettle, the Church has been deprived of a member who was universally beloved for the clear and steady consistency of his character; and the public of one of our most philanthropic and estimable citizens. The loss of such a man at such a time càn ill be spared either by the Church or by Society. 'Help, Lord, for the godly man ceaseth; for the faithful fail from among the children of men.' The lesson taught by the example of his active and well-spent life, and the parting admonition of his calm and hopeful death, find meet expression in the weighty sentence with which he closed the printed address to the families in

his Sabbath school district thirty years ago—'Many
are the opportunities of spiritual improvement that
God is giving us; they are all talents that must be
accounted for.   Let us, therefore, work while the day
lasteth, taking care lest any of us fail of the grace of
God, watching with prayer against all sin, seeking
daily to Christ for life, light, and strength, that every
day may find us advancing toward the heavenly Zion;
and when the night of death cometh upon us, as come
it will, may it be followed to us by the bright glories
of eternal day!'"

On Monday, 29th March, amidst a vast concourse of
mourners and onlookers, his remains were committed
to their resting-place in the Glasgow Necropolis.

"Into this most romantic burial-ground," says the
Rev. William Reid, "perhaps the most beautiful
in Europe, there have been carried the remains
of some of the most distinguished of Glasgow citizens.
Seldom, however, has such a funeral procession crossed
its 'Bridge of Sighs,' and ascended by its over-
shadowed pathway, as that which Monday, the
29th March, 1852, beheld.   The eyes of a spec-
tator must at once have marked that no ordinary
corpse was being borne along.   Not only were there
the usual attendance of immediate friends, but group
after group following them.   Nothing of state bespoke
honour done to departed rank, and yet seldom are
funereal trains composed of so much that is eminent in
piety and exalted in station.   Civic authorities,

ministers of various sects, men foremost in all great movements, were there; but chief of all, the men who constitute the heart and sinews of the temperance cause. Well nigh two thousand mourners, brought by the simple attraction of goodness, is a tribute which emperors might envy."

Over his honoured grave, in a prominent part of the Necropolis, a granite monument has been erected by a few friends and fellow-citizens, bearing the following brief inscription:—

ERECTED BY FRIENDS IN MEMORY OF
ROBERT KETTLE, MERCHANT: ·
AN EMINENT CHRISTIAN PHILANTHROPIST.
Born at Kintillo, Perthshire, 18th December, 1791:
Died at Glasgow, 23rd March, 1852.

Robert Kettle was in every respect a remarkable man. His great element was strength of character—a resolute and indomitable will. Decision of character in itself, as Foster shows, is real and rare power. Look what it accomplishes in the little ant, which, with small strength and size, performs such marvels of industry and skill, by sheer strength of resolution. And how many a man, humble in circumstances, narrow in understanding, and limited in information, has yet done great things, simply because he had so *willed* to do. Without much, or any, of what is called learning, he had read very extensively. When a boy he devoured all the books within his reach,

"Exhausted shelves, and then imagined new."

He read not books only, but men. Business brought him in contact with innumerable living volumes of all varieties—many bound in sheep, some in calf, some lettered, and some unlettered, and a good many *gilded*, and these he soon learned to rate at their true value. A friend of mine, a distinguished public man, informs me that he, when a mere boy of some 14 years of age, met Kettle once in a friend's house in Glasgow, and remembers to this day his gentlemanly appearance; his sagacious countenance, his sensible yet humorous conversation, and the deference that was paid him by the little circle. He remembered that evening afterwards, and speaking to the friend about Kettle, said, among other things—"I mind that during the evening he was on every chair in the house!" Mr. Kettle had a great deal of wit and pointed remark in his conversation. After joining the Temperance Society, a lady said to him—"You're not so fat as you were, Mr. Kettle?" "Oh, I'm glad you say so, for *fat's* a disease," was the prompt reply.

Common sense was, probably, his ruling intellectual faculty. And, morally, his benevolence and conscientiousness seemed to struggle in him for the mastery. He did not parade his charities, nor did his left hand always know what his right was doing. His beneficence was an underground river of good, and while in Glasgow he had many pensioners. The far-off village of his early days was not forgotten, and not a season passed without some drops from the shower of his bounty falling upon it. He took a special interest in the promotion of such institutions as the Glasgow Royal Infirmary, the Eye Infirmary, the Blind Asylum, the Night Asylum for the Houseless, and, above all, the Glasgow City Mission, of which he for many years acted as one of the Secretaries. Indeed, as has been well said, the range of his philanthropy was only bounded by the extent of human wants and woes. His religion, while very sincere and very ardent, was not one-sided, starched, or exclusive. It hung about him in easy folds. It co-existed in his mind with good humour, broad charity, and warm human sympathies. Hence the universal respect with which he was regarded not only in Glasgow but far beyond. The teetotallers hailed him as their champion; the general religious public admired him for his consistent and catholic piety; the poor loved him as their bountiful benefactor; and the intellectual respected his public spirit, wide information, and excellent sense. To such men as Chalmers, Irving, Wardlaw, Heugh, Anderson, and other leading clergymen, he was a most valuable ally, and was even more than this—"a brother beloved." They were highly cultivated men, but he was a natural sage, and added to this the elements of the Christian character in very high measure.

The Rev. William Reid has annexed to his valuable memoir a selection of Kettle's "temperance memorials," which form not the least excellent and characteristic part of the volume. They are, even to those who may differ occasionally from some of his views, exceedingly interesting productions. They reveal that strong sagacity, that natural untaught logical power, that racy humour, and that fervid spirit of philanthropic piety and zeal, which were so characteristic of the man. Here and there, indeed, he may allow his ardour to run away with him, and at times may use rather homely expressions, which, perhaps, he would not employ were he living and writing now-a-days—but, after subtracting this, no impartial reader can deny the great merits of the writing, the strength of the case he makes out, the variety of illustration he employs, and the astonishing general knowledge of books and of life which he discovers. Altogether, Glasgow is not likely soon to forget the name or to ignore the achievements and the merits of one of the most modest, but most meritorious, of her departed citizens —ROBERT KETTLE.

CHAPTER XV.

WILLIAM MARTIN AND FATHER MATHEW, OF CORK.

IN February, 1848, I visited Cork, under the auspices of the Scottish Temperance League, .and at the request of the Cork Total Abstinence Union. At that time I wrote some notes respecting the early history of the movement in Cork, and with special reference to Father Mathew, which appeared in *The Scottish Temperance Review*, and what follows is substantially the same. In order to avoid misapprehension, it may be stated that the two worthies, whose names I have placed at the head of this chapter, have since then been called from this to a higher sphere of bliss—William Martin in 1853, after having reached fourscore years and six, and Father Mathew on 8th December, 1856, in his 66th year. To begin at the beginning, I must refer to an interview I had with William Martin, the gentleman who had the honour of first directing Theobald Mathew's attention to the subject of temperance. William Martin was an esteemed member of the Society of Friends, and took an active part in every praiseworthy effort to benefit the human family.

At the commencement of 1830, business called Wm. Martin to England. On his way thither he happened to dine, in company with the steam-boat passengers, at an inn in Holyhead. After the substantial part of the dinner had been duly honoured, one of the party said,—"Well, gentlemen, what shall we have to drink?" "I suppose," said William, "there's no good Irish whisky to be had here?" "Have you no temperance society in Cork?" said another. "No," replied William; "and if there was, I would not be likely to join until the spirits in the cask are finished." "Would you not," continued the gentleman, "unite in a cause which was likely to do your fellow-creatures good?" "I ought to do so," said William; and here the conversation dropped. By and by William returned home, and for a time thought seriously on the question. One day after dinner he stood up, and, addressing his family, said—"I'll take no *punch* (whisky and sugar diluted with water) to-day." "It's not like a dinner without it," observed Sarah, his wife. "Then," rejoined William, "thou can make some for thyself and the boys." "I'll not make any," said Sarah, "unless thou take some." "I'll not take any," said William. "Then thou wilt lose thy health," said Sarah. "I don't think I will," replied William. At the same time he quietly left the room, and took a final leave of that which has ruined thousands of Ireland's children—whisky punch. Shortly after William had taken this initiatory step, he began to look about for temperance companions, and continued to do so for nearly twelve months. About April, 1831, three or four agreed to meet him one evening in the Friends' Meeting-house, when a society was established, and regulations were adopted. In a short time a meeting was held in the room where the Anti-slavery Committee occasionally took breakfast together. Other meetings were subsequently held, and a number of individuals were quite ready to join, providing that one tumbler of punch was allowed at dinner. This was strongly protested against. "What gentleman," it was asked, "at the head of his own table, would stop with a single glass as an example or signal to those who had been invited to partake of his hospitality?" Occasional meetings were held in a room adjoining the theatre, but they ultimately became so crowded that a loft in an unoccupied store was taken and fitted up, where many excellent meetings were held, and much good was accomplished.

On St. Patrick's eve, 17th March, 1835, a temperance tea-party was held, for the purpose of showing the public that people could enjoy themselves without intoxicating liquors. After several reformed characters and others had spoken, William arose and said,— "Well, after all, the only sure way to prevent the reformed drunkard from again falling into his evil habits is to abstain from *all kinds* of intoxicating drinks, as well as ardent spirits; and the best means of preventing the rising generation from becoming drunkards is for every man who occupies a house not to allow anything that can intoxicate to come into it." Strange to say, this common-sense speech was too strong for even

M

a number of the zealous friends of the cause present. No one, however, attempted a reply; but in a day or two an influential gentleman, who had taken part in the meeting, met William, and said—"O, you wounded my feelings very much the other night." "How so?" said William. "If you had," said he, "run a sharp instrument through my flesh, you could not have given me greater pain. Why, you want to do away with every kind of drink, as well as spirits. I could not eat my dinner without a couple of glasses of wine; and if I felt ever so inclined to do without it, my mother would not allow me." "I don't doubt," replied William, "but thou hast been a dutiful child; but thou art old enough now to judge for thyself. Thou knowest very well that when any of the members get tipsy they say that they don't break the pledge—it was only porter, etc., they drank, not ardent spirits. It is quite evident, therefore, that there is no safety in anything short of abstinence from all intoxicating drinks." The gentleman was also recommended to give up his two glasses of wine as an experiment, and, if not injured thereby, to continue the practice. He tried the plan for a time, and acknowledged that it was both safest and best.

On an early day in April, 1838, Father Mathew sent a message to William Martin, stating that he wished to see him in the evening. William attended at the hour appointed. Father Mathew said—"I have sent for you to assist me in forming a temperance society in this neighbourhood.   You may remember that a considerable time ago you spoke to me on the subject at the House of Industry."   "I remember it very well," said William. "I could not," said Father Mathew, "see my way clear to take up the question then, but I can do so now.   How shall we begin?"   "Appoint a place to hold a meeting, fix a day and hour, and we shall begin."   "Will Tuesday next," said Father Mathew, "at 7 o'clock, in my school-room, answer?"   William replied in the affirmative. Father Mathew accordingly took the chair on Tuesday evening, the 10th of April, 1838, and stated that he had called that meeting for the purpose of forming a society on total abstinence principles.   "No person," said he, "in health, has need of intoxicating drinks.   My friends, you don't require, nor do I require them, *neither do I take them.*   Any persons wishing to join the society may write their name in the book which lies on the table."   Father Mathew having first signed the declaration himself, was then followed by 56 others, amongst whom were William Martin, George Cox, Rodger Olden, James Kenna, and others.   In the course of the evening, William rose to address the meeting, and, amongst other things, said—"If it pleased the Almighty to take him out of the world soon, he thought he would go with more satisfaction than if he had been taken some years ago, because he felt the weight going off his shoulders and (laying his hand on Father Mathew's) *falling here.*"

Thus ended the first total abstinence meeting which was honoured by the presidency of the most successful temperance reformer that ever lived. The subsequent meetings in Cork soon became so popular that the original place of meeting had to be abandoned and another obtained, capable of holding about 2000 people. In a short time great numbers commenced to flock in from the country to take the pledge; and, ere long, the movement assumed not only a national character, but became a subject of deep interest throughout the civilised world.

FATHER MATHEW VISITS GLASGOW.

Passing over many interesting results of Father Mathew's labours in Ireland, England, and America, I shall only refer to his visit, in August, 1842, to Glasgow, which was urgently solicited and eagerly looked forward to. On Tuesday, the 16th, his arrival was celebrated by a grand teetotal procession, composed of abstainers from all parts of Scotland. After the procession had returned to the Green, Father Mathew administered the pledge to a large number of people.

At five o'clock, a banquet was given to him in the City Hall, by the Executive Committee of the Western Scottish Temperance Union. Mr. Ebenezer Anderson occupied the chair, and called upon Mr. Robert Kettle to read and present an address to the distinguished guest of the evening. That address was prepared, I

believe, by Mr. Kettle himself, and I cannot proceed
without transcribing part of it for the benefit of the
reader :—

"Reverend and respected Sir,—The Western Scottish Temperance Union have great pleasure in bidding
you a hearty welcome to their head quarters, the commercial metropolis of Scotland, and in presenting you
with their warmest congratulations as the distinguished
champion of a cause in the prosecution of which they
also have the honour and happiness to be engaged.

"We have long heard of your name, admired your
character, and rejoiced in your eminent success. Your
zeal has often stimulated ours, when, in the midst of
discouragement and disappointment, we have heard of
your abundant labours, and the rich reward attending
them ; and often have the kindly spirit and intelligent
character of the sentiments expressed by you called forth
our admiration and esteem.   We conceive it, therefore,
our duty and our privilege to take this opportunity—
and we thank you for so kindly allowing it—of
acknowledging our past obligations to you, expressing
our happiness in seeing you among us, and assuring
you of our most ardent wishes for your future well-
being and continued prosperity.

" When an individual becomes famous, and acquires
reputation as a reformer of morals, the very fact of his
having done so indicates that he is possessed of certain
principles, and is actuated by certain motives, in the
exercise of which he has been enabled to achieve those

very things which have gained him celebrity. Any course of conduct, therefore, on the part of his friends and admirers, which is calculated either to weaken these principles or to taint these motives, must be alike imprudent and improper. A person can only become and continue great in this department of excellence, by the constant and increasing exercise of humility, unwearied perseverance, self-denying zeal, and prayerful dependence on the divine blessing, and that man is not his friend, nor the friend of the cause in which he is engaged, that would do or say anything calculated to weaken or destroy the very foundation upon which rests all his greatness, and along with it the successful issue of all his philanthropic efforts. With such views, your fellow-labourers in Scotland, in place of expatiating on that brilliant career of beneficence by which you have made a large portion of your once-degraded countrymen an example worthy of the imitation of the whole British empire, would rather lift up their hearts in gratitude to the Fountain of all blessing for having put it into your heart to begin these labours, and for having sustained you in the prosecution of them.

" The undertaking in which we have unitedly embarked is worthy of our efforts. We have spent much of our time and strength in advancing its interests, and although our success has not been on the same scale as yours, it has been sufficient to animate our hopes, energise our efforts, and confirm our determination to live and die in its prosecution. The work is one in which all parties may harmoniously engage; the means by which it is accomplished are so pure and simple, that even enmity cannot impeach them; and the end, when attained, brings with it unmixed good to all who honestly hold by it. A strong coalition of all sects and parties exists in practical opposition to our measures. Custom and prejudice have leagued their millions against us; they have had long training, and are a firm, united body. Let us, who have reason, benevolence, and virtue on our side, be alike united and steadfast, feeling a brotherhood of aim and action, a community of interest rejoicing in each other's prosperity, and never resting satisfied till intoxication, with its madness and manifold miseries, be banished from the British dominions, and from every place where the voice of truth and kindness can be heard.

"May you be long spared, Sir, as a blessing to your country, and a benefactor to our common humanity, and having already learned, may you long enjoy, ' the luxury of doing good !'"

Father Mathew, in acknowledging the address, said,—"He received with unbounded pleasure the address from the members of the Western Scottish Temperance Union. He felt very much indebted to the writers of this address that they had spoken the truth, and had not given him credit for qualities which he did not possess, or for services which he had not performed. On this head he might appropriately quote the words of sacred authority, and say that Providence always selected the foolish things and weak things of this world to serve His purposes, 'that no flesh should glory in His presence.'   .   .   .

"He was convinced that, though differing in features, opinions, customs, or religion, they were the same people. He had seen nothing in Scotland to make him think that they were not natives of Ireland. At all events they were the children of one common Father—born to the same rights—redeemed by the same Saviour—believers in the same blessed gospel; and oh! that the sweet and beneficent spirit of the gospel of Jesus were diffused from pole to pole, uniting and making all happy, pure, and guileless. The world would then be a pleasant habitation, and its children worthy of heaven. Though naturally timid and desponding, he felt new vigour arise within him to see so many of different religious professions—for it was not likely that they could all have unity of faith, but they could all meet in unity of affection—banded together in behalf of so great and good a cause.

"However, he thought he heard some one saying, 'Now, Father Mathew, this is making fine speeches to delude the people of Glasgow: perhaps these are not your sentiments in your own country.' For five-and-twenty years he had entertained these views, and if any man could say that his heart had been shut against his neighbour because of differences in religion—if any man could say that the needy had been turned from his door in consequence of an opposite belief—that the tenant had been dismissed from his holding, or the servant from his place, because of a difference of religious belief—he would allow them to say that his actions did not correspond with his words. In that time he had done what lay in his power to reconcile and harmonise the warring principles of faction—to sweeten the cup of woe—to exalt the downtrodden and unfortunate, and if another voice were required at his hands, still he would repeat, 'A new commandment I give unto you, that ye love one another.' He ought, perhaps, to apologise for thus alluding to himself, but heaven forbid that he should do so from a spirit of paltry egotism, but for the glorious cause in which they all laboured. It was for this purpose that he wished to exhibit to them the inmost recesses of his heart, and to show it glowing with love for the whole human family. This was a cause in which they should all unite ; it was the cause of their common humanity, the cause of their common country, and the cause of God."

It is unnecessary to say that these noble sentiments were most cordially responded to by all present. In the remaining part of the speech he gave a rapid sketch of the progress of the movement in Ireland. On the following morning, at 10 o'clock, he resumed his labours in the Cattle Market, and continued administering the pledge until nearly six in the evening. I visited the memorable spot—for such it has been since that time—in the course of the day, and there saw the good man pleasantly receiving company after company, whilst the perspiration trickled down his face like water.

RESULTS OF FATHER MATHEW'S VISIT TO GLASGOW.

His visit to Glasgow, in 1842, told beneficially, not only on the prisons, but also upon some of the more depraved parts of the city. It is well known that John Barleycorn is no respecter of persons. He leads the ardent Irishman as well as the calculating Scotchman into difficulties. Previous to Father Mathew's visit, a fair proportion of the sons of the Green Isle found their way into the then "drunkards' hall" of the Central Police Office. About one-half of this hall was supplied with a bench, which answered all the purposes of a lounge, a seat, or a bed. One Sabbath evening it happened to be pretty full, and amongst others a patriotic Scottish baker honoured the "hall" with a visit. As he had been more frequently there than at a place of worship, he began to search about for a seat, and finding one Irishman here and another yonder, the consequential baker began to lose patience, and making a bold effort to retain the perpendicular, he said with an air of importance, "Why, I wish you folks would keep to your own country ; we can't get the use of our own premises for you." After Father Mathew's visit, however, the baker, together with his "brither Scots," had the police office almost exclusively to themselves. When distributing tracts after this on Sabbath, amongst the prisoners, I very seldom met with a person from Ireland, charged either with intemperance or with theft.

But the result of the good man's labours was still more visibly seen in the lower parts of the city. For example, in the district I visited as a city missionary, there was a close off High Street, which contained about eighty families, the majority of whom were Roman Catholics. The people were so uproarious that they almost required a policeman constantly amongst them. On a Wednesday morning, however, most of the adults, and a number of the juveniles, set off in a body to the Cattle Market and took the pledge from Father Mathew. From that day till May, 1845, when I left the district, there was not a quieter close, considering the number of inhabitants, in the city.

During my few weeks' residence in Cork, I had several pleasant interviews with Father Mathew at his own house. Although his health was impaired by incessant labour, he was evidently as deeply interested in the cause as ever. He was so busy with temperance meetings during my sojourn in Cork, that two-thirds of his time was actually spent from home. Every visit that I paid to his unostentatious residence I observed a number of persons either wishing to take the pledge or to converse with "the poor man's friend." The room on the first floor was entirely set apart for the accommodation of those who desired to become total abstainers. After the pledge had been taken, the person's name was entered by the clerk into a huge roll-book. The total number of individuals enrolled from 10th April, 1838, till 3rd March, 1848, I found on investigation, was five millions seven hundred and eight thousand and seventy-eight.

In this necessarily brief tribute to Father Mathew, I have designedly confined my remarks to his visit to Scotland, but for the sake of those who may desire a full account of his manifold labours in Ireland, England, and America, I have much pleasure in referring to an admirable Biography of Father Mathew, by John F. Maguire, M.P., from which I quote the following letter addressed to the biographer by the Right Hon. W. E. Gladstone, M.P. :—

HAWARDEN, CHESTER,
Jan. 14th, 1864.

MY DEAR SIR,—I have enjoyed an unmixed pleasure in perusing your Biography of Father Mathew. I am ashamed to think that, before you thus instructed me, I had, in common perhaps with many others, but a vague idea of his great excellence; and I did not know the great height of virtue and of holiness to which he had attained. The "pledge" must, I think, be judged not so much upon its abstract merits as with reference to the frightful evil it was designed to meet: and thus Father Mathew himself is to be regarded, with reference to the chief cause of his public celebrity, rather in the spirit than in the letter of his acts. But, so regarded and so understood, what a glorious career it was of apostolic labour and self-sacrifice! And, even apart from the whole subject of temperance, what a character have you shown us, in its simplicity, its earnestness, its deep devotion, and, above all, in that boundless love which caused him to show forth, in deed and truth, the "beauty of holiness," and to present to his fellow-creatures so much of the image of our Blessed Saviour! I can truly congratulate you on having known and loved him; on having been able to write of him in a spirit of such intelligent sympathy; lastly, let me presume to say, on having composed your able book, from one end of it to the other, as a true continuation of his living work, and in the very temper as towards God and men which he would have himself desired.—I remain, my dear Sir, very faithfully yours,

W. E. GLADSTONE.

J. F. MAGUIRE, Esq., M.P.

CHAPTER XVI.

JOHN LAING, OF KIRKCONNEL.

JOHN LAING, unlike those early heroes whose names have occupied a more prominent place in preceding pages, was a member of the agricultural class, and, as such, did not a little to advance the temperance cause in his neighbourhood.

He was born at Blagannoch, Dumfriesshire, in 1796, and died at Guildhall, Kirkconnel, in his native county, on Tuesday, the 24th of June, 1862, aged sixty-six years. "John Laing," says the Rev. Dr. Robert Simpson, of Sanquhar, "is a lineal descendant of the ancient family of Blagannoch, in the Moors, which had been the residence of the Laings for about four hundred years. The Laings of old were staunch Covenanters, and afforded shelter to the wanderers who, in the dreary days of persecution, were driven to the upland wilds. It was in the house of Blagannoch that the youthful Renwick often found a hiding-place from the fierce storms of the inclement winter, and from the still fiercer blasts of a relentless persecution. In modern times David Laing, the father of John, denominated 'The Patriarch of the Desert,' woned also in Blagannoch, and was a perfect specimen of the piety and nobility of the preceding generation of the hosts of the martyrs, many of the bodies of whom sleep in the mosses and the wilds around. He had about him all the qualities with which, in imagination, we feel disposed to adorn the worthies who lived, and prayed, and suffered, in thé desert, when the crimson car of persecution was driven over the breadth and length of a bleeding land."

John's forefathers followed the humble and honourable occupation of the shepherd, which also occupied the early part of his own life till he married, in April, 1817. After his marriage he turned his attention to road-contracting, and in a few years to agricultural farming. John lived for upwards of forty years at Guildhall, which is beautifully situated on the banks of the Nith. Inheriting as he did the noble virtues of his ancestors, he resolved to devote a part of his time to the elevation of his fellow-creatures. The temperance reformation very soon attracted his attention, but he did not, for a time, see it to be his duty to go the length of total abstinence. A somewhat "interesting" event, however, soon occurred, which materially altered his views, and led him to a satisfactory decision on the subject—the birth of a son in 1831. John Inglis, then an intelligent, plodding stone-mason, happened to call at Guildhall just when Laing had got orders to proceed without loss of time to Sanquhar, a distance of from four to five miles, for the doctor. The two Johns jogged on together at a quicker pace than usual to Sanquhar. This was too good an opportunity for a zealous teetotaller of 1831 to lose, and Inglis set to work to try and make a convert of Laing, and presented as clearly and tersely as possible a few of his best arguments. Laing was not in the best mood for defending himself; and feeling, too, that the Miniaive stonemason had the best side of the question, he listened as attentively as possible to what was advanced, and the two having reached Sanquhar, with a hasty shake of the hand, parted.

For the benefit of our younger readers, it may be stated that, shortly after this, John Inglis—Hugh Miller-like—pushed himself forward, and entered Glasgow University, was ordained for the ministry, spent some ten years as a missionary in Aneityum, South Seas, and returned to Scotland in 1860 for the purpose of superintending the printing, for the first time, of the New Testament in the Aneityum language. In the month of May, 1862, as Moderator of the Reformed Presbyterian Synod, he preached the annual sermon, in the Rev. Dr. Symington's Church, Glasgow, and he returned before long to resume his important labours as a missionary in the New Hebrides. The Rev. John Inglis has done more than most men, at home and abroad, to advance the temperance cause, and is deservedly held in high esteem by a large number of the older members of the total abstinence movement.

The happy results of this unexpected wayside interview between Guildhall and Sanquhar soon appeared. The child was born, and, for the first time at Guildhall, no intoxicating liquors were used. The whisky bottle, as formerly, had been filled, and placed upon the table —the doctor receiving orders to use it if necessary, but no one besides was to partake of it except as a medicine. The children looked for their accustomed "wee drap, wi' sugar;" but the father, with an expressive look, and a quiet, significant movement of the hand, said, "Na, na, bairns—nae mair o' that fiery stuff—you shall soon have something better." The children were not at all disappointed, and his noble-hearted wife, as soon as she understood what her husband meant, cordially coincided with him; and from that day till the present no intoxicating liquors as a beverage have had a place under the roof at Guildhall.

In 1831 John Laing threw himself heartily into the temperance movement, and laboured from that time till his death for its advancement, with a zeal, perseverance, and disinterestedness which are beyond all praise. To use one of his own favourite verses—

"If I had talent, lear, and time,
 And walth o' cash my pouch to prime,
 The temperance cause I would proclaim
 Across the sea, as weel's at hame."

It is well known that from thirty to forty years ago travelling was not so convenient as now; and in those

N

days many a long, weary, fatiguing journey did John Laing cheerfully undertake to serve the cause. For many years he was a regular visitor at the temperance soirees in Darvel, Newmilns, Lorn, Ochiltree, Old and New Cumnock, and in other places in the South of Scotland. "When he became acquainted with the League meetings," said my beloved departed friend, Robert French, M.A., "before railways were opened, he used to travel on foot to Glasgow and return home by the coach. His route lay by Muirkirk, past Darvel, and thence to Glasgow. During the most stormy season of the year he travelled across the black, heathery hills between Kirkconnel and Muir-kirk to their annual temperance soiree. Sometimes he would walk to Dalmellington at this inclement season, a distance of upwards of twenty miles, along a wild, dreary, uphill road. About this time of the year he would be absent from home fourteen or fifteen nights, never once under his own roof, but here, and there, and everywhere, attending temperance soirees. He sometimes travelled to Leadhills, to their soirees and other meetings. The road to this place is up a wild, romantic glen. The place is situate almost upon the top of the hills, and the storms of winter are at times so severe as to render it almost inaccessible; yet he feared not for being overtaken in a storm—with a heart full of temperance zeal, he feared nothing."

A friend, writing after Mr. Laing's death, observed —"We will not soon see his like in Nithsdale. I

regard his death as one of the greatest losses which
the abstinence cause has met with in this district for
a long period. I have been present at the annual
soiree of the Kirkconnel Society every year since I
came into this district. He was the soul of the meeting, and I know not how we shall succeed without
the presence of our dear departed friend. May his
decease remind us that our working day will soon be
over also; and may we be stirred up to augmenting
activity in the Master's work!" About this time,
Mr. Robert Rae, London, in a note to myself, said—
"I remember John walking all the way from Kirkconnel to Old Cumnock—a distance of twelve miles
—to attend a meeting I had there in 1847. In his
removal the cause has lost one of its best and most
devoted friends. Verily our veterans are fast departing!"

Although the demon Strong Drink had never entered John's own soul, he, nevertheless, pitied the poor
drunkard. Many a publican's outcast he picked up
in a state of helpless insensibility, fed and sheltered
them, and, when sober, sent them away with a seasonable word of advice. On one occasion he carried a
drunk man, whom he found by the wayside, upon his
back for a quarter of a mile, and brought him in safety
to his own dwelling at Guildhall. On another occasion, while on his way home with a horse and cart, he
found a drunk man lying on a heap of stones. With
some difficulty he got the man into the cart, and then,

blending waggery, irony, and humanity together, he actually drove up to the door of every public-house in Kirkconnel, and asked the publicans to look upon a specimen of their handiwork! but urged them in vain to take charge of the man; and John, good Samaritan-like, took him to his own house and treated him kindly.

The first time I met John Laing was at Kirkconnel, in June, 1844, when on a short lecturing tour through the south of Scotland. As soon as the coach had stopped, an open, honest, genial face presented itself, and a voice was heard calling out, without the least ceremony, "Is Mr. L., the teetotal lecturer fre' Glasgow, here? My name is John Laing." In a few minutes John and I were busily discussing the best plan to get up an open-air meeting. A hand-bell was procured, and John, with his usual considerate kindness, said, "Now, you must not accompany me—the folks all know me in Kirkconnel—sit ye down in a friend's house here, and rest yourself—it's an easy matter for me to do the noisy part of the business;" and off John set to ring the bell and call the meeting, which was to take place "immediately" at a certain part of the village; and a first-rate bellman he made. The inhabitants of the village turned out in large numbers, by far the greater portion being females, all remarkably clean and tidy, every one seeming to vie with each other who should appear in the neatest snow-white piped cap, and the well-known small-checked Scottish plaid, most gracefully thrown around the shoulders, especially by the mothers with babes in their arms. The meeting was an interesting one, and after a few pointed closing words from John, at the close of my address, urging the men, but especially the mothers and the boys and girls present, to adopt the teetotal pledge, we wended our way to Sanquhar, and talked over the past and present, and, as John termed it, "the bright and blessed future of the great temperance movement." "Of the future triumphs of the cause," said he, "I have no more doubt than that God's sun (pointing to that luminary overhead) is now shining in the heavens! Only let its friends prove faithful to their sacred trust." That encouraging and stimulating wayside interview I shall think of with pleasure as long as memory lasts. On reaching the ancient town of Sanquhar we met with a cordial reception from Mrs. Ballantyne, Mr. Thomas Shaw, Mr. Thomas Lawrie (now one of the directors of the Scottish Temperance League), and other temperance worthies.

Whilst John Laing felt deeply interested in the temperance cause as a whole, he took a special interest in the juvenile department. He was a great favourite with the boys and girls. It was somewhat rare to meet him in the street without a number of young people clustering around him. Even at the public school the children were frequently divided into two general classes, the distinction being "The Laingites" and "The Moderates," and by this simple designation each youth had no difficulty in understanding his schoolmates' views on the drink question. During the summer he arranged for small excursion parties— in the winter held regular meetings, and when he could muster teetotal ice-players, the lads were treated to a game at the ice, under the superintendence of their kind leader. Once in the year he invited the male and female members of his Band of Hope out to his own house, where they were supplied with bread and milk in the barn, after which they spent a pleasant hour or two singing temperance melodies and romping on the green fields by the banks of the Nith. For twenty years or more, no face was more familiar than that of John Laing at our annual temperance gatherings in Glasgow, where he was a general favourite.

Only six weeks before his death he delivered, at the anniversary of the Scottish Temperance League, in Glasgow, one of his original speeches in rhyme, full of mother wit, blended with sturdy common sense and fine touches of pathos.

Not a few well-meaning people looked upon John Laing as a teetotal enthusiast, who made rather too much of his "teetotal hobby," as they were pleased to term it. John had been a diligent and admiring student of the Bible, and was, moreover, a keen observer of what was transpiring in the world. He had strong faith in Christianity as the grand regenerator of the human family. He felt thoroughly convinced that the drinking system in this country was the great enemy of God and man, and, as an honest man, he could not but feel intensely interested in the advancement of the temperance enterprise. Would to God that we had, as temperance reformers, more of plain, honest John's intelligent enthusiasm amongst us! There would then be less time, and far less inclination too, for snarling and wrangling with each other upon mere questions of temperance policy.

Our friend was seized with rheumatic fever a little more than four weeks before his death. The temperance cause was not overlooked by him when nearing the end of his earthly journey. Two days before his death he charged a young abstainer, in whom he felt interested, " to persevere in the good cause of temperance." He also expressed a wish to a friend that another promising young man, a student at the University, might be engaged as a temperance missionary, to advocate the cause and to visit and converse with every family in the parish. The very night before he died, he tendered to a "reformed character" his most earnest advice, entreating him to resolve, in God's strength, to remain faithful to the abstinence pledge till death, and also to give his heart to Christ.

Mr. Laing's funeral was a highly respectable one, being attended by upwards of one hundred individuals, many of whom had come from a distance of several miles. A few of his old, attached temperance friends were present from Old and New Cumnock, Auchinleck, Ochiltree. and Glasgow. In the funeral procession I observed a most touching yet encouraging sight—several boys, members of the Kirkconnel Band of Hope, walking two-abreast, and holding each other by the hand. At the good man's grave, none, with the exception of the relatives, seemed more deeply concerned, or more anxious to get a last look of the coffin, than these intelligent, thoughtful lads.

In front of these Band of Hope boys walked the student in whom John Laing, on his death-bed, had expressed such interest. That student was Robert French, who was ordained at Queen Anne Street Church, Dunfermline, in October, 1870. He occupied a prominent place at the annual public meeting of the Scottish Temperance League, in the City Hall, Glasgow, in May, 1872, and in August of the same year, after a brief but very useful and promising ministry of some eighteen months, was translated to Bootle, Liverpool, where, in six weeks afterwards, he was taken from his Master's service on earth to nobler work above. His attachment to the temperance cause remained firm to the last; and within a few days of his end, he spoke to myself of the necessity of increased zeal on the part of its friends.

CHAPTER XVII.

MALCOLM MACFARLANE, GLASGOW.

I AM indebted to my old friend, Mr. Robert Reid, Glasgow, for the following sketch of the late Malcolm Macfarlane, which appeared in the *Journal* of the Scottish Temperance League, of March 1st, 1862:—

Another distinguished friend of humanity has been removed. Amongst those who have, during the last thirty years, laboured for the moral elevation of the masses, there is no name better known or more justly respected than that of Malcolm Macfarlane. He belonged to the working class, and was one of its greatest ornaments. While possessed of abilities which might easily have raised him to another sphere, he was content to remain where he believed Providence had for wise purposes placed him. Proud of his order, he ardently devoted himself to the furtherance of every scheme calculated to promote the interests of his fellow-workmen. He began his career of usefulness as a Sabbath-school teacher; and when the Glasgow Christian Instruction Society was formed (an institution which had preaching stations in nearly all the suburban villages), he became one of the gratuitous preachers, and performed the duties devolving on him with much earnestness and acceptance. His attachment to the principles of civil and religious liberty led him to take an active part in the voluntary controversy.

During the Chartist agitation he was one of the most formidable opponents of the physical force party. Perhaps the most remarkable public appearance ever made by him was at a densely-packed meeting of the promoters of physical force, held in the City Hall, Glasgow, to receive Feargus O'Connor, who was then at the height of his popularity. Feargus, satisfied that he had the meeting completely with him, challenged any one present to controvert the statements he had made. Mr. Macfarlane, to the amazement of all present, stood forth, his modest demeanour, and slender make, contrasting strangely with the boisterous manner and powerful frame of his antagonist. Looking calmly at his opponent, and then at the tumultuating mass before him, his soul seemed stirred to its very centre; and yielding to the inspiration of the moment, he grappled with the sophistries of O'Connor in a manner so masterly and overwhelming, that the storm was hushed to a calm, and the unruly crowd convinced that their favourite had for once met with more than his match.

During the political agitation to which we have referred, a chapel was opened on the Sundays, where many hundreds of those who never before attended public worship resorted, and here our friend eagerly availed himself of the opportunity thus presented to preach the glorious gospel. Those who listened to his appeals know with what power and purity he proclaimed the unsearchable riches of Christ. These meetings resulted in the formation of a church under the designation of the Christian Brotherhood, of which our friend was one of the pastors up to the day of his death. He was by trade a cabinetmaker, and always had the reputation of being a first-class workman. And while his hands were busily employed at his bench, his head was no less busy making sermons and speeches, which for correctness of diction, fervour of delivery, and soundness of sentiment, were at least equal to the average of those delivered by better educated men. When that excellent man, Joseph Sturge, of Birmingham, originated the movement for securing the complete extension of the suffrage, our departed friend, true to his nature, devoted himself to its promotion. In fact, every scheme calculated to benefit the masses had his instant and hearty support. Baths for the working-classes, Building Societies, Mechanics' Institutions, Peace and Anti-slavery Associations, came all alike to him. He took part, along with the late Rev. Dr. Bates, at the first meeting held in Glasgow for securing a day of rest for the cabmen.

He was a successful competitor for one of the prizes offered by the late Prince Consort, Earl of Shaftesbury, John Henderson of Park, and others, for the best essays on the Sabbath; and was twice called to London to address large audiences in Exeter Hall on the subject of Sabbath observance. The Earl of Shaftesbury, who presided on both these occasions, was struck with the eloquence of the simple-looking, unpretending working man that stood before him, and was so pleased with Mr. Macfarlane's appearance and conduct, that he volunteered his aid and influence to assist our friend in bettering his condition in life. But while he appreciated the kindness of the worthy nobleman, he preferred returning from the plaudits of Exeter Hall to work at his bench, and labour as a working man for working men, to any other position in life that could be offered him. At the Social Science Congress, held in Glasgow in 1860, he was appointed one of the speakers for the meeting of working men held in the City Hall, at which Lord Brougham presided; his Lordship passing a high eulogium on the creditable manner in which the representatives of the people had acquitted themselves on that platform.

As might have been expected, he was an early friend of the temperance cause. The old society had his hearty co-operation; and when the total abstinence movement was originated, he became its warm promoter and devoted advocate, directing the attention of the masses, with whom he was so justly influential, to the grand truth that there could be no political or social advancement for them so long as they indulged in drinking habits; and he lived to see a great and glorious, though partial, change effected in their condition through this instrumentality. Mr. Macfarlane, like all others actively engaged in temperance work, had his impressions of its importance deepened and strengthened by the progressive experience of its blessed results. He was satisfied that the future welfare of this country was closely identified with the political and social advancement of the people, and that there could be no such advancement without the cultivation of the domestic virtues in the homes of our working men. He knew many who, by the sheer force of character, had risen from a very low position in the social scale to comfort and usefulness, and argued justly, that what had been attained by hundreds was within the reach of all, if only the proper means were employed. The adoption of the total abstinence principle he regarded as the first grand and essential step towards the attainment of this end. It therefore required little persuasion to induce him for a time to relinquish his trade, and become one of the lecturers of the Scottish Temperance League. In this capacity he laboured for several years, and was eminently successful in promoting the cause. His correct, chaste, and eloquent style of address, coupled with that modesty, zeal, and kindliness of manner which characterized his conduct, made him a welcome visitor wherever he went, and the intelligence of his death sent a pang of sorrow to many a heart.

He was to working men what Robert Kettle was to the class among whom he moved. In purity of life, in soundness of judgment, in largeness of benevolence, in style of oratory, in readiness for every good work, there was a striking similarity. Nor was the pleasing analogy broken in their death. When the messenger came, he found them prepared and waiting for the great change. They both died in the firm belief that they had been about their Master's work, trusting in a risen Saviour, and rejoicing in the hope of a glorious immortality. There is this peculiarity about Malcolm's career which invests it with a double charm. He was a working man, and never had more than a working man's wage. He provided honestly for the support and education of his family, was most faithful in the performance of every domestic duty; and yet he found time for an amount of public labour which few men, even of independent means, have accomplished. He was little more than 52 years of age, having been born on October 29, 1809, comparatively young in years, but old in labour.

We know of no better model for our rising workmen than he whose loss we deplore, and who was so deeply interested in everything pertaining to their welfare. There was nothing dazzling in his career; worldly greatness he did not attain ; he knew its value, and did not desire its possession. To do good, to love mercy, and walk humbly with God was the chief end of his being, and he nobly fulfilled it.

The circumstances attending his funeral evinced the high esteem in which he was held. A very large assemblage, composed of all classes, met—without any special invitation—in the hall of the Free Church, Anderston (the Rev. A. N. Somerville's). The procession from thence to the place of sepulture (a distance of two miles) attracted considerable notice, and remained unbroken till the mournful services were completed. With a saddened spirit we followed the remains of our departed brother to their last resting place—saddened with the thought that we should no more behold the face of him who for the better part of a long life had laboured with us in a noble work, spreading sunshine on our path. But, after all, it is only the separation we regret; he bravely did his work, and is now entered on his rest. The seeds of the truth he scattered with a liberal hand, and though he is dead and gone, they will yield an abundant and enduring harvest. He espoused our cause in its infancy, and left it in its strength. A valuable treasure has he bequeathed to posterity in the example of his life, and in the testimony of his death.

An obelisk, bearing an appropriate inscription, has been placed on his grave, in the Southern Necropolis of Glasgow, by those friends who had been associated with him in his labours of love.

CHAPTER XVIII.

JAMES MITCHELL.

AT my request, the following sketch of James Mitchell has been kindly furnished by my friend, Mr. Robert Reid, Glasgow:—

The name of James Mitchell is inseparably and nobly associated with the early struggles of the abstinence enterprise. In the year 1837, when following his calling as an Officer of Excise, in the town of Stirling, intelligence reached him of the new movement, and of its marvellous results. He was charmed by the simplicity and reasonableness of its principles, and, without hesitation or delay, espoused them. The difficulties Mr. Mitchell had to encounter in giving effect to this resolution would have discouraged and driven back to drinking practices any less resolute man. He was living in the very midst of the liquor manufacture, and in daily intercourse with the men who were making rich by the drinking habits of the people. An exciseman at best was considered a nuisance at a distillery, but of two evils, the one who drank freely of the product of the still was greatly to be preferred to the one who preserved his senses, by obstinately refusing to partake of it. Indeed, up to

Mr. Mitchell's conversion to abstinence principles, it was not considered by those interested in the traffic, that the anomaly of an abstaining exciseman could possibly exist; and when convinced to the contrary by an example concerning which there could be no mistake, they felt it to be an intolerable outrage, which they were called upon by every means in their power to resist. He was accordingly warned by the traffickers to desist from his teetotal crusade, but his courage was not to be shaken by their threats, and he defied them to do their worst; which they did, by requesting his superiors to remove him from the service. Having nothing to urge against him but his abstinence, they failed in the attempt, and were informed by those to whom they applied, "That they had frequently been under the necessity of dismissing officers for drinking, but saw no reason why they should do so on account of their abstaining."

I have much pleasure in giving an extract here from a letter of Mr. John Dunlop's respecting Mr. Mitchell, dated April, 1862 :—

" Many years ago I had frequent occasion to travel past an oak tree in Strathblane, which they called the Blair Loch Oak. Opposite was a small distillery, the very sight of which made me shudder. One day while I was presiding at a temperance meeting, on a visit from London to Glasgow, a strong, middle-sized, respectable-looking individual addressed the audience in a speech replete with good sense and power. In

o

those days small encouragements in our cause were
precious. I got a most joyful surprise when I was
informed that this was actually the Exciseman at
the aforesaid distillery. The idea of temperance
agitation and recommendation issuing, as it were, from
the mouth of the Alcoholic Tartarus itself, was most
unexpected and amazing."

Nor must we overlook here the fact that Mr.
Mitchell was one of those happy, generous-hearted,
jovial men who are the very life of a social
gathering; and as all social gatherings in these
days were drinking ones, his adoption of abstinence
was certain banishment from those circles in which he
was accustomed to move. Then, among the educated
classes, and more especially among the ministers and
the doctors, the abstinence movement had no really
earnest friends, but was everywhere condemned as unscriptural and unsound. But comparatively few of those
who at first became abstainers had resolution enough
to resist the influences which drinking practices and
interests brought to bear upon them—influences of
the power of which abstainers of the present generation
cannot form any adequate conception. In Mr. Mitchell's
case, however, persecution only added fuel to the flame
of devotion that was burning within him. He had
correctly counted the cost of the undertaking. He had
faith in the work before him. His mind was possessed
simply by one grand idea. Opposition, as well as encouragement, served the same purpose of fixing it

more deeply there, and how firmly it had laid hold of his spirit is evident from the fact that the rescue of his race from the slavery of drink was from then till the hour of his death—a period covering more than a quarter of a century—the one absorbing thought of his life. He was a man of deep religious feeling, and consequently, to his mind, the abstinence movement appeared as a necessary means to the attainment of a greater end. He saw that the whisky influence was terribly powerful in the Church, impairing her purity and usefulness—that all efforts for the salvation of the world, abroad as well as at home, were rendered next to abortive through this cause—that the drinking practices of Christian people were an insuperable barrier to the progress of Gospel truth, and therefore he laboured with the zeal of an apostle to remove it out of the way.

Mr. Mitchell was about forty years of age when he entered on the great work of his life. He was a burly, middle-sized active man, of pleasing manners, possessing great power of endurance, a clear intellect, a sound judgment, and tremendous energy. He was admirably adapted for the rough work he was called to perform. The merits of the question he soon mastered. Judging alcohol by its fruits, he unhesitatingly pronounced it a poison. Having obtained this good foundation principle, he was prepared for his work, and no sophism, however skilfully constructed, could divert him from it. At first his platform labours were confined to localities within twenty miles of his residence. This, however, was too limited a sphere for his force of character. There was no rest for him till almost every town and village in the kingdom had listened to his heart-stirring appeals. From the nature of his occupation his place of residence was changed every few years, and this circumstance afforded him opportunities of opening up new fields for temperance action, of which he eagerly availed himself. Wherever his home chanced to be—at Stirling, Burnfoot, Lochside, or elsewhere—it was always regarded as one of the great centres of temperance influence. Mrs. Mitchell, a most superior and energetic person, was quite as earnest and laborious as himself. Theirs was a charming family circle, and for many years the favourite resort of the leading spirits in the movement, where many a scheme was originated, and many a disheartened labourer at temperance work received encouragement and strength.

His style of oratory was well suited for the work he had to do. In the earlier part of his career abstinence meetings were composed almost entirely of the working classes. His addresses, while characterised by sound reasoning and depth of thought, were always illustrated by telling facts, and presented with a rough-and-ready earnestness that never failed to attract the attention, if not to convince the judgment. When urging his audiences to abstain, there was a fatherly tenderness about his manner which was exceedingly pleasing; but when he came to speak of the traffic and its doings, his impetuous, fiery spirit seemed stirred to its very depths, as he hurled out against it the most withering denunciations. The following remarks by one who knew him well are very characteristic :—"When he rose to speak on this subject he felt that he was burdened with a subject of solemn and terrible importance. As he proceeded, his short, square figure quivered with the depth of his earnestness, and his honest Scotch face flushed, and his dim and almost sightless eyes flashed with the intensity of inmost feeling. His voice, when speaking, chorded with his appearance, and when his feelings were aroused, pealed over his audience in accents of thunder. A man of this fiery and impetuous character, so bold and so honest, so sincere and so inflexible, was not the man to trim an unpopular doctrine to suit the popular taste."

The Western Scottish Temperance Union, which was founded in 1839, had in Mr. Mitchell one of its ablest and most devoted leaders. He was also one of the earnest supporters of the Scottish Temperance League from its commencement, and until the year 1850 took a deep and active interest in the proceedings of that Association. At the annual meeting of the League, held that year, the delegates present declined to commit the institution to the movement then rising into importance for the legislative prohibition of the manufacture and sale of intoxicating drinks. He strongly dissented from that decision, and, along with others, withdrew, with the view of devoting their attention more exclusively to the legislative aspect of the question. At that time he was residing in Edinburgh, carrying forward the work with his usual zeal. From thence he removed to Glasgow, resolved to devote his entire time to the movement. There he became the mainspring of the Glasgow Abstainers' Association. He visited from house to house, scattering around him the blessings of temperance, and employing his Sabbath evenings in eloquently and earnestly pleading with the crowds gathered on the Glasgow Green. In 1856 he was appointed agent of the United Kingdom Alliance, and did good service in connection with that institution. Two years later he was appointed Secretary of the Scottish Permissive Bill Association, the duties of which office he continued faithfully to discharge up to the day of his death. Mr. Mitchell was not merely a powerful speaker, but during the whole of his public life was a constant contributor to the temperance literature of the country, and the productions of his pen were not less powerful than his spoken addresses.

Whatever may have been his views concerning the relation between the moral suasion and the legal prohibition aspects of the question latterly, there can be no doubt that during the earlier part of his public life he believed that any measure of traffic restriction or prohibition would be worthless, unless based on an enlightened public sentiment regarding the pernicious nature of the liquor. The following words, written by him in 1843, are worthy of record :—

" *Let me not be misunderstood here.* What I assert is, that in the present state of society no power exists to enforce such a law, and that the very attempt to do so would only be followed by a state of things represented by the casting out of one devil to be repossessed by seven others worse than the first. It is painful to hear good men ignorantly crying out, 'Stop the distilleries, and you cut up the iniquity by the roots; shut up the dram shops, and you close the fountains of death.' No; you must change the national taste— you must alter the tone of public opinion, which now so fearfully preponderates in favour of strong drink— else laws which seek to deprive men of their beloved lusts will be trodden under foot. Let the punishment of death be this hour annexed to the furnishing of intoxicating liquors, and there are thousands in this country ready to brave it night and day. That national taste which we and our forefathers had helped to form must be changed before strong legislative enactments can be made available to remove or keep down intemperance; and the first and imperative duty of every man and woman who fears God or loves their fellow-creatures is to labour with untiring energy to change the national taste and overthrow the drinking customs—resolving, in the strength of God, never to cease until public opinion has been so wrought upon that it shall become enlightened enough and patriotic enough to render Government strong enough to seal for ever the downfall of all intoxicating agents."

Nor was he less clear regarding the condition of the Church through the drink evil. As far back as July, 1841, we find him at a meeting of the Western Scottish Temperance Union proposing that that Association should " take every opportunity to impress upon Christian brethren the sinfulness of continuing to make, sell, or use an article looked upon by millions of our fellow-Christians as a curse, and who are praying daily for its destruction." In supporting this motion, he said—" Some say, don't agitate the Church ; but my motto would be, agitate, agitate, till the foul blot of drunkenness be for ever wiped from her escutcheon. She must be pure before she can enjoy peace ; and he most truly seeks the peace of Zion who tries to purge her. Is it reasonable to expect that we shall sit down quietly, and see men who are the salt of the earth expelled from the Church—cast out like an unclean thing —for refusing to drink intoxicating drink in the ordinance of the Lord's Supper, while distillers and spirit-dealers are retained in membership, and allowed unquestioned to sit down at that most holy table and shew forth the Lord's death ? It is not. There is a limit to forbearance, and abstainers must now give no rest till the Church is purified, and such a defence be formed around her that none shall be allowed to fall away from her by the temptations of strong drink."

Mr. Mitchell died on the 18th January, 1862, rejoicing in the hope of a blessed immortality. He was in harness to the very last, actively engaged in his favourite work. Over his remains, in the Southern Necropolis of Glasgow, has been placed by his late fellow-workers a monumental column, bearing the following inscription :—

"In affectionate remembrance of JAMES MITCHELL, one of the early, disinterested, unwearied, and successful advocates of the temperance reformation, who died at Glasgow, 18th January, 1862, in his sixty-sixth year, in the faith and hope of a blessed immortality.

"Erected by friends resident in various parts of the country."

This departed labourer in the cause of human progress was a remarkable man. He possessed the true spirit of a reformer, and has not passed away without leaving the noble impress of his character on the age. The temperance enterprise is destined to be the greatest of all moral reformations ; and let it not be forgotten that he to whose memory we pay this tribute was one of those earnest workers, the aim of whose life was to secure for it a solid foundation.

CHAPTER XIX.

JAMES STIRLING.

JAMES STIRLING was one of the most remarkable men I ever met with in connection with the temperance movement. Like not a few he had been a victim to strong drink, and, after having been sorely bitten, was brought seriously to reflect on the course he had been pursuing by the following touching incident. One night on his return home, after having spent a whole day in the public-house, he found his wife engaged, as usual, in reading a chapter to the children. The portion of Scripture read was the twenty-fifth chapter of Matthew's gospel, in which these words occur:—" When the Son of man shall come in his glory, and all the holy angels with him, then shall he sit upon the throne of his glory: and before him shall be gathered all nations: and he shall separate them one from another, as a shepherd divideth his sheep from the goats: and he shall set the sheep on his right hand, but the goats on the left." His youngest boy, then about four years of age, was lying with his head on his mother's lap, and just when she had read those striking words, he looked up earnestly in her face and asked—" Will father be a goat then, mother?" " This," says Stirling himself, " was too strong to be resisted. The earnest, innocent look of the child, the bewilderment of the poor mother, and, above all, the question itself, smote me to the heart's core. I spent a sleepless, awfully miserable night, wishing rather to die than live such a life. I was ashamed to go to church on the following Sabbath. I stopped at home and read the 'Six Sermons on Intemperance,' by Beecher, which had found their way into the house, but how I never knew. But so it was, that when looking about the house for some suitable book to read on Sabbath, I laid my hands on them, and they seemed as if written and printed and sent there for me alone. I was now decided. My resolution was taken, as it had never been before. All the men on earth could not tempt me to drink, clear or brown, thick or thin."

After the occurrence of this incident, Stirling naturrally looked around him for assistance, and immediately found it in the temperance cause, which is, and has been, ever ready to lend a helping hand and restore to the paths of sobriety. In the spring of 1830, a temperance society was formed at Milngavie, near Glasgow, where Stirling then resided. A meeting was called for the purpose, greatly to the astonishment of the old wiseacres about the village.

" The Rev. Alexander M'Naughton," says the Rev. Dr. Wallace, Glasgow, "ever anxious to promote the temporal and eternal well-being of his fellow-men, came manfully forward and took the chair, and at the

close of the meeting was the first to enroll his name
as a member of the new society.   In the original list
of names, now lying before us, the third name on that
list, written in good round ploughman style, is that of
James Stirling.   As soon as he had publicly enrolled
his name, one of his sons, then a boy, who was present,
ran home as fast as a pair of the nimblest feet in the
village could carry him to tell his mother, who was
lying unwell, the glad news.   'Mother! mother!'
he cried out in eager haste, as the door flew open and
he rushed to the bedside, 'father has put down his
name, and the minister has put down his, and they're
all putting down their names!'

"'Thank God!' ejaculated the broken-hearted wife,
who had passed through a long night of weeping, and
on whom light was now breaking at last, 'Thank God!'
But she could say no more till she found relief in
tears.   And such tears!   It was the first time in her
married life that tears had started from the long-sealed
fount of joy.   'Thank God!' she said, after a pause;
'if he has signed it, he'll keep it.   Yes, he'll keep it,'
she added, with still greater emphasis, and her pale
face was flushed as it had not been for many years,
with the pride of early love.   'Thank God! he has
signed it, and I'll sign it too, and ye must all sign it,
for, oh, surely the time, the set time, to favour us, and
mony puir families, has come at last!'"

Mr. Lauchlan Mackay, Glasgow, one of the early
earnest workers in the cause, and who has for many

years been a director of the Scottish Temperance League, has furnished me with the following account of Mr Stirling's first temperance lecture in Glasgow:— I remember, on my first visit to Milngavie, in 1837, being much struck with the originality of James Stirling's character, his excellent conversational powers, his great acquaintanceship with our national poets, Burns, Shakspeare, Cowper, Wordsworth, &c., long pieces of whose poems he readily recited; but, above all, his deep religious feeling and evident piety, and his prayer at family worship, had on me (a young lad) such an impression that even yet that little family gathering is vividly before me. "The old man eloquent" poured out (evidently from the heart) such a prayer, for deep humility, for grandeur of expression, for pathos and sublimity of conception, and all in such broad homely Saxon language, that it completely touched my young heart, and made me feel as if I had got into the company of one of the worthy old patriarchs.

At one of my subsequent visits, learning he had been a total abstainer for some time—I having just joined the cause—I urged upon him to come into Glasgow and address one of our temperance meetings. I had from the first become a member of committee of the Total Abstinence Society. We held our meetings then in Spreull's Court, Trongate. After much persuasion and entreaty, I got him to consent; and, that he should not be put to any expense, he was to share

my bed in my parents' house.   Well do I remember
his first lecture in Sproull's Court.   The place, as
usual, was crammed to suffocation, as at that time the
novelty of total abstinence attracted many friends and
many opponents.   As the old man rose to speak—
being a new face (for our speakers were not very
plenty), unknown to any of the committee except
myself, and as I had all the responsibility of intro-
ducing him, having heralded him as "a wonderful old
man"—there was considerable interest excited among
the audience.   There was a dead silence, but the first
few sentences at once rivetted the attention of the
meeting.   It was evidently felt by all that no ordinary
speaker stood before them, and as he warmed with his
subject, which was the "Three Crafts,--"Witchcraft,"
"Priest Craft," and "Still Craft," the three crafts that
for ages had ruled the world—dwelling more particularly on the last head, alternately he had the people
weeping and roaring with laughter.   His description
of a drunkard's house was inimitable—its wretchedness and misery, from its being devoid of all furniture
and comfort, and the sufferings entailed on the helpless
wife and children, were depicted in such language and
with such feeling as to draw tears from almost every
eye; but the grotesque description of the drunkard's
bed and bedding, of his getting out of it in the morning, of his legs and arms peeping through all the holes
in the only blanket, and of his exertions to free himself, like a fly running off with a spider's web on his

back, was given in such a graphic manner that I have never heard it equalled except by Gough.

Mrs. Stirling I knew intimately, and she may well be classed among the temperance heroines, for a more excellent and godly woman I have never met. She was a helpmate indeed, and it is possible that, but for her exertions and earnest prayers, the temperance cause might never have been blessed with the powerful advocacy of James Stirling. In the days of his folly, he occasionally neglected his business, which was a good one for a country district, as he had often six to eight men in his employment; it would, I have no doubt, gone completely to wreck but for the unremitting care and attention bestowed upon it by his self-sacrificing wife. When, in after years, it was proposed that James should give up his business, and devote himself entirely to lecturing on the temperance cause throughout the country in connection with the Scottish Temperance League, it was at first a hard struggle for her to consent, to feel that in her declining years she should be ofttimes separated from his presence and company; but she yielded at last, saying, "What a blessing total abstinence has been to him and myself! Go, James; I would have liked to have had more of your company, but as we have been blessed by the temperance cause, God may make you the instrument of like blessings to others."

Mr. John Dunlop, when writing to myself, about fifteen years ago, thus refers to the "Scientific Cobbler," as Stirling was often called:—"Sometime after the beginning of my temperance career, I was greatly encouraged, amid serious and permanent hindrances, by the artisans of Johnstone, in Renfrewshire, honouring me with a soiree (then a novelty), and when I arrived, I was told that a 'famous new han',' from Milngavie, was to attend. By and by he came, and was introduced to me with some little form. There stood before me an athletic old man, with a majestic, but modest countenance; and a noble head of matted, wavy hair, nearly white. The tones of his voice and mode of pronunciation were singular; but his ordinary talk was melodious and powerful; yet leisurely, as if flowing from a deep well of thought. I could not help smiling at the commencement of his speech to the audience. 'Ma freens,' said he, 'when I came here to present my old white head, I did not expect to find my 'father' in your midst' (meaning me, a youth compared to him)."

It was in 1842 that I first heard James Stirling address a total abstinence meeting in Glasgow. His reasonings and appeals, especially to the working classes, were always powerful. We often met each other in the prosecution of temperance work; and I can truly say, that I never listened to a more zealous, useful, and indefatigable friend of the cause.

After what has been so graphically described of Stirling's Life and Labours, by the Rev. Dr. Alex. Wallace, Glasgow, in that charming little volume of his, "The Gloaming of Life," of which many thousands have been circulated, any further entrance into detail on my part is quite unnecessary. I shall therefore close by quoting from Dr. Wallace's remarks on the "evening" of Stirling's life :—

"The last time," says the Doctor, "we had the pleasure of seeing Mr. Stirling was in June, 1855, in Glasgow. He looked feeble and worn-out, but the old spirit was there, and even then he cherished the idea that he would yet be able to accomplish a tour to the north, and see and address his friends once more at Aberdeen. He took a deep interest in the young, and his last public appearance at any meeting was at a soiree held in Milngavie on the 1st January, 1856, when he delivered a most earnest address to the youths who were present. Early that year he was seized with a complaint which ended in paralysis, and his naturally robust frame was soon reduced to a state of great weakness. From the nature of his disease he was subject at times to great mental depression, when ' he was made to possess the sins of his youth,' and the memory of his drinking days came up like a dark impenetrable cloud between him and the sunshine of Christian peace and hope. He was cast into 'depths,' and from these he could not even at times cry for help. On such occasions his aged and faithful minister, who frequently visited him, acted the part of a wise counsellor and a faithful friend.

"The Directors of the Scottish Temperance League,

P

to their honour be it recorded, felt a deep interest in him all along, especially during the closing days of his life, and generously provided for all his wants.

"Two of his faithful friends from Glasgow, Robert Rae and William Logan, paid him a visit a few days before his death, and to them we are indebted for the following particulars :—

"'We found him confined to bed. He had had a slight paralytic stroke on the previous day, which affected his left side and also his speech. He was, however, able at once to recognise us, and said, 'I am very glad to see you both.' Immediately after we entered the house, the Rev. A. M'Naughton, his venerable pastor, called to see him. Mr. M.'s remarks were brief and to the point, and his prayer most appropriate and impressive.

"'After the minister left, we said, 'James, you will now find Christ to be your best friend.' In reply he said in a firm tone of voice, and with great impressiveness and fervour, 'Christ is a friend to whom we can all go at all times. He is ever ready to receive *all* who come to him in *faith*,' laying special emphasis on the words *all* and *faith*. That comforting passage in Isaiah xli. 10 was repeated, and was evidently relished by our dying friend—'Fear thou not; for I am with thee: be not dismayed; for I am thy God: I will strengthen thee ; yea, I will help thee ; yea, I will uphold thee with the right hand of my righteousness.' During our visit another minister of the district called, and, among other things, he asked our friend if he was now ready to give up his spirit to God who gave it. The reply, uttered in a distinct voice, was—'Yes, I really am ready—quite ready.' One of us said, 'We are glad to find you trusting in Christ as your hope for heaven. We expected this; you often expressed it when in health. And now that you seem to be dying, we have no doubt you still feel some interest in that movement to which you have devoted so much of your time.' He replied, with great emphasis, 'Yes, sirs, I feel a keener and a keener interest in the great cause of temperance than ever.'

"'The movement,' one of us replied, 'is now in a more hopeful condition than when you entered the field some twenty-five years ago; and your labours have done something to bring this about.'

"Our old friend's voice for a few moments seemed to resume all its former well-known expressive tone, and he said, with an earnestness that would have impressed the largest audience he ever addressed—'If ever I were able to lift up my voice in public again, I—I—I—.' He could say no more at the time; but there was no difficulty whatever in comprehending what he meant. We were deeply moved. One of us broke silence by remarking, 'James, you have done your part faithfully.' After a brief pause, during which he seemed in deep meditation, he said, 'Mr. Wallace urged me during last summer to write more on the subject; but I always found great difficulty in

writing.' These were the last words which fell from
his lips on the great temperance enterprise in our
hearing. He evidently in these words referred to a
short sketch he had written of his own life, and which
the Rev. A. Wallace had been urging him to extend."

" He had all along," continues Dr. Wallace, " been
an ardent admirer of nature, and a few days before
his death, when the breath of spring was again
renewing the face of the earth, he asked his daughter,
one morning at six o'clock, to open the window
shutters, so that he might see the light, and then
he desired her to lift the window a little, that he
might hear the early song of birds. The ruling
passion was strong in death. At that instant he
heard the mellow piping of a thrush from a neighbouring tree, and he said, with much rapture,
'Oh, that's the voice of nature! Sweet nature has
spring coming to renew her charms, but no coming
spring will on earth revive the cold, cold ashes of the
urn!' . He was in a desponding mood that morning.
The nature of his complaint tended to produce that,
but happier thoughts ere long came to his relief, and
he was enabled to cling to Him who is the Resurrection and the Life, and through whom it can so
truly be said, 'Awake and sing, ye that dwell in dust;
for thy dew is as the dew of herbs, and the earth shall
cast out the dead.' The voices of nature could not
comfort the departing soul, but the voice of the Elder
Brother did—' He that believeth in me, though he

were dead, yet shall he live;' and in the full faith of this our aged friend fell asleep, on the 20th March, 1856. He was loosed from his infirmity. His severe conflict and weary wanderings were brought to a close. The harness was ungirt, and he went to rest.

"On the memorable evening when he joined the temperance society along with a few others, some put down their names with the understanding that they might withdraw them in six, twelve, or eighteen months. The Rev. A. M'Naughton, who stood by, turned to Mr. Stirling and said, 'Well, James, for how long have you signed?' 'For evermore, sir, with God's help,' was the reply, and with that help he nobly '*worked his way*' through many difficulties, before which any ordinary man would have quailed; and he never ceased to do battle with the great curse of our country, till he heard the voice saying, 'Come up hither!' and the old warrior exchanged his battle-sword for the palm, and entered upon that land where there is 'no curse, and nothing to hurt or destroy.'

"His remains were conveyed by many faithful friends to their final resting-place, in the quiet churchyard of New Kilpatrick. The day of interment was one of the brightest and most genial in the opening spring, and the fresh flowers and the bursting buds, and the many voices of nature, as well as revelation, gave strength to the assurance, which friends were warranted to cherish, that 'earth was committed to earth,

ashes to ashes, dust to dust,' in the well-founded hope
of a blessed and a glorious immortality.

"At the request of the directors of the Scottish Temperance League, the Rev. William Reid, of Edinburgh,
preached to a crowded audience in the City Hall,
Glasgow, an appropriate and heart-stirring sermon, in
which he paid a high and well-merited tribute to the
worth and labours of the departed veteran. What a
change! Thousands assembled, and hundreds could
not obtain admission, to hear a funeral oration for
a man who, thirty years before, might have been
found intoxicated, ill-clad, and in danger of being
frozen to death in the dead of winter, not very many
yards from the magnificent hall where a funeral
oration was delivered in honour of his untiring and
invaluable labours as an advocate of that cause which
was instrumental, through the blessing of God, in
plucking him as a 'brand from the burning,' and
which made him the means of blessing many homes,
and of making many hearts sing for joy."

"His friend, Mr. Logan," says Dr. Wallace, "who
was with him in Dunoon on a beautiful Sabbath
evening in the summer of 1848, has still a vivid
recollection of a meeting held on that occasion
near the pier, and of the impression which was then
produced. The far-flashing radiance of the setting sun
gilded the noble Firth, and bathed with its golden
light the majestic peaks of Arran, the Cumbraes, and
all the giant hills of Argyle, and the softly-undulating

plains of Ayrshire. It was one of those sunsets, when earth seems to put on for a time the lustrous loveliness of the better land. He could not allow such an occasion to pass unimproved; and as there were very many out of doors enjoying the fragrance and beauty of that delightful hour, he proposed to hold a meeting by the sea-shore. A large crowd soon assembled, and his venerable appearance, his broad, earnest face, his massive forehead deeply furrowed with age, his silvery locks trembling in the breeze, his eye beaming with affection and intelligence, his peculiar phraseology, his thick and guttural articulation, as he read with emphasis the psalm to be sung, awakened at the very outset the interest of the crowd. But this was greatly increased when he rose up, bent and hoary with age, and in that vast temple poured forth a prayer, replete with the most striking and apposite allusions to nature, and the most gorgeous imagery which scripture language furnishes upon the same subject;—and then passing from the beauty of such a scene to the ravages of sin, every heart seemed melted, as he lifted up his own in gratitude to the Father of mercy for his redeeming love, in the gift of the Saviour, who came to seek and to save that which was lost. That prayer will long be remembered by those who heard it. Then followed an address as striking and as memorable, and which, doubtless, owed much of its peculiar power to the inspiring influences of that glorious sunset, and the magnificent panorama of unrivalled scenery that lay all around.

Whatever motives brought the crowd together, and however differently affected they might be at first, all retired at last most favourably impressed, and under the conviction that they had listened to a man not only actuated by Christian earnestness, but moved by expansive philanthropy, and gifted with genius and imagination, which could press into his service the scenes and events of the passing hour, and make them all tell with effect upon the great object for which he lived and laboured.   His company was greatly relished by the intelligent and the pious, in the higher as well as the humbler walks of life.

"Such a man, notwithstanding all the imperfections of his education, and all the drawbacks of many wasted years, and his humble position in society, could not but exert a very widely extended influence for good even in the '*gloaming*' of his life.   He was highly esteemed by the leading benevolent men of his day, and their estimate of his character and labours may be gathered from the following words of John Dunlop, author of the well-known 'Exposure of our Drinking Usages':—

"'Our excellent friend, "Old Stirling," is worthy of being denominated a hero, if good sense, energetic eloquence, and untiring good-will to his kind, can bestow this title.'

"Substantial and public expression has been given to this sentiment in the monument which has been erected over the grave of the veteran reformer in

New Kilpatrick churchyard. It is a lovely sequestered spot, in keeping with that strong love of nature which glowed so warmly in his breast, whilst the monument, in its plain simplicity, is no less appropriate to the memory of one who assumed so little and yet did so much.

"The monument is in the form of an obelisk. Near the top there is a carved bridle, an ingenious device of the sculptor (Mr. Stewart M'Glashen, Edinburgh), to represent temperance or restraint, of which the departed was such a remarkable instance. The following is the inscription:—

IN MEMORY OF
JAMES STIRLING,
The first agent of the Scottish Temperance League, and one of the most distinguished advocates of the Temperance Reformation.

Born, 6th March, 1774. Died, 20th March, 1856.

His noblest monument is to be found in the many once-wretched homes that he made happy; and the highest testimony to his Christian character and personal worth, his stirring eloquence and self-denying labours, is expressed in the warm gratitude of hundreds whom he rescued from the crushing grasp of Scotland's greatest curse.

The blessing of those who were ready to perish came upon him, and he caused many hearts to sing for joy.

ERECTED BY A FEW FRIENDS."

CHAPTER XX.

ROBERT SMITH.

WHEN glancing over the proofs of the last of the preceding pages, I received an intimation of the death of Mr. Robert Smith. In common with Temperance Reformers throughout Scotland, and far beyond its bounds, I deeply mourn the departure from amongst us of this honoured and worthy friend of the cause. It was my privilege very frequently to call on Mr. Smith during the last twenty years, to solicit his aid in behalf of benevolent objects, when I invariably met with a cordial reception, and, after answering his few discriminating questions regarding the case, never left empty-handed. The thought suggested itself to my mind that a sketch of Mr. Smith's life might be appropriately embodied in this little volume; and for what follows I am indebted to my esteemed friend, the Rev. John Guthrie, M.A., Glasgow.

After long-protracted illness, Mr. Smith died at Hafton House, on the Clyde, on the 26th July, 1873. He was a native of Saltcoats, in Ayrshire, where he was born on the 25th July, 1801. He had, accordingly, just completed his 72nd year. He was a partner in one of our leading merchant firms—that of Messrs. George Smith & Sons; and up to the time that he was overtaken within the last twelve months by what has proved to be his last illness, he was daily and actively engaged in the management of its concerns.

Of Mr. Smith's general position in Glasgow, no one resident in it, or near it, needs to be informed. No names arc more familiarly associated with the river and its expanding traffic than those of his and of kindred firms. Their ships or steamers float on every sea. If less prominent than his brother, Mr. George Smith, in public business, especially relating to tho port in which the latter wields great and just influence, he was not less in his own department an eminent and thorough man of business. Prompt, discerning, and direct, his mind was speedily made up, and the judgment thus formed resolutely maintained. On this same principle he acted with objects of benevolence. He instinctively sympathized with them all as a humane and Christian man, and liberally contributed to their support; but he was no blind contributor. He must be satisfied, not only as a matter of course in regard to the object, but to a fair extent as to what else it might be wise and needful to know about. Hence, we have heard of instances in which applicants for aid to some scheme have come away disappointed, or received less than they anticipated. But contrariwise, we have known cases (and some of them have transpired since his lamented decease) in which friends have left him rejoicing with much larger donations than they ventured to expect. The one principle above noticed alike explains both.   In his giving, as in other matters, Mr. Smith acted as a man of principle, and as a man of business.   Predisposed to everything that was good, and originating and carrying through, with his like-minded brother, not a little in that line within their own domain, when any object was pressed on him from without, his method was not to get rid of an unwelcome visitation, either by undiscriminating facility or by a trifling pittance, but to satisfy his mind in regard to it, and then adhere to his judgment.   For many years Mr. Smith subscribed £100 annually to the Scottish Temperance League.

In the earlier stage of his career, while yet the centre of their business was in London Street, near the Cross, and as far back as the pastorate of the late Dr. Heugh, Mr. Smith was elected to the office of eldership in that church, but, with characteristic diffidence, declined acceptance.   Ere long, the body, or part of that church in East Regent Street, removed westward, and founded the United Presbyterian Church in Renfield Street, under the Rev. Dr. James Taylor, now Secretary to the Board of Education in Edinburgh.   There he was again chosen to the office of elder, which he at this time accepted, and worthily occupied and fulfilled till the summons, "Go up higher," "Come up hither!" called him away to serve and enjoy his Master in a more exalted sphere.

In his civic or secular relations, his career, like that of his relatives in the well-known firm, was one of steadily advancing influence and respect. He was chosen a member of the Town Council at the election in November, 1845, at a time when the honour was more an object of ambition and of difficulty than it is now; and after acting as Councillor for one year, he was, in November, 1846, elected a Magistrate of the city, and honourably fulfilled the duties of that office for two years while the late Mr. Hastie, M.P., was Lord Provost of Glasgow. After a triennium of civic duty, Mr. Smith retired from the Town Council in 1848. During that brief term of public life, Mr. Smith commanded universal respect for the admirable manner in which he harmonized those functions with unflinching fidelity to his temperance convictions. Without referring to the conventional calls upon him in the matter of official hospitality—the due claims of which, and of hospitality in general, he ever delighted to honour—delicate publican cases could not but occur in the course of his magisterial duties. From that quarter, as might be expected, querulous utterances would occasionally make themselves audible in our public journals, demanding that no abstainer should be held qualified to sit in judgment on cases in which the drink-vending interest was concerned. But though these complaints were made with direct allusion to Mr. Smith—just as they have since been with others like-minded—they never ventured beyond the *possible* to any insinuation of the *actual*, or mooted the faintest charge against him of biassed administration.

MR. SMITH AS A TEMPERANCE REFORMER AND LEAGUE PRESIDENT.

It was in the year 1843 that Mr. Smith threw in his lot with the total abstinence movement, which, in its more perfected and extended organism, he was soon after to head.   It is interesting to find men in their youth or early prime, destined to rise to highest social position in the city, gradually attracted, as by a way they knew not, to a common focus of benevolent effort, which, in its turn, was destined to rise into a great social and moral power.   Mr. Smith was then in ripe manhood. Mr. John M'Gavin was much younger, but already active and energetic in the cause; and it was only a few years later that we heard one remark who had good reason to know, that the latter already exerted a commanding influence in the councils of the young but growing League.   Over many trying years, Mr. Smith was President of the League, and Mr. M'Gavin Chairman of the Board; and under their shadow, and that of others, it has grown to what we see.

Mr. Smith expired in the very month in which, many years before, he had been elected President of the Scottish Temperance League.   That was in 1852; so that his tenure of office extended over a period of twenty-one years.   No face and figure were more familiar than his at our anniversary meetings; for none were more regularly and punctually present; and none, we may be permitted to add, were more

genial and ornamental. His *personnel* could not but
attract attention. His features, expression, and
bearing were exceptionally pleasing. An air of
geniality, benevolence, and placid dignity, which could
be firm and resolute without ceasing to be kind, pre-
eminently distinguished him. This he had no need to
put on as an official "robe and diadem;" it was part
of himself, and could not be put off. The period of
his presidency embraced some stormy years, in which
flank fires were too often interchanged between large
temperance organizations that needed rather to have
all their energies combined and directed against the
common foe. For a good few years in succession the
annual meetings of the League were clouded and
convulsed by these inter-organizational strifes. The
thoughts of many minds were revealed; and in the
freedom of our representative constitution, as well as
in the proverbial vigour of our teetotal vitality, these
thoughts were not always vented in parliamentary
language. But no regrettable language ever escaped
the President's lips. He could be, and often was,
inflexibly firm; but it was invariably in the direction
of order and fair play. Amid all crimination and
debate, never a word fell from any, so far as we ever
heard, implying the least reflection on the procedure
of the President.

This was the more to be admired that, tested by his
own individual sentiments, Mr. Smith must have often
had a good deal to bear. What his own leading views

of temperance policy were, he occasionally indicated with characteristic honesty and business precision in his opening addresses on annual or other public occasions. But these were all expressed with deference, and as general principles, and were never obtruded when any of the questions involved were in actual debate. He never attached much importance to temperance legislation. In prohibitory legislation, as things are, he never had any faith; in restrictive action, such as we have in Scotland, and more partially in England, he had some little faith, but, we have reason to believe, not very much. Often, indeed, did he preside at League and other meetings got up in promotion of our restrictive legislation, and especially while the conflict was in process in which, for nine years, the Forbes Mackenzie Act had to be defended against the machinations of the publicans for its modification and repeal. On those occasions he did his duty with an earnestness and impartiality which thoroughly harmonized with the general sentiment, and befitted the gravity of the conjuncture. But the one article of his temperance creed to which he attached prime importance, was that of total abstinence from all that intoxicates, in strict accordance with the original and fundamental principle of the Scottish Temperance League and of all its affiliated societies. In this he justly felt himself to be on ground which was both practical and safe. Leaving it to others to see further if they could, and prosecute what action they thought best in the line of their convictions, he felt it enough that total abstinence was the only sound and solid basis of the temperance reformation throughout all its departments, and that progress in this line, as one individual after another was brought to abstain, was vital progress in all that pertained to temperance reform.

Though a man of invincible gentleness and suavity of tone, Mr. Smith, as we have said, could, on occasion, be faithful and formidable. His strength of temperance principle was such as to brook no attack on our movement that emanated from any quarter worthy of notice. On these occasions he would appear in the local press, and administer a rap on the knuckles to those whom it might concern. As an instance of this faithful vigilance of what was passing, we recall the following morsel from a speech of his at the annual meeting of the League in 1862 :—

"For myself, I may say that hitherto I have had little faith in making people either religious or sober by Act of Parliament; but when I find one of our city members stating in Parliament that '*nothing was more common than for a man to entertain his friends, and for some of them to get drunk,*' I begin to think that some police regulations may be found necessary to put an end to the practice of drunkard-making out of pure friendship. If our members of Parliament, our magistrates, our ministers, and the editors of our daily press, were to adopt our practice, and recommend it in their

Q

various circles, it is difficult to estimate the amount of good they might do."

MR. SMITH AND HIS FAMILY CIRCLE.

Mr. Smith by no means stood alone in temperance zeal in his family circle. That family circle is remarkable for its longevity. His venerable father predeceased him only a few years ago at the age of 91. His revered father-in-law, William Service, of Culcreuch, a zealous and devoted temperance reformer from the very first, and a living monument of the life-prolonging influence of abstinence, still survives him at that same patriarchal age, being now in his 92nd year. Mr. Smith had by no means "attained unto the days of the years of the life of these, his fathers, in the days of their pilgrimage;" but for all that, neither " few nor evil have the days of the years of his life been," for he had entered his 73rd year, a period exceeding the "allotted span," and his hoary head has gone down in peace and honour to the grave, having always been found " in the way of righteousness."

A saddening memory is here called up in contrast to these ample life-terms—the image of Mr. Smith's brother-in-law, Mr. William Service, son and namesake of the venerable nonagenarian above-named, who, it will be remembered, died in his early prime in May, 1869, at the very date of the League Anniversary for that year, being consigned to the tomb on the day of the annual meeting. Under such congenial home influences as those referred to, he had been a temperance reformer from his youth, was early prominent in the work, and acted through many of .those early years as Treasurer of the League.

There are too many cases in which the removal of a noted temperance reformer means the extinction of the family influence in relation to the movement. Happily, this in the present instance will not be the case. With Mr. Smith and his immediate circle it was a family principle and practice heartily embraced and consistently carried out. Mrs. Smith's interest, let us rather say her fervid zeal and energetic, albeit unobtrusive, action in furtherance of the cause, is well known to all who are conversant with its history and progress in the West of Scotland. And those exertions were most abundant at that stage of its development when they were at once most needed and least belauded—in the period of early struggle, when results that have since been reaped in joy had often to be sown in tears. "Yes," exclaims Edward Morris, in chronicling the early fortunes of the movement in Glasgow and these western bounds, "we have many Miriams in our teetotal bands, who 'have done virtuously,' and rescued not a few drunkards from fiery ruin in both worlds, under God, and saved others from the awful vortex; and by it have mightily strengthened the hands of the sterner leaders. We give a few names;" and among the names he gives is that of "Mrs. Robert Smith." Though in later years her interest evinced itself in other modes, it never betrayed the least abatement—as many can witness who have been present at the hospitable gatherings in Woodside Terrace on anniversary or other special temperance occasions, when, in unreserved freedom at her own table, her conversation showed how well her zeal was sustained, and how thoroughly her intelligence was posted up to the last phase of the movement.

We need hardly add that in the line of their only daughter the same temperance interest and principle continue, and are destined, we trust, to continue and descend. Though from habit and temperament, and no doubt also from the demands on his time as partner in a firm that owns one of our leading commercial fleets, Mr. Alexander Allan's voice is little heard on our temperance platforms, his presence and influence are never wanting on any occasion of importance, and a more staunch and consistent abstainer could not be named.

Mr. Smith was not more conspicuous as a temperance reformer, than he was, on the larger scale, as a devout, earnest, and consistent Christian man. His temperance zeal was but a cluster, though a very goodly one, on the fruit-bearing tree of his personal religion. As an elder in the Renfield Street United Presbyterian Church, as a magistrate, as a leading Glasgow merchant, as President of the Scottish Temperance League, as a citizen, as head of a family, in all his relationships he sought simply to translate his religious faith into appropriate action and influence, with what result none who knew him need to be told.   Let every temperance head of a household bethink himself at such a moment, and be animated by his example to do his utmost to leave that best of all legacies—a well-transmitted, well-embodied, and well-devoted Christian influence.   The sight of a well-ordered, well-principled, and prosperous Christian family, is one of the fairest to be found on earth.   But let no one suppose that it is a result that can be commanded or improvised. There could be no greater mistake.   It is the harvest of long and "patient continuance in well-doing."   It is the fruit of good principle early received, assiduously cultivated, faithfully embodied in family duty, and persistently prosecuted to the end.   It is, as our familiar temperance motto has it—"Be faithful unto death, and thou shalt receive a crown of life."

At the annual meeting of the League, in May, 1873, Mr. Smith was unable to attend. This was the one shadow that clouded its anniversary. There was but one sentiment of sympathy and regret; and no little foreboding was irresistibly felt. On the motion of the Rev. William Reid, of Edinburgh, who, along with the present writer, who seconded the motion, gave fitting expression to the common sentiment, the following resolution was adopted at the business meeting :—"In view of the long-continued illness of Robert Smith, Esq., this meeting expresses its high appreciation of the valuable services which he has rendered to the cause of temperance and the Scottish Temperance League by his high Christian character, social position, consistency, liberality, and efforts during the twenty-one years that he has held the office of President; its deep sympathy with him and his partner in life and family circle under this affliction; and its earnest prayer that, if it be the will of the Sovereign Disposer of all events, his health may be restored, and he be permitted again to take the place among us which every member of the League has ever been delighted to see him occupy." If this expression of sympathy was deep and heartfelt then, how much more, now that the stroke has fallen, —may the mourning widow and family assure themselves of the profound sympathy of many more than can be named in a loss which, though most intensely felt within the family concerned, is realised in its measure in wider circles beyond. The loss of a husband and parent like Mr. Smith is no commonplace sorrow, and calls for the sympathetic interest and prayer of friends in no ordinary measure; but we intrude no further into the sanctuary of private grief.

MR. SMITH'S LAST APPEARANCE AT THE
LEAGUE ANNIVERSARY.

At the Anniversary Meetings of the League in 1872, Mr. Smith was for the last time at his post, and spoke with his usual interest and vigour. When we revert to the records of that year, two features of tender and

instructive interest impressively appear. Both of these
are found in the public meeting in the City Hall.
Over that meeting, Mr. Robert Smith, venerable in
years, presides, and the Rev. Robert French, M.A., in
his young enthusiasm, speaks—both of them at the
last League Anniversary they were destined to see.
At that Anniversary Mr. Smith seems to have been
unusually interested in the juvenile gathering on
Saturday evening in the City Hall. "He thought
he never saw such a galaxy of flowers as was before
the platform at the meeting on Saturday." This he
said in his few congratulatory words at the close of
his duties which terminated with the business meeting.
At the public meeting on Monday, his opening speech,
after a word of greeting, and an admirable *resumé* of
the League's condition and operations for the year,
closed in the following animating terms, in which the
young buds of temperance promise were also referred
to :—"From this short statement, my friends, you
will see we have a great and a good work on hand,
one to which every Christian and philanthropist must
say God-speed. I would therefore call on every one in
this meeting to use his influence in changing the customs of society. Exercise a little self-denial, banish
the bottles from your tables, decline the use of wine
and spirits at the tables of your friends, and you will
soon feel quite at home without these stimulants ; and,
better than all, by so acting you will put it out of the
power of any one who has fallen to say that your

moderate example caused him to slide.   In recommending this course, I only ask you to do what I did myself some thirty years ago, and which I have not yet seen reason to regret.   I hope that ere another thirty years pass away, abstinence will stand on a much broader platform than it does at present.   The Band of Hope meeting in the City Hall, on Saturday evening, gives good promise in that direction.   It was one of the most charming I have seen, and the hall literally crammed."

Here is as appropriate a parting word as our friend could have bequeathed to us.   Let the young especially, who are so prominently named in it, ponder and lay it to heart.   He carries them back over the course of a generation to the time when he first became an abstainer, and after thirty years, and as with his dying breath, he pronounces that act "one which he has not yet seen cause to regret."   In his last moments, we may be sure, when descending into the death-shade, that act was one which he did not regret; and least of all, will he now look back upon it from the clear light of heaven with any feeling of regret.   From this retrospect he turns to what might be looked for in the future after the lapse of another thirty years, if due zeal be shown in the promotion of the movement.   It is for the young especially to take up this challenge and appeal, and translate it in due time into history. And it is for those who, like Mr. Smith, have grown hoary in the service, and may be soon called away, to hear in these parting words of his the warning, "Work while it is day, for the night cometh." "Whatsoever thy hand findeth to do, do it with thy might."

Young men may see from such examples as that of Mr. Smith (and they are by no means rare) how benign are the influences of the temperance reformation in conducting its adherents, if not often to elevations like that reached by our lamented friend, yet, in numberless instances, to positions of competence, affluence, and social weight. Towards this goal total abstinence ever directly tends. Proverbially and demonstrably it promotes health, already the best of earthly fortunes; and health imparts and maintains the spirit and vigour which give mercantile ability its best chance in the keen wrestle of trade, and, better still, gives it credit and respectable position. In nothing is the sapping and undermining, the enervating and muddling influence of indulgence more felt than in the shop, the mart, the counting-house, or the Exchange, when the business man puts in what appearance he best can, after a previous evening of free-drinking, with languid muscles, oppressed brain, dulled nerves, dimmed vision, and a mental vision more blunted still. Above all, the divine benediction may be most surely counted on in the line of personal purity and sobriety, and self-sacrifice undergone in behalf of our fellows, especially when prompted and directed by Christian principle, whose ways are pleasantness, and whose paths are peace.

Mr. Smith's funeral took place on Friday the 1st August. The body, on being brought tö Glasgow, was taken to the United Presbyterian Church, Renfield Street, to which the deceased had belonged; and at two o'clock a solemn service was held, conducted by the Rev. Dr. Taylor, the former minister of the church, the Rev. J. G. Scott, its present minister, and the Rev. Dr. Black, minister of the United Presbyterian Church, Wellington Street. There was a large attendance. Besides a full representation of the ministers and friends of the temperance cause in the West of Scotland, and of the leading citizens of Glasgow, among whom he held a position of such influence and respect, there were present a considerable number of the leading friends of the temperance movement in Edinburgh, both lay and clerical, including his first predecessor in the presidency of the Scottish Temperance League, the Rev. William Reid of that city. The procession was a very long one. As the body was lowered into its silent resting-place in the Glasgow Necropolis, many were the tributes we heard and overheard—some of the foremost of the citizens declaring, at that solemn moment, that "in all Glasgow he had not left behind him a more truly excellent man." Not a few, we believe, will echo that tribute, and be reminded, in connection with his history and influence, of the beautiful words: "When the ear heard me, then it blessed me; and when the eye saw me, it gave witness to me: because I delivered the poor that cried, and the fatherless, and him that had none to help him. The blessing of him that was ready to perish came upon me : and I caused the widow's heart to sing for joy.   I put on righteousness, and it clothed me : my judgment was as a robe and a diadem."

Farewell, honoured name, and ever welcome presence! Long fragrant will be thy memory, and long indelible thy image!   Being dead thou yet speakest, and art still, we trust, thus destined long to speak.   Our best wish for the Scottish Temperance League is that it may be privileged to have for thy successor one as like to thee as may be !

"The memory of the just is blessed."

Seventh Edition, 18th Thousand, 472 pages,

WORDS OF COMFORT for BEREAVED PARENTS.

EDITED BY
WILLIAM LOGAN,
WITH A HISTORICAL SKETCH,
BY THE REV. WM. ANDERSON, LL.D., GLASGOW.

OPINIONS OF THE PRESS.

Dean ALFORD, in the *Contemporary Review*, 1869.—This charming book . . . originally sprung out of a bereavement, which has indeed brought forth choice fruit. Mr. Logan has brought together an ample collection from writers, English and foreign, in prose and verse, of passages which could bear on this subject; and has prefixed to all an Historical Essay, by Dr. Anderson, of Glasgow, on Infant Salvation. The large diffusion of the volume is of itself testimony of the truth of our recommendation. When we say that it is one which would form a precious gift to bereaved friends, and would be admitted into counsel with the wounded heart, at a time when almost all words, written and spoken, are worthless, higher praise could hardly be given.

British Quarterly Review, July 1, 1867.—Mr. Logan puts forth an enlarged edition of a precious little book, consisting of a selection of pieces, both in prose and poetry, from various authors, concerning the death of children, which will speak tenderly, piously, and soothingly to the hearts of bereaved parents.

London Quarterly Review, April, 1869.—A most beautiful and blessed book. Here are treasures of consolation, in prose and poetry, for all that are bereaved. The volume has no rival, and is one which no Christian should lack.

The Westminster Review.—We might say a word or two theological on the "Words of Comfort," by William Logan, but prefer to direct attention to it on account of the appropriateness of the collection, for its kindly purpose, and especially because of the great beauty of the short pieces of poetry which it contains.

Rev. Dr. JOHN CAMPBELL, in the *Christian Witness*, 1861.— Here is opened up a fountain of consolation sufficient to meet the case of bereaved Christian parents in millions through all the world to the close of ages! The book may be entitled the "Cyclopædia of Sympathy."

Evangelical Magazine.—Its lessons are full of healing balm, enriched with truth, and clothed in beauty; they cannot fail to relieve, console, and gladden.

The Sword and the Trowel.—Rev. C. H. SPURGEON, Editor.— We have aforetime mentioned, with much approbation, this well-stored treasury of comfortable words. A very valuable compendium of the opinions of divines, and a choice collection of the songs of poets.

(Wesleyan) *Methodist Recorder.*—It seems to contain almost everything on the subject of the safety of little children that is to be found in the whole range of literature.

English Independent.—There is certainly no corresponding collection of words of consolation in our language. They are extremely varied and beautiful, and are admirably suited to the end the compiler has in view.

The Freeman (Baptist newspaper).—There must be tens of thousands of families to which this volume needs but to be known to prove a most welcome boon.

Liverpool Mercury.—Mr. Logan's volume has our very honest and very warm recommendation.

Public Opinion (London).—A very beautiful collection of Words of Comfort. We can easily understand how such a charmingly written work should become popular.

Literary World.—Quite an encyclopædia of passages upon the touching subjects of which it treats.

Glasgow Herald.—It will help to wipe away those tears which, we suppose, are well nigh the hottest that gush out even in this sad and sorrowing world.

North British Daily Mail.—The opening essay, by Dr. William Anderson, is one of the most strikingly characteristic papers he has ever written, and this is saying much, not only for the writer but for the book.

Evangelical Repository.—Never before—at least in this country—has love entertwined so lovely and so sweet a wreath—a true *Immortelle*—to lay on the grave of departed childhood.

Dundee Advertiser.—Cordially do we wish that it may find its way into every room of the vast house of mourning, and do there its benevolent mission as a portion of the grand ministry by which God is yet to wipe "away tears from all faces."

Paisley Herald.—It is truly a golden treasury of comfortable words for all who delight in the little ones of society. None can resort to it without benefit and delight.

United Presbyterian Magazine.—Once more we heartily commend this work to the acceptance of the universal church, as pre-eminently fitted to bind up the wounds of those who weep because their children are not.

Londonderry Standard.—Dr. Anderson contributes a delightful introduction on the "Salvation of Deceased Infants," which we commend to the attention of every thoughtful reader. The great value of the work is its intense practical tone.

North American (Quarterly) *Review.*—A richer treasury of consolation in human words could hardly be compiled.

In the Prefatory Note to the American Edition of "Words of Comfort," published by Robert Carter and Brothers, New York, in 1870, is the following:—

"That its lessons, so full of healing balm, so enriched with truth, so clothed in beauty, may relieve, console, and gladden many a stricken heart, is the hope of the American publishers."

LONDON: JAMES NISBET & CO., AND BOOKSELLERS.

TEMPERANCE WORKS

PUBLISHED AT THE OFFICE OF THE

Scottish Temperance League,

108 HOPE STREET, GLASGOW.

Single Copies, when the price is 4d., or upwards, sent Post Free, on receipt of Postage Stamps to the amount mentioned.

Demy 8vo, in Paper Covers, Price 1s., Post Free; Post 8vo, Fine Paper, in Cloth Boards, with a Portrait of the Author, 3s., Post Free,

ALCOHOL: ITS PLACE AND POWER.

With an Appendix, containing the Resumé and Conclusions of MM. Lellemand, Perrin, and Duroy, in their recent work, *Du Role de l'Alcool;* together with an Account of Experiments by Dr. E. Smith, London. By James Miller, F.R.S.E., F.R.C.S.E., Surgeon in Ordinary to the Queen for Scotland Professor of Surgery in the University of Edinburgh, &c., &c.

Fcap. 8vo, in Paper Covers, Price 6d.; in Limp Cloth, 1s., Post Free; Post 8vo, Fine Paper, in Cloth Boards, Price 3s., Post Free,

NEPHALISM

THE TRUE TEMPERANCE OF SCRIPTURE, SCIENCE, AND EXPERIENCE.

By JAMES MILLER, F.R.S.E., F.R.C.S.E., Surgeon in Ordinary to the Queen for Scotland, Professor of Surgery in the University of Edinburgh, &c., &c.

Price, in Paper Covers, 1s.; in Illuminated Cloth Boards, 2s., Post Free.

BRITAIN'S SOCIAL STATE.

By DAVID LEWIS,
One of the Magistrates of Edinburgh.

Price, in Paper Covers, 1s.; in Illuminated Cloth Boards, 2s., with Portrait, Post Free.

AUTOBIOGRAPHY OF JOHN B. GOUGH.

With Twenty-six Years' Experience as a Public Speaker.

TEMPERANCE WORKS—continued.

704 pp., Crown 8vo, Price 5s., Post Free,

THE TEMPERANCE CYCLOPÆDIA.

By the REV. WILLIAM REID, Edinburgh.

This Work comprehends a large and classified selection of Facts, Opinions, Statistics, Anecdotes, and Comments on Texts of Scripture, bearing upon every Department of the Temperance Question. New Edition.

Price, in Paper Covers, 1s.; Cloth Boards, 2s. 6d.

SCRIPTURE TESTIMONY AGAINST INTOXICATING WINE.

By the REV. WILLIAM RITCHIE, D.D., Dunse.

In a Handsome Volume, Price, Cloth Boards, 2s., Post Free,

THE TEMPERANCE PULPIT:

A SERIES OF DISCOURSES BY MINISTERS OF VARIOUS DENOMINATIONS.

(For separate Sermons, see List of Pamphlets).

Price, in Paper Covers, 1s.; in Cloth Boards, 2s. 6d., Post Free,

GEORGE EASTON'S AUTOBIOGRAPHY.

Just Published, Price, in Paper Covers, 1s.; in Cloth Boards, 2s., Post Free,

SKETCHES OF LIFE AND CHARACTER.

ILLUSTRATED WITH A PROFUSION OF WOOD ENGRAVINGS.

By REV. ALEXANDER WALLACE, D.D.,

Author of *The Desert and the Holy Land*, &c.

Crown 8vo, in Paper Covers, Price 1s.; Post Free, 1s. 1d.; Post 8vo Fine Paper, in Cloth Boards, Price 4s. 6d., Post Free,

£250 PRIZE TALE.

BY THE TRENT.

By MRS. OLDHAM, Stroud, Gloucestershire.

Price, in Paper Covers, 1s.; in Extra Cloth Boards, 2s. 6d., Post Free,

DUNVARLICH; OR, ROUND ABOUT THE BUSH.

By DAVID MACRAE, Author of *Harrington*.

TEMPERANCE TALES—continued.

Price, in Paper Covers, 1s.; in Limp Cloth, 1s. 6d.; on Fine Paper and Extra Cloth Binding, 2s., Post Free,

GEORGE HARRINGTON.

A Temperance Tale of great Power, replete with Incident and striking Illustration.

By DAVID MACRAE.

Price, in Paper Covers, 1s.; in Limp Cloth, 1s. 6d.; in Extra Cloth Boards, 2s., Post Free,

RACHEL NOBLE'S EXPERIENCE.

By BRUCE EDWARDS.

Price, in Paper Covers, 1s.; in Limp Cloth, 1s. 6d.; on Fine Paper and Extra Cloth Binding, 2s., Post Free,

RETRIBUTION.

By MRS. C. L. BALFOUR, Author of *Burnish Family, Drift,* &c.

Price, in Paper Covers, 1s.; in Cloth Boards, 2s., Post Free,

THE COVENTRYS.

By STUART MILLER.

Price, in Paper Covers, 1s.; in Cloth Boards, 2s., Post Free,

THE FIERY CIRCLE.

By the REV. JAMES STUART VAUGHAN, A.M.,
LATE VICAR OF STOCKLAND.

Price, in Paper Covers, 1s.; in Cloth Boards, 2s., Post Free,

KINGSWOOD;
OR,
THE HARKER FAMILY.

By EMILY THOMPSON,
Author of *The Montgomerys and their Friends.*

Price, in Paper Covers, 1s.; in Cloth Boards, 2s., Post Free,

REV. DR. WILLOUGHBY AND HIS WINE.

By MARY SPRING WALKER.

TEMPERANCE TALES—continued.

Price, in Paper Covers, 1s.; Cloth Limp, 1s. 6d.; on Fine Paper, in Cloth Binding, 2s., Post Free,

£100 PRIZE TALE.

DANESBURY HOUSE.

By MRS. HENRY WOOD.

Being the Temperance Tale for which the Prize of One Hundred Pounds was unanimously awarded by the adjudicators.

Price, in Cloth Boards, 1s., Post Free.

NELLY'S DARK DAYS.

With six full page Illustrations.   By the Author of *Jessica's First Prayer; Little Meg's Children; Alone in London; &c. &c.*

Price, in Paper Covers, 1s.; in Limp Cloth, 1s. 6d.; in Extra Cloth Boards, 2s., Post Free,

TROUBLED WATERS.

By MRS. C. L. BALFOUR, Author of *Burnish Family.*

Price, in Paper Covers, 1s.; in Limp Cloth, 1s. 6d.; on Fine Paper and Extra Cloth Binding, 2s., Post Free,

DRIFT:

A STORY OF WAIFS AND STRAYS.

By MRS. C. L. BALFOUR, Author of the *Burnish Family, &c., &c.*

Price, in Paper Covers, 1s.; in Limp Cloth, 1s. 6d.; in Cloth Boards, 2s.; Post Free,

GLENERNE.

A TALE OF VILLAGE LIFE. By FRANCES PALLISER.

Price, in Paper Covers, 1s.; in Cloth Boards, 2s., Post Free,

THE CURSE OF THE CLAVERINGS.

By MRS. FRANCES GRAHAME, LONDON.

Price, in Paper Covers, 1s.; in Cloth Boards, 2s., Post Free,

ISOBEL JARDINE'S HISTORY.

By MRS. HARRIET MILLER DAVIDSON.

Price, in Paper Covers, 1s.; in Illuminated Cloth Boards, 2s., Post Free,

SYDNEY MARTYN; or, TIME WILL TELL.

By MRS. WILSON.

TEMPERANCE WORKS.

Price, in Paper Covers, 6d.; in Cloth Limp, 1s.; in Cloth Binding, 1s. 6d.; in Fancy Cloth, Gilt, 2s., Post Free,

THE CITY: ITS SINS AND SORROWS.

BY THE REV. DR. GUTHRIE.

Price, in Paper Covers, 6d.; in Limp Cloth, 1s.; in Cloth Boards, Gilt, 1s. 6d.,

THE GLOAMING OF LIFE:

A Memoir of JAMES STIRLING, the League's First Agent.

BY THE REV. ALEXANDER WALLACE, D.D., GLASGOW,
Author of *The Bible and the Working Classes.*

Price, in Cloth Boards, 2s.; Extra Cloth, Gilt, 2s. 6d., Post Free,

KILWUDDIE, AND OTHER POEMS.

BY JAMES NICHOLSON.
With Introductory Notice by the REV. A. MacLEOD, of John Street
U.P. Church, Glasgow.

Price, in Paper Covers, 6d.; in Cloth Limp, 1s.; in Handsome Cloth Binding, 1s. 6d.; in Fancy Cloth, Extra Gilt, 2s., Post Free,

OUR NATIONAL VICE.

BY THE REV. WILLIAM REID, EDINBURGH.

Price, in Limp Cloth, 1s. Post Free.

THE ADAPTATION OF TEMPERANCE.

A Series of Twelve Addresses by various Authors.
For separate Addresses, see List of Pamphlets.

Price, in Limp Cloth, 1s., Free by Post for Thirteen Postage Stamps.

PICTORIAL TRACT VOLUMES.

Nos. I. II. III. IV. V.

Those are profusely Illustrated Volumes of Temperance Tracts.
(See Page 10.)

The following, Price 2d. Each. Two Copies sent Post Free for Four Stamps, or in a Handsome Volume, "THE TEMPERANCE PULPIT," Price 2s., Post Free.

THE WORKERS AND THEIR WORK; or, Christian Duty in Relation to Drunkenness and Drink. By the REV. WILLIAM ARNOT, B.A., Edinburgh.

NEHUSHTAN; or, the Principles of Hezekiah's Reformation applied to the Temperance Reformation. By the REV. DR. BROWN, Glasgow.

ABSTINENCE: A Special Service for a Special Need. By the REV. ALEX. MACLEOD, Birkenhead.

SCRIPTURAL AUTHORITY FOR TOTAL ABSTINENCE; or, What the Bible says about Intoxicating Drinks. By the REV. T. C. WILSON, Dunkeld.

PATIENCE NEEDED; or, the Duty of Temperance Reformers at the present Crisis. By the REV. WILLIAM REID, Edinburgh.

THE BANE AND THE ANTIDOTE; or, Intemperance and its Double Cure. By the REV. JOHN GUTHRIE, A.M., London.

THE DRINK SYSTEM AND THE REVIVAL OF RELIGION. By the REV. NORMAN L. WALKER, Dysart.

THE CITY, THE PLAIN, AND THE MOUNTAIN; or, Intemperance, Abstinence, and Religion. By the REV. J. P. CHOWN, Bradford.

ANCIENT AND MODERN HIGH PLACES OF IDOLATRY. By the REV. ALEXANDER WALLACE, D.D., Glasgow.

NEHEMIAH: A Study for the Modern Worker. By the REV. ALEXANDER HANNAY, London.

Price One Penny Each—Four Copies Sent Post Free for Four Stamps.

THE PUBLIC HOUSE AGAINST THE PUBLIC WEAL. By the REV. WILLIAM ARNOT, Edinburgh.

DR. LIGNUM'S SLIDING SCALE: A Temperance Story. By MRS. C. L. BALFOUR.

SIX SERMONS on the Nature, Occasions, Signs, Evils, and Remedy of Intemperance. By the REV. DR. BEECHER.

The following are the Addresses in "Adaptations of Temperance." (See Page 6.)

CHRISTIAN WITNESS-BEARING AGAINST THE SIN OF INTEMPERANCE. By the REV. HORATIUS BONAR, D.D., Kelso.

"LOOK BEFORE YOU LEAP:" An Appeal to Young Men. By JOHN STEWART, ESQ.

BETTER DWELLINGS FOR THE WORKING CLASSES, and How to Get Them. By ARCHIBALD PRENTICE, ESQ.

A WORD BY THE WAY TO THE WIVES OF WORKING MEN. By the REV. DUNCAN OGILVIE, A.M., Edinburgh.

THE WORKSHOP AND THE DRAMSHOP; or, a Bag with Holes. By the REV. ALEXANDER WALLACE, D.D., Glasgow.

THE WORKING MAN'S HOME. By J. H. DAWSON, ESQ.

CHRIST OR BACCHUS; Which ought the Church to Help? By the REV. WILLIAM REID, Edinburgh.

PAMPHLETS—continued.

HEALTH—THE ABSTAINER'S HOPE:—DISEASE—THE SPIRIT-DRINKER'S DOOM. By DAVID BRODIE, ESQ., M.D., Edinburgh.

THE FOLLOWERS OF THE YOUNG MAN TIMOTHY. By the REV. JAMES MORISON, Glasgow.

THE HOUSEHOLD BLESSING. By MRS. CLARA LUCAS BALFOUR.

TEMPERANCE AS AFFECTING THE INTERESTS OF EMPLOYERS AND EMPLOYED. By ARCHIBALD PRENTICE, ESQ.

JUVENILE DELINQUENCY THE FRUIT OF PARENTAL INTEMPERANCE. By MARY CARPENTER, author of "Reformatory Schools," and "Juvenile Delinquents; their Conditions and Treatment"

Price One Halfpenny Each.

APPEAL TO MISSIONARY SOCIETIES and their Agents, on behalf of the Abstinence Movement.

THE TRAFFIC IN INTOXICATING LIQUORS. By the REV. ALBERT BARNES, Author of "Notes on the New Testament," &c.

COMMON-SENSE: A Word on the Temperance Reformation. By the REV. W. WIGHT, B.A.

AN AFFECTIONATE APPEAL to all who Love the Lord Jesus Christ in Sincerity. By the late ARCHDEACON JEFFREYS.

THE DRUNKARD'S BIBLE. By MRS. S. C. HALL.

TEMPERANCE TRACTS.

PICTORIAL TRACTS.

Issued Monthly, Price 1s. 8d. per 100, Post Free. 500 Tracts sent, carriage unpaid, for 6s. 3d.

Packets containing 25 Tracts assorted—Nos. 1 to 25, 26 to 50, 51 to 75, 76 to 100, 101 to 125, 126 to 150, 151 to 175, and 176 to 200—Price 6d. each, Post Free.

Also in Volumes, bound in Cloth Limp, each Volume containing 36 Tracts—Nos. 1 to 36, 37 to 72, 73 to 108, 109 to 144, 145 to 180—Price 1s. 1d. each, Post Free.

TRACTS WITH SPECIAL HEADINGS.

Where 500 Tracts are ordered Monthly, and for a series of Months in advance, the Name of the Society is printed on the Tract, thus:—

"PERTH TOTAL ABSTINENCE SOCIETY'S MONTHLY PICTORIAL TRACT."

and, when it can be done without interfering with the Plates, Meetings are announced.

Tracts already issued can be had in any quantity, but cannot be printed with special Headings, unless 5,000 copies of the same Tract are taken.

Societies must give Four Months' notice previous to the discontinuance of their Orders, since the large quantity circulated necessitates printing considerably in advance.

TEMPERANCE TRACTS—CONTINUED.

Pictorial Tracts Already Issued.

1 Three Village Worthies.
2 The Doctor's Devotee.
3 The Confessions of a Drunkard.
4 Who drains the Sap out of us?
5 The Washing-Day.
6 Strike for a Cheap Loaf.
7 Bonnie Bessie Stewart.
8 Tag Rag; What He Was, and What He Is.
9 The Beginning of the End.
10 Who Killed the Man?
11 What Twopence a Day will do.
12 "Hold to the Right."
13 "The Mother's Boon."
14 Moderation.
15 The Two Soldiers.
16 My Brother's Keeper. A New Year's Tract.
17 I did it for You; or, the Brothers' Reply.
18 Love is Strong as Death.
19 The Public-House *versus* The Savings Bank.
20 The Doctor.
21 Strong and Weak.
22 Past and Present.
23 Mary Nicol; or, the Downward Path.
24 Hugh Hart; or, the Pleasures of Drinking.
25 Supper in Chambers.
26 The Deacon and the Dog.
27 Little Mary.
28 Dissolving Views. A New Year's Tract.
29 Words and Deeds.
30 Example.
31 The Only Son of His Mother.
32 The American Lady's Story.
33 Temptation.
34 The Tradesmen's Sons.
35 Roger Bell.
36 Your Health, Sir!
37 George Thomson.
38 The Buffalo Club.
39 A Year's Experience.
40 Drop the Subject. A New Year's Tract.
41 Cause and Effect.
42 John Laing.
43 The Widow's Son.
44 Turning over a New Leaf.
45 The Head-Ache and the Heart-Ache.

46 The Downward Course; or, the Shepherd Ruined.
47 The Two Mechanics.
48 The Curse of the Village.
49 The Two Johns of Rochdale.
50 My Mother's Funeral.
51 The Publican's Signboard, and what became of it.
52 Prayers and Pains. A New Year's Tract.
53 Who is Safe?
54 Upwards and Onwards.
55 The Reform Bill.
56 The Convict's Story.
57 Glasgow Green.
58 What Makes a Happy Fireside.
59 The Lost Brother.
60 The Lost One.
61 The Sisters.
62 I Don't Care for it.
63 William Halkett; or, the Danger of Irresolution.
64 A Word in Season. A New Year's Tract.
65 Richard Weaver.
66 The Willow Bed.
67 The Rescued Brand.
68 The Price of a Pot.
69 The Battle for a Soul.
70 Little Lizzie.
71 Good Counsel.
72 A Morning Glass.
73 The Wife's Secret.
74 The Image of His Father.
75 Bright Hopes Blighted.
76 The Contrast. A New Year's Tract.
77 The Bridal and the Burial.
78 What will my Sons be?
79 The Ruined Banker.
80 The Towncrier of K——.
81 The History of John M——.
82 The Two Brothers.
83 Social Shipwrecks.
84 My Last Glass.
85 A Night at Inch-Mnigh.
86 Foster Cochran, M.D.
87 Love without Wisdom.
88 Who Slew All These? A New Year's Tract.
89 The Greengrocer's Story.
90 It's Quite Safe, Sir!
91 "Can Nothing be done?"
92 Mary Millor.

TEMPERANCE TRACTS—CONTINUED.

PICTORIAL TRACTS—continued.

93 How I became an Abstainer.
94 Gilbert Gray; or British Human Sacrifices.
95 The Shady Side of Village Life.
96 He Never could be his own Master.
97 What the Cheap Wine did.
98 Kindly Counsels for Young Abstainers.
99 Three Times he Did it.
100 The Unwise and the Undone. A New-year's Tract. Two Woodcuts.
101 The Ship Steward.
102 Only a Sweep.
103 G. G.'s Experience.
104 A Race for the " Corner."
105 Not Dead, but Sleeping.
106 The Tender Chord.
107 A Dangerous Employment.
108 The Pirn Winder.
109 The Meridian Men of Moxton.
110 Hearts and Homes.
111 Mrs. Timberhead's Legacy.
112 The Ice Slope and the Crevasse. A New-year's Tract.
113 Good Standing in the Church no Safeguard.
114 Annie's Husband.
115 Blasted Trees; or, Dying at the Top.
116 Joe.
117 The Secret Foe.
118 Killed, Wounded, and Missing.
119 The Bunch of Rags.
120 The Broadford Fair.
121 How they became Partners.
122 The Briggate Flesher.
123 The Father and the Son.
124 The Rhine and the River of Death.
125 Life in Death.
126 Mrs. Richmond's Visit to Liverpool.
127 The Briggate Blackbird.
128 The Whirl of the Strom.
129 The Story of a Short Street.
130 The Moulders.
131 The Stairhead Club.
132 The Cowardice of Abstinence.
133 The Two Burials.
134 Gin Toddy.

135 My First Ministerial Difficulty.
136 My First Funeral.
137 What will you Have?
138 The Close-mouth Gathering.
139 A Memorable Trip to a Certain Island.
140 George Easton's Autobiography.
141 Feeding the Swan.
142 Our Young Minister.
143 The Three Bars.
144 Pleasure Trips.
145 Hereditary Intemperance.
146 Our Village Struggle.
147 The Pawn and the Blighted Home.
148 The Public-House versus the Mission Church.
149 The Gled's Grip.
150 The Experience of a Village Missionary.
151 From Sire to Son.
152 The Clock in the Corner.
153 M'Ian's Daughter.
154 The Fatal Flower.
155 The Doctor's Mistake.
156 Almost Rescued.
157 Madame Duchot's Testimony.
158 Off the Rails.
159 Hetty's Folly.
160 Old Sam's Advice.
161 Clearing the Houses.
162 Roland Bruce.
163 Under the Surface.
164 Mony a Job has I got by a Gill.
165 Lost Hopes.
166 The Ruin of Souls in a Cask.
167 Lizzie's Sacrifice.
168 The Minister's Story; or, Try Again.
169 Katie's Good Work.
170 Bob. Taken from Life.
171 The Confession of an Old Publican.
172 A New-year's Day Tract for Boys and Girls.
173 Andrew Macdonald.
174 Grace Darling.
175 The Dangerous Leap.
176 Mavlstock.
177 Seven Reasons for Abstinence.
178 The Poor Man's Club.
179 The Village Flower Show.

TEMPERANCE TRACTS—CONTINUED.

PICTORIAL TRACTS—continued.

180 Prince and his Master
181 One Glass; A Glass too many
182 Highland Hospitality
183 Notes of One Day's Visits
184 The Reason Why
185 Poisoned Arrows in Modern Warfare
186 A Pic-Nic worth more than it cost
187 "Whose End is Death."
188 The Nest-Egg
189 One Sinner destroyeth much good
190 On Broken Ice
191 The Dry Rot
192 The Non-Excluded Church Member
193 Professing Christians and the Temperance Movement
194 The Tempter and Victim
195 Never Begin
196 After the Spree
197 A Fatal Venture
198 Thirty-five Years' Experience of a Medical Practitioner
199 How to Arrest and Cure Drunkenness
200 A Teetotal Exaggeration
201 The Haunted House
202 The Law of God written on the Body
203 Love and Liberty
204 The Law of God written in the Bible
205 Queens of Society

TEMPERANCE TRACTS—CONTINUED.

CROWN 8vo SERIES.

Price 6d. per 100, *Post Free, for 2-Page Tracts;* 1s. *per* 100, *Post Free, for 4-Page Tracts;* 2s. *per* 100, *Post Free, for 8-Page Tracts.*

When large quantities are ordered for gratuitous distribution, the 4-page Tracts are supplied at 7s. 6d. per 1,000, carriage unpaid. 2-page and 8-page Tracts at a proportionate reduction.

A Packet containing One of Each sent Post Free on receipt of One Shilling in Postage Stamps. Also, in a Volume, Paper Covers, 1s.

No.		Pages
1	What are the Principles of the Abstinence Movement?	4
2	Characteristics of Total Abstinence,	4
3	Why should Working-Men become Teetotalers?	4
4	Total Abstinence a Health Question,	4
5	Abstinence: its Claims on the Christian,	4
6	Objections to Teetotalism,	4
7	Moderate Drinking Examined,	4
8	A Word with You,	4
9	A Word to the Drunkard,	4
10	A Word to Females,	4
11	The Traffic in Intoxicating Liquors,	4
12	Dialogue between a Minister and one of his Elders,	4
13	The Church in a False Position. By the Rev. W. Reid,	4
14	Moderate Drinking Christians on the side of Intemperance,	4
15	Drinking and Sabbath Desecration. By the Rev. W. Reid,	4
16	Total Abstinence an Essential Element in the Moral Training of the Young. By the Rev. W. Reid,	4
17	Ought Parents to Encourage their Children to become Members of Juvenile Abstinence Societies,	4
18	A Kind Word to Working-Men,	4
19	The Principle and Practical Operations of Teetotalism,	4
20	The Short Pledge. By Robert Kettle, Esq.,	4
21	An Address to Christian Professors. By S. Bowley, Esq.,	4
22	The Best Men are sometimes in Error,	4
23	Testimony and Appeal on the Effects of Total Abstinence. By Edward Baines, M.P.,	4
24	It's Never Too Late. By Mrs. S. C. Hall,	4
25	Tom Rudge. By Mrs. S. C. Hall,	4
26	An Auxiliary to the Gospel,	4
27	"Look not every Man on his own Things." By the Rev. James Morgan, D.D., Belfast,	2
28	A Word to Working-Men. By the Rev. William Johnston, Belfast,	4
29	A Voice from Jamaica,	4
30	The Test of the Liquor Traffic. By the Rev. I. N. Harkness, Stewartstown,	4
31	Why should Working-Men give up the Use of Beer?	4
32	The Story of a Wife's Endurance. By the Rev. W. Reid,	4
33	The Double Fall. By James M'Kenna, Esq.,	4
34	A Highland Village; or, the Dark and Bright Side of the Picture. By the Rev. A. Wallace,	4
35	John Jasper as He Was, and as He Is,	4
36	Count the Cost. By the Rev. Dr. Simpson, Sanquhar,	4
37	A Warning. By the Rev. Dr. Simpson, Sanquhar,	4
38	Lost in the Crowd,	4
39	Strong Drink in the House,	4

TEMPERANCE TRACTS—CONTINUED.

CROWN 8vo TRACTS—continued.

No.   Pages

40 The Best Diggings. By the Rev. A. Wallace, - - - - 4
41 The Ruined Artisans. By the Rev. A. Wallace, - - - - 4
42 Sally Lyon's First and Last Visit to the Alehouse, - - - 4
43 Charles Simpson; or, One Half-pint at Supper Time, - - 4
44 Drummer Dickie. By the Rev. Duncan Ogilvie, A.M., - - 4
45 A Lost Life, - - - - - - - - - - 4
46 The Loss of the Ferry-Boat, - - - - - - - 4
47 Harry Vedder; or, Look on This Picture and on That, - - 4
48 The First Meeting and the Last. By the Rev. Alex. Wallace, - 4
49 On the Self-Imposed Taxation of the Working-Classes of the United
     Kingdom. By J. R. Porter, Esq., - - - - - - 4
50 The Statesman's Son. By Lucius Markham, - - - - 2
51 The Coral Insects; or, What Good can I Do? - - - - 2
52 My Wife Won't Sign. By a Wife, - - - - - - 2
53 Cold-Heartedness of Temperance, - - - - - - 2
54 The Public-Houses Act, a Necessary, Just, and Beneficent Law. By
     the Rev. Wm. Arnot, Edinburgh, - - - - - 8
55 The Sabbath Clause of the New Public-Houses Act, - - - 4
56 Friendly Suggestions to Working-Men. By the Rev. W. Johnston,
     Belfast, - - - - - - - - - 2
57 The Glasgo' Buchts; or, the Lost Horse, - - - - 4
58 The Temperance Island, - - - - - - - 4
59 Pleasure Trips. By the Rev. Alex. Wallace, - - - - 4
60 Scenes Around Us. By a Lady, - - - - - - 2
61 The Bright Half-Crown. By Uncle Tom, - - - - 2
62 A Word to Workmen in behalf of the New Public-Houses Act, - 2
63 The Drunkard's Bible. By Mrs. S. C. Hall, - - - - 8
64 The First Year of War. By the Rev. John Ker, M.A., Glasgow, - 4
65 Cruelty of the Strong Drink Traffic, - - - - - 4
66 Intemperance at Sea. By Mrs. Sigourney, - - - - 4
67 True Temperance Cordial. By Mrs. S. C. Hall, - - - 4
68 Why the Poor are Poor? - - - - - - - 2
69 Temperance and Missions. By a Missionary, - - - - 4
*70 Adam Dingwall; or, the Broken Pledge, - - - - 4
*71 Asleep above the Rapids, - - - - - - - 4
72 One Hour in a Police Court; or, How Police Rates are Expended, - 4
73 Be Steadfast: an Address to Members of Temperance Societies. By
     Rev. L. E. Berkeley, Faughauvale, - - - - - 4
74 A Word to Ministers of the Gospel, - - - - - 4
75 Friendly Letter to all who call on the Name of Jesus Christ, - 4
*76 The Weak Brother: a Tract for Sailors, - - - - 4
*77 James Harley: a Tract for Young Men, - - - - 4
*78 The Old Woman's Appeal, - - - - - - - 2
*79 Saturday Night, - - - - - - - - 2
80 Responsibility; or, Who are to Blame for the Sin of Intemperance?
     By the Rev. S. J. Moore, Ballymena, - - - - 4
81 The Drunkard's Doom. By S. B. Loudon, Esq., - - - 4
82 Appeal to Ministers of the Gospel. By the Rev. W. B. Kirkpatrick,
     D.D., Mary's Abbey, Dublin, - - - - - 4
83 Nabal; or, The Dangers of Drink. By the Rev. J. Hall, Armagh, - 4
84 Alcohol: its Place and Power, - - - - - - 4

Those with an * are illustrated.

PUBLICATIONS FOR YOUTH.

Price, in Paper Covers, 6d.; in Cloth Limp, 1s.; in Cloth Boards, 1s. 6d.; in Extra Cloth, Gilt, 2s.,

THE PRIZE JUVENILE TALE,

COUSIN ALICE.

Price, in Paper Covers, 6d.; in Limp Cloth, 1s.; in Cloth Boards, Gilt, 2s.,

RITTER BELL, THE CRIPPLE.
A JUVENILE TALE.

Price, per Volume, Post Free, in Paper Covers, 9d.; in Extra Cloth Limp, Gilt Edges, 1s. 6d.; in Fine Cloth Boards, Gilt and Gilt Edges, 2s.

THE ADVISER,

For 1862, 1863, 1864, 1865, 1866, 1867, 1868, 1869, 1870, 1871, and 1872.

A BOOK FOR THE YOUNG.

Illustrated with beautiful Wood Engravings.
(*See Page 7.*)

THE ADVISER ALBUM OF HYMNS AND TEMPERANCE Songs, with music in the Tonic Sol-Fa Notation, Arranged for Band of Hope Meetings and Children's Classes. Price 2d; Two Copies Post Free for Four Stamps.

THE SCOTTISH TEMPERANCE LEAGUE HYMN-BOOK. Arranged by the Rev. T. C. WILSON, Dunkeld. Price 2d.; Post Free on Receipt of Three Stamps; or 12s. per 100.

A CATECHISM FOR JUVENILE SOCIETIES. By the Rev. GEORGE PATERSON, East Linton. Profusely Illustrated, price One Half-penny, or 3s. per 100. Eight Copies sent Post Free on Receipt of Four Stamps.

THE CRYSTAL FOUNT. A COLLECTION OF HYMNS AND Temperance Songs for Juvenile Meetings. Price 1d.

THE CRYSTAL FOUNT. SECOND SERIES. A COLLECTION of Hymns, Temperance Songs. and Recitations. Price 1d.; Four Copies Post Free for Four Stamps.

PUBLICATIONS FOR YOUTH—continued.

BAND OF HOPE SERIES.

Price One Penny Each, Four Copies sent Post Free on Receipt of Four Postage Stamps.

No. 1.—RECITATIONS. No. 2.—RECITATIONS, by George Roy, Author of *Generalship*, &c., &c. No. 3.—MELODIES. No. 4.—BRIEF HINTS FOR THE FORMATION AND MANAGEMENT OF BANDS OF HOPE. No. 5.—TEMPERANCE SONGS, by Alexander Maclagan.

TRACTS FOR THE YOUNG. Illustrated with Engravings on Wood. Assorted in Five Packets, Price 6d. each, Free by Post. Each Packet containing 6 Copies each of 12 different Tracts.

PACKET No. 1 contains:—1. The Whirlpool. 2. Strong Drink. 3. The Drunken Shepherd Reproved by his Dog. 4. Total Abstinence in the Palace. 5. Abstainers among the Prophets. 6. Little Drops. 7. The Dying Son. 8. The Banished Wife. 9. Walking Crooked. 10. No. 11. A Great Army. 12. The Good Abstainer.

PACKET No. 2 contains:—13. Thomas Williamson; or, a Mother's Reward. 14. Frank Faithful; or, the Trials and Triumph of a Young Abstainer. 15. The Jug. 16. The Two Fatherless Schoolboys. 17. The Serpent's Bite. 18. The Cure for the Serpent's Bite. 19. Whose "Creature" is it? 20. The Pylorus. 21. The Balance. 22. A Father's Letter to his Son. 23. Delirium Tremens. 24. A Drunkard's Family.

PACKET No. 3 contains:—25. "Wee Jamie;" or, the Fatal New Year. 26. The Half-Way House. 27. The Murder of the Innocents. 28. Uncle Gray; or, the Short Leg. 29. The Boy Blacksmith. 30. The Snake in the Grass. 31. Should Girls as well as Boys be Abstainers? 32. Peter's Pot. 33. The Minister and his Pony, Cow, and Pig. 34. Johnny Jackson. 35. The Two Little Children whose Mother was Dead. 36. The Temperance Meeting.

PACKET No. 4 contains:—37. A Story of a Robber. 38. The Boy who Saved his Comrade. 39. The Patent Lock. 40. The Destruction of the Crocodiles. 41. Signboards and their Lessons to Little Folks, No. I. 42. Tom and Puss. 43. The Devil's Blood. 44. Signboards and their Lessons to Little Folks, No. II. 45. Trying to Look Big. 46. The Sober Horse and the Drunk Man. 47. What does it mean to be Drunk? 48. The Voyage.

PACKET No. 5 contains:—49. Hot Corn. 50. The Child Stripper. 51. The Empty Arm Chair. 52. The Arm Chair Filled. 53. The Ragged School Boys. 54. The Spark in the Throat. 55. The Fleeing Deer. 56. Little Peter. 57. The Red Lion. 58. Little Mary. 59. The Golden Spur. 60. Anecdotes: Will you take a Sheep? The Man and the Thieves.

AGENTS FOR THE LEAGUE'S PUBLICATIONS.

LONDON: Houlston & Sons, and W. Tweedie. EDINBURGH: W. Oliphant & Co., South Bridge; Religious Tract Depot, St. Andrew Street; J. Menzies & Co., Princes Street, and Oliver & Boyd. ABERDEEN: W. Lindsay, and Lewis Smith. MANCHESTER: Tubbs & Brook, and John Heywood. LIVERPOOL: Philip, Son, & Nephew. YORK: J. C. Booth. BELFAST: The Bible and Colportage Society for Ireland, and W. E. Mayne. MELBOURNE, AUSTRALIA: George Robertson. TORONTO, CANADA: James Campbell & Sons. MONTREAL: F. E. Grafton.